IN THE DARK NIGHT

Wyoming's Double B Ranch
Book 1

V P FELMLEE
vfauthor.com

IN THE DARK NIGHT

IN THE DARK NIGHT

Published by TCS Publishing

ISBN: 979-8-9911602-0-9

IN THE DARK NIGHT

OTHER BOOKS BY V P FELMLEE

The Abandoned Trilogy

Prince Tadpole and Princess Clara

Good Boy Ben

Autumn and The Silver Moon Stallion
Silver Medal Winner, 2024 WILLA Literary Award
Young Adult Fiction and Nonfiction

In The Dark Night

Coming soon

The Color of Fire

Sunset's End

DEDICATION

To the many devoted and hard-working volunteers, professionals,
and scientists working to save all animals from abuse, neglect,
horrible circumstances, starvation, and death.
There has to be special places in heaven for all.

IN MEMORIAM

Leland Dirks
The coyote misses you.

IN THE DARK NIGHT

THANK YOU

As with so many works of art, literature, creation, so many people along the way have helped, encouraged and provided so much hope.

Thank you to my wonderful writing group, Kimberly, Carolyn, Karima, Carolee, and Skye. You keep me on the steep and narrow path that defines what I do and how I do it.

My editor, Jude DeLorca, is one of the keys to any success I might achieve. I am grateful for her skills, professionalism, and expertise.

And, thank you to the person who has become one of my biggest fans, my mother-in-law, Elma Martinez.

IN THE DARK NIGHT

"Her (Wild Horse Annie's) advocacy was not based on saving all wild horses and burros. Nor was it in allowing carte blanche control of the "public" lands by the livestock and hunting industries. By 1950 when Annie's campaign began, the western rangeland was already in terrible condition, and there was plenty of blame to be shared on all sides of the issue of range conservation. Rather, her campaign was based on respecting the heritage the wild horse and burro brought to the expansion and development of the West. Few industries, communities, or transportation systems could have developed without having a wild horse or burro involved. The footsteps of man generally followed the hoof prints of a wild equine."

Wild Horse Annie: Velma Johnston and Her Fight to Save the Mustang by Alan Kania

Reprinted with permission from the author.

IN THE DARK NIGHT

Mustangs, the wild horses of the West, are considered an invasive species, like weeds, giving the U.S. government the reason and purpose to systematically dispose of all of them. We are racing against time to prove them wrong, to show that horses, in some areas, perhaps in many others, are indigenous, living in remote valleys, along tropical rivers, foraging at the foot of tall mountains, even while Columbus was "discovering" America in 1492.

— Dr. Faith Jergens, speaking at the International Symposium of Environmental Ethics, Paris, France, June, 2021.

IN THE DARK NIGHT

CHAPTER 1
IN THE DARK NIGHT

Autumn shifted her weight from one leg to another, trying to find a balance against the pain shooting up from her stomach to her back, and failing. With a loud moan, she collapsed into a soft patch of sand by the shadow of a large rock. A warm breeze ruffled her mane and tail.

Juno, her sister mare, grew closer, concern in her eyes. "This is the third night," she snorted.

"I know." Autumn tossed her head impatiently. It hurt to talk. She looked up at the black sky. Only a few stars pierced their way down to earth, waiting for the full moon to finally make its way over the mountains. The two horses were in the depths of Silver Moon Canyon. Away from the other horses in their family, there was seclusion and privacy here.

There hadn't been any problems when she'd given birth the year before, at least any Autumn could remember. This time was different, and not in a good way. The pains in her abdomen were coming more often, each one more severe. Night after night she struggled to keep standing, the pain never letting go, and getting worse.

Now she struggled to breathe, and was getting more frightened by the hour.

"Go back up to the meadow," Autumn told Juno. Juno's foal, Peggy Sue, stood several feet away. "Take your daughter. I'm sure she's hungry. Let our stallion know I will be all right."

"Are you sure? I can stay here with you." Juno gruffed. "You shouldn't be by yourself."

Autumn knew Juno's concerns. While wolves and coyotes often announced their presence in the night air, mountain lions relied on silence and stealth before they attacked. A lone horse, especially one in distress, made an easy target. Autumn still bore the scars of one of those encounters. The big stallion, Silver Moon saved her then. She knew there was nothing he could do for her this night.

"I'd rather be alone, this is a good place. Quiet. I feel like my baby will come anytime."

"I'll stay near the top, ready to come down if something finally happens." Juno turned to make her way up the trail, and out of sight.

Now alone, Autumn's sharp eyes pierced the gloom of the canyon. It eventually led to a flat place near the river, a place where she might find the help she needed.

Autumn stood up and began to pick her way carefully over rocks and around bends. The canyon floor was steep in spots; she stumbled a few times. Often the pain forced her to stop, catch her breath. Her whole body seemed to heave with the effort of every step.

She smelled the river and knew the flat spot was ahead.

Stepping out of the canyon, her fears almost overwhelmed her. She still had so very far to go. Another sharp pain. She shook her head to clear it.

It wasn't too late to turn back. The little horse was taking a big risk. The certainty she'd felt earlier waned. Would she be remembered? Would she be helped? And if she wasn't, could she make her way back to the meadow where her family was? She didn't think she could.

At last, the silver moon rose, lighting her way.

Corky growled, whined, and growled again. He jumped down from the foot of the bed and padded his way to the window overlooking the yard.

He whined again, louder.

"Ah, come on, Cork, let me sleep a little longer," Becky MacKendrick mumbled, half awake. She glanced at the bedside clock. Seven o'clock in the morning.

She needed a full night's sleep in her own bedroom, maybe even sleeping until noon. Between college classes, labs, and researching the latest veterinary techniques, it seemed she never got any sleep.

Last night, she texted her boyfriend, Phillip, "*Please*, don't wake me up. Maybe ever. Kidding. I'll see you tomorrow afternoon."

Now, the sun barely up, she tried to pull the blanket over her head, willing the dog to come back to bed. The border collie remained by the window. He began to bark.

"OK, something's going on." Becky gave in and stepped onto the floor, bunching her long, red hair into a ponytail. "Probably some raccoons." When she got to the window, her breath caught in her throat.

In the early morning light, there was a horse, a palomino, head down almost to the ground, legs splayed like she might fall anytime.

"Autumn," Becky whispered, grabbed her phone, and flew out of the room, Corky behind her.

Her parents' bedroom door was open. Carl, her father, was out of town. Her mother, Tess, was still in bed, planning on taking the day off from working at her organic grocery store and adjoining coffee shop to spend time with her daughter.

"Mom, get up, Autumn's here!" she shouted.

Becky was in the courtyard seconds later, approaching the horse as calmly as she could, even though her heart was beating wildly.

Corky hung back. The dog sensed the horse was in trouble.

"Hey, little girl," Becky soothed, reaching out a hand. "Good to see you."

Autumn couldn't raise her head, a bad sign. Becky touched Autumn's muzzle, stroked it. It was plain to see the horse was gravid. Her classes in Animal & Range Sciences were giving her an experienced eye. The mare's abdomen was extended much larger than it should be for a horse her size.

Tess struggled into a robe as she ran across the deck and down the stairs. "Oh, dear," she breathed, "she's barely able to stand up."

"Mom, can you go get my medical bag?" Becky asked, then stroked Autumn's neck. "Come on, sweetheart," she coaxed, and led the way to the barn.

The barn held stalls for each of the family horses Dot and Max, an empty one still haunted Becky. Her prize champion horse, Slash, had been "put down, out of his misery." A magnificent black, Slash was too young to die, and his death destroyed a lifetime of Becky's dreams.

It was ironic this horse, coming to her for help, had once given Becky new hope, new purpose, new dreams. And a new love.

Once in the vacant stall, the horse's legs gave out and she fell into a thick bed of soft straw. In the barn's light, Becky saw how her eyes were shot through with pain and fear.

Tess rushed into the barn with the black leather bag. The bag held rudimentary equipment for treating large animals such as horses and cows.

Taking a deep breath, Becky placed her stethoscope on the horse's chest. A good heartbeat. She moved the instrument down to the abdomen where the foal's heart should be.

Nothing.

Another spot closer to Autumn's back.

Nothing.

Now Becky moved it towards the tail.

"Can you hear—" Tess started to ask. Becky raised a hand.

Moments passed, the stethoscope was pressed harder into Autumn's stomach. "I think I hear something, but the foal isn't in a good position."

Becky and her mom used straw to wipe down Autumn. The horse's back was flecked with foam. "I can't imagine she walked all the way here, by herself," Tess mumbled.

"She knew she was in trouble." Becky pressed the stethoscope against Autumn's chest again.

"Her heart is racing, but her lungs sound clear.".

"Good. No pneumonia. She's probably dehydrated." Tess drew a bucket of fresh, cool water from the barn's tap, took a clean sponge from a shelf, handing both to her daughter.

Autumn's mouth opened to the sponge, she seemed to like the

water against her gums and tongue.

"We're going to take care of you, nothing's going to happen to my girl. We love you so much," Becky whispered into Autumn's ear.

Taking her phone from a pocket, hands shaking, Becky keyed text messages to two people:

Dr. Shultz. Phillip.
Autumn's home and we need you now!!!

CHAPTER 2
K STREET, WASHINGTON, D.C.

Tab Taggart eyed the two suitcases near the open front door. He had packed the night before, realizing he didn't have much to show for his year in the Capital, working for one of the most prestigious law firms in the country. A couple of expensive suits with matching expensive ties, and five expensive dress shirts.

Laughter made him turn around. Two of his housemates—*former housemates*—brushed past him. It was clear they didn't want to make eye contact. He was an outcast, a pariah, all because of a simple misunderstanding.

The day before, his boss, a sanctimonious, over-weight and over-bearing moron (in Tab's opinion), called him into his office. The man was clearly envious of Tab's youth (he was thirty), his height (almost six feet), his good looks (often compared to Justin Timberlake), and his mother's money (a good divorce is better than a bad marriage).

Tab sat comfortably in the chair opposite the desk, and his boss blurted out a question: "Did you send this text message to Congresswoman Gorminder's aide?" He pushed a printout across his desk.

Ha ha, you're out of touch. We're going to get that oil and gas bill passed next week and I'm gonna love watching your head explode. I'll get you fired.

Tab took the paper and shrugged. "Yes, and I meant every word of it. Gorminder doesn't know what she's doing and her staff is a bunch of idiots."

"In this law firm, we don't threaten people," Tab was told. "You've embarrassed us. Get out. You're fired."

Tab wasn't part of the "in" crowd and didn't have a contract, so he could be fired anytime, for anything. Just like then, and just like that.

So much for the guaranteed future his Harvard law degree was supposed to confer.

Shocked at the aide's betrayal (in his opinion), and doubly shocked his boss didn't give him any more time or opportunity to defend himself (he was certain he could explain his way out of this) he wasn't given a choice. He cleared out the desk in his cubicle and faced the sneers and scorn of his fellow attorneys and the various legal aides, including Julia, a blonde he was dating.

He looked in her direction. She turned away, her face a bright red. Embarrassed for him or embarrassed for herself? Hard to say.

But what hurt most was how fast the word spread in the D.C. law community. He returned to his apartment on K Street, when he got a text ordering him to pay for his room six months in advance. He was given twenty-four hours to come up with the money, or he was evicted. Twenty-four hours. Ridiculous.

K Street apartment, what a joke. Barely bigger than a closet, he shared it with two others. The expensive address to show he "belonged" with "prestige." It was all a show, and a bad one.

He keyed his phone, looking for the next flights out of D.C. to New York City. No reason to stay here. He found a commuter leaving the next morning and booked a ticket with one of his many credit cards.

One more night in this swamp. As usual, he'd sleep alone.

Now in the morning heat and the noise of the city, he hefted his suitcases and walked out the door, refusing to give a backward glance at the three-story old brick building.

His ride to Reagan International was waiting for him. The heat and noise from the busy street traffic hit him all at once. The driver told him there was an accident ahead, they'd have a slight detour of only a few more minutes.

The D.C. tourist trap landmarks and monuments scrolled past his window. The White House, the Mall, the Lincoln Memorial, a glimmer of the Potomac River, finally getting close to the airport. More statues, more memorials.

Had he ever been truly excited to work and live here? The United States capital was the center of the world's attention. Had he ever really felt a part of it, stuck in a cubicle on the third floor? Would he miss it?

Tab Taggart, in the top ten percent of his law class, didn't think he would. He was expected to do great things, born to do great things. Even though he was humiliated, maybe in some ways he was relieved. He'd never have to see these idiots again.

The case holding his laptop was clutched firmly in his hands. There were files, a few notes, meetings he'd sat in on. For the next few days, he'd nurse his wounds in his mother's Central Park townhouse and go over those files, looking for something, perhaps far away, where he could find a new road, a better one.

He would certainly never come back to K Street.

CHAPTER 3
GROWING PAINS

"Welcome to the Double B Wildlife Science Center. Beautiful morning, not a cloud in the sky." Phillip Ebbers extended a hand to the woman stepping from the minivan.

Phillip hoped he sounded excited. Showing off the science center, talking about his plans, used to be one of his most favorite things to do. But now he always felt exhausted.

Knowing "good PR" was valuable, Phillip was often asked for interviews. The fact he was tall, well-built with long, blond hair he usually wore in a braid, added to the appeal.

Today, he was being interviewed by one of the most famous photo journalists in the country, Nan Whittier.

"I've been looking forward to this for weeks," Nan told him. "Thanks for inviting me." She was a petite thirty-five-year-old. A camera was strapped around her neck and she carried a notepad.

She specialized in high-quality photos of wildlife, especially mustangs. Her work appeared in many national publications, documentaries, and television shows, winning numerous awards.

Here in Wyoming, she liked to photograph and write about several dozen wild horse families, from McCullough Peaks to Salt Wells Creek. Her favorite was Silver Moon's family, and the Double B was the key to understanding the mustang's history.

Phillip led the way inside.

"This is a beautiful room," she said, admiring the woodwork and leather furniture.

"My grandfather built it, spared no expense." He went on to explain the ranch house was Al's crowning achievement. "He added on to it several times, remodeled it, from its imposing native rock exteriors to the gleaming timbers on the ceiling.

"I know you have lots of questions, thought I'd show you around a bit."

They walked outside to the large deck. A long line of Ponderosa Pines stretched out into a field, the air pleasant with a breeze carrying the scent of pine cones.

"You missed Lacaria and Joe Ruiz," Phillip told her. "Our ranch managers. Couldn't do any of this without them. They're in Jackson, picking up their niece this morning, she's spending some of her summer with us."

"Summer on one of the biggest ranches in Wyoming," Nan smiled. "I think I could do that."

"It's not really a ranch anymore, not in the way people think. We used to graze hundreds of cows, we have only a few left as the ranch changed course. Adjacent fields are fallow, to allow alfalfa to grow without grazing, give the soil a rest.

"The east field will be a sanctuary to dozens of horses, all rescued from brutal government holding pens, destined for slaughterhouses."

"Do you have all of the approvals for the sanctuary?" Nan asked.

Phillip shook his head. "The paperwork and red tape for the government's approval has been arduous, expensive, and time-consuming. We have a former Bureau of Land Management on our team, Carl MacKendrick. With his help, it was finally submitted. A permanent approval should be coming soon, perhaps in a few days."

They passed a large barn and several outbuildings for storage skirting the fence line. Further on was a stable for quarter horses mostly used for pleasure riding.

"You have thousands of acres?" Nan asked. "This land must dominate the landscape, and the local economy."

Phillip nodded. "My grandfather, Al, was the third in his generation to own it, and he made sure everyone knew he was the one who built it into a centerpiece of power and influence."

Al's sole purpose was to entertain Very Important Guests, politicians and officials from the State House to the United States Capitol. Lakes were stocked with trophy fish. Elk hunting was a big draw to get those men and women out of their offices and into Al's palm.

"He wanted the Double B to thrive as a cattle ranch, but he had other schemes, plans he kept hidden from others, revealed only after his sudden death."

"I appreciate you being so candid," Nan complimented him. "Many people would rather keep their family skeletons buried deep in a closet."

Phillip laughed. "Unfortunately, it would do me little good trying to keep it all a secret. Almost everybody in these parts know what Al did, might as well be upfront about it all. Including how he died two years ago."

"It was an accident?"

"We don't know what happened, nobody was here when he left on the ATV. It was raining, the road muddy. He might have over-dosed on some of his medications, fogged up his mind. Took a turn too fast and fell into Silver Moon Canyon."

"After he was gone, did you know what you wanted to do with the ranch right away?"

"My degree is in Archaeology. I was getting ready to head back to Europe for more field work, research." He shrugged. "I realized I could do something here, maybe make a small difference."

Nan smiled. "Small difference? You're only twenty-seven, your accomplishments are impressive. You've turned your grandfather's massive ranch into a science center. It's already attracting some of the most famous wildlife experts in the nation."

"I have lots of help." Phillip was sincere. "Especially from Dr. Faith Jergens."

"Ah, Dr. J." Nan wrote on her notepad "The most famous equine geneticist in the country. Full professor at the University of Colorado. She's your partner, correct?"

"We each have our own foundations, keeping them separate for legal reasons. It's working out well.

"Let me show you the conference center. A lot of this was her idea."

They walked down a flagstone pathway. The two-story building loomed in front of them. Construction workers hurried back and forth, carrying boxes and tools.

Phillip pointed out details as they went. It was an ambitious project, especially for this area of Wyoming with small towns and challenging construction requirements, from getting materials to arranging contractors and employees. Cost overruns doubled the initial estimates.

"A few growing pains, to be sure," Phillip said. "This building will serve as a testament to what we are doing, a symbol to the naysayers and doubters, and our enemies. We're here, we're staying."

He handed Nan a brochure describing the conference's features. The main conference room could seat three hundred people with five rooms for smaller groups and sessions. Another room would provide several computers for attendees. The building also housed a small kitchenette.

They took the stairs to the upper floor. "Our elevator isn't working yet," he smiled, "an unexpected addition." He opened a door. "This is something we're particularly proud of."

They stepped into a large room with counters set up on two walls.

"Our studio will have several computers dedicated to video and audio production." He walked across the room. "Through this door, is our broadcasting booth."

Nan's eyes grew large. "This is state of the art," she exclaimed. The walls were white sound-proofing material. In the center was a large table that would hold microphones and laptops. Three large cameras were already mounted on the walls.

"As you know, we have a pretty popular podcast," Phillip smiled. "We've been limited in the ranch house, this will give us what we need to reach our members, our audience."

Back in the hall, Phillip said, "We all get our own offices. Joe, Lacaria, Carl, Dr. J."

Nan interrupted him. "Dr. J will have an office here?"

"She plans on dividing her time between here and her office at the university."

Nan wrote more notes. "I was hoping to meet her today."

"She and Carl are in Iceland now, I can set up a meeting with her for you in the next couple of weeks? If you're available, that is."

"I'll make myself available!"

Relax.

When could he do what he wanted? Lots of spinning plates in the air. A thousand moving parts. Hectic.

When did he get so easily bogged down?

Only two years ago, he was traveling to ancient sites to look at petrographs, trying to discern their meaning, talking with experts, staring at those cryptic messages.

Then he met Becky, and she set him on an unexpected path. They discovered a shared passion for wild horses, the mustangs of the American West, and the region's environment and ecology. They fell in love almost without knowing it, certainly without planning it.

Days later, the unexpected death of his grandfather gave him a vision and purpose he never could have imagined.

Becky began college in Montana, studying to be a veterinarian. She was home for the summer; he wanted to see her, but his stomach pulled at him. Did she want to see him?

Over the holidays she'd said some things, gave him doubts. He was hurt, making him wonder about their future together.

Her text to him last night confused him. She was home, but tired, sleeping in, don't call her, she'd see him later in the day. Firm instructions, perfunctory.

Which was why he was surprised when his phone pinged, a text from Becky.

Autumn's home and we need you now!!!

Thirty seconds later, doubts or no doubts, future or no future, he was out the door.

CHAPTER 4
THERE'S NO ONE LIKE YOU

Dot and Max, the MacKendrick family horses, came closer to the large opening leading to the field. These warm nights the horses were allowed to stay outside where there was plenty of grass for grazing and fresh water.

They looked inside and saw Autumn on the floor. Her belly looked bloated and she didn't move.

Corky jumped up on the window sill, excited to share his news. "Look who's back."

Max shook his head. "Who? What are you talking about?" The big gelding had a short memory.

"Autumn, of course," Dot reminded him.

"Oh, the antsy one," he mumbled, "always pacing back and forth, back and forth. Never content, was she."

They peered through the opening and saw Autumn on the floor of the stall.

"She's in trouble," Corky told them. "Becky's worried."

"The humans will take care of her." Max turned to saunter back to the field.

Dot was inclined to stay where she was. "Maybe I can help, let her know we're here. I sense this might be bad."

Phillip arrived before Dr. Shultz, his truck skidding to an abrupt halt in the yard. He hurried into the barn to find Becky sitting on the stall's floor, cradling Autumn's head in her lap, stroking her neck.

"She's in trouble." Becky tried to choke back her tears.

He knelt down.

"She's probably been trying to have her foal on her own. She came to you, Cowgirl." Phillip reached over to squeeze Becky's shoulder.

They heard the gravel crunch of another truck. Seconds later, the county veterinarian stepped in. He was not a large man, his years showed in the white hair and beard, but everybody who knew him could attest to the strength he often showed picking up an ailing calf or lamb, pulling out a stubborn foal from its mother's womb, or pushing and pulling a frightened animal into a place where it could be treated.

He was also one of the most respected vets in the state of Wyoming.

Dr. Shultz joined Becky and Phillip on the floor. He ran a hand over her stomach and back. Autumn's big brown eyes, filled with pain and fear, watched him.

"Hey sweetheart, we've been here before, do you remember? It's been a few years." His fingers traced the faint scars on the horse's flank from a mountain lion attack.

Becky handed him her stethoscope. He listened to Autumn's heartbeat, then moved down to the large bulge. He moved it back and forth, up and down before settling on one area for several seconds.

He pressed his hands over Autumn's abdomen, coming to her rear and gently probing those areas. He finally looked up. "I hear another heartbeat."

"I thought I heard it, too. Does that mean it's OK?" Becky could only hope at the answer.

"I'm not sure I want to put my hands in at this point. He might be breech, but I'm thinking she's not able to push him out. Such a little horse."

"She gave birth to Sandy last year, on her own." Tess interjected.

"Sandy was smaller, this foal is larger, perhaps too large."

"What can we do?" Phillip asked.

"In the wild, both of them might die. But here, there are two things. I can inject oxytocin, to stimulate her hormones and hopefully induce labor. If it doesn't work," he hesitated, "we can perform a caesarean. I've done a few over the years." Dr. Shultz shook his head. "One mare didn't make it, the others did, it's a long recovery, several weeks, maybe three or four months. And," he looked around, "these are not the most sterile of circumstances. The risk of infection would be large.

"Autumn was domestic, then she chose to be wild. Now she's back here on the farm. I might be breaking some rules treating her."

Tess put her hands on her hips. "We won't tell if you don't." There was nervous laughter all around. "But we don't want you to get in trouble, either."

The vet blew air out of his cheeks.

"Carl and Dr. J might know what to do. Are they still in Iceland?" he asked.

Tess nodded. "They won't be back for a few days."

Dr. Shultz bit his lower lip. He was still kneeling next to Autumn, stroking her neck. He made his decision.

"Autumn's special. She came to us for help. We're not going to let her down."

Decision made, Dr. Shultz and Phillip left to gather equipment from the vet's clinic. Becky stayed with Autumn while Tess filled various pots and pans with hot water and collected old, clean towels. She also found a large blanket. Even though the barn was warm, she knew the blanket would provide a measure of comfort for the horse.

A short time later, all were in attendance for Autumn's procedure. These were horse people, born and bred on ranches and farms, and were ready to do what needed to be done.

"Can't ask for a better team," Dr. Shultz said.

Phillip was asked to hold Autumn's front legs: "I'm going to give her a low-dose muscle relaxant. I want her to be awake, not active. I've been kicked by horses, kind of a reflexive motion, so let's be sure her legs don't move."

To Tess: "I think we have enough water, keep an eye on it, we might need more. I'm going to ask you to keep her tummy and back wiped down with straw, it will help her stay warm and relaxed.

"Now I'm going to tell you all about the tricky part." He looked up and chuckled. "Of course, all of this is going to be tricky." They all smiled, appreciating his barnside humor.

"The baby could come out in a few minutes, or it could be an hour or two. Can't predict. As soon as it's out, we'll have to make sure its airways are cleared, so it can breathe. Phillip, I'd like you to do that. You might have to give it mouth-to-mouth resuscitation. The rest of us will wipe it down with straw, get it warm and get the birth sac away. Those few seconds will be crucial."

The vet inserted an IV line into one of Autumn's legs to keep her hydrated and administer the relaxant. A metal tray filled with various surgical tools was ready at his side.

Becky was instructed to keep Autumn's head up and make sure she didn't asphyxiate. "Pretty sure she hasn't eaten anything for some time, so her tummy's empty. I can't be positive."

The oxytocin was injected through the IV line. Within seconds, Autumn's stomach began to spasm. Becky looked up, concern in her eyes.

"Normal," the vet assured her.

Nothing else happened, although Autumn's breathing seemed to be more regular.

The minutes dragged. Tess gave Dot, still in her post at the window, some much-deserved attention for being such a good "midwife" to Autumn's labor.

A full hour later, Autumn's stomach began to distend to what seemed like an impossible size.

"Here it comes," Dr. Shultz breathed. "I hope."

With a mighty "sploosh" the large amniotic sac filled with a gleaming, wet mass was discharged onto the barn floor.

Everybody immediately sprang into action, all efforts and energies concentrating on the newborn.

Phillip tore the amniotic sac from the foal's head. He opened its mouth clearing blood and mucus away. The foal twitched and appeared to take its first breath.

Becky and Tess cleared the rest of the amniotic sac away and began to vigorously clean the back and legs with handfuls of straw, massaging and wiping at the same time. The wet coat glistened from the attention. The foal's eyes gradually opened, tiny slits of life.

"A little boy." Phillip smiled, glancing at Dr. Shultz. "And a good-sized one, like you said. Autumn didn't have a chance pushing him out on her own."

Dr. Shultz kept an eye on the team's progress, nodding and encouraging with a "Good job." Several times he listened to Autumn's lungs and heart: He reported both sounded good and strong. "She's young, she has that going for her."

He then moved to the foal, who was still lying on the floor. "Heart a little weak, he's been through a lot. I'm sure it'll even out. I am going to take a blood sample, get it tested. Want to make sure there aren't any issues we're overlooking."

"How long before Autumn can stand up?" Tess asked, bringing him a warm bucket of water to wash his hands.

"Hopefully soon, let's don't force it," was the answer. "I want to keep her hooked up to the IV as long as possible. Becky, I'm giving you the next few days off," he chuckled, "but only because I want you to keep an eye on our star patient." Becky's summer job was working at the vet clinic, getting in hours of valuable "real time" veterinary work.

She smiled. "Thanks, boss."

"I'll come back this afternoon. We'll see about taking her off the IV."

"Will you give her a sedative? Keep her quiet?" Phillip asked.

"I'd rather not, I'm hoping she'll doze off a time or two. She'll have to stay in the barn, of course." He looked around. "You have bales of straw outside?" he asked Becky, who nodded.

"I'd like you to stack them up in here, make a barrier for her, wide enough for her to get up or lie down if she wants or needs to. I don't want her to move around."

Becky understood.

The veterinarian continued. "Now the big steps. One Two Three."
All of them knew the routine.

One: A foal should stand up in the first hour.

Two: A foal should begin to nurse in the second hour.

Three: A foal should release any placental material still left in his stomach.

They also knew the foal would not be able to nurse from Autumn for a day or two, perhaps longer. Dr. Shultz carried "baby horse formula" in his truck.

Mother and son could not be left alone during the day or night. Shifts were arranged to not only keep an eye on Autumn, but to also feed the foal every hour. Tess would take the evening hours, Becky would come in after midnight, and Phillip would arrive at five a.m.

"Joe and Lacaria will be back later today. I know they'll want to help, too," Phillip said.

Dr. Shultz was ready to leave, then he turned back. "Should we talk about daddy?"

They all knew he was referring to Silver Moon. "He's going to come looking for her sooner than later. You better be prepared."

Phillip looked outside to the field. "He's not going to be happy."

Becky nodded. "He's such a drama king. He'll put on a show for the heck of it to prove he's the boss."

"What do you think he'll do?" Tess asked. "The fence is sturdy, surely he can't break through?"

"I'll check the gates," Phillip promised. "We'll reinforce them if we need to. One kick and he'll be in here, you won't be able to stop him."

A chill ran through Becky. She had been "up close and personal" with Silver Moon a couple of times. His size and strength were impressive, and frightening.

Tess took her phone out to take pictures of Autumn and the foal.

"I'll text Carl and Dr. J later. Tease them a little. I want to see the look on their faces."

Becky laughed. "I'll call Joe and Lacaria, too. Ask them to come by." She stood up, her legs cramped and her back ached.

"What a way to start summer vacation. Mom and I were planning a quiet day, sleeping in, maybe ride the horses over to the Double B. Have some lunch, catch up." She looked expectedly at Phillip.

Phillip avoided her glance, looked down at his phone. "I gotta get back to the ranch, contractors have some questions for me." He looked up. "I'll return for my shift."

Had he even listened her? She watched him leave the barn, heard his truck start. Yes, he'd shown up quickly after getting the text about Autumn, eager to help.

Now he seemed equally eager to leave, not interested in talking to her, asking even nominal questions:

How did final exams go?

Have you decided which vet school you're going to?

Or, even, *sure glad you're home. I missed you.*

She frowned, chiding herself. *He's busy, there's been so much to do at the Double B, he's been working long hours making it all happen. This is his vision.*

His vision. Where did she fit in?

Or, did she?

Tess left to get them something to eat. Alone in the barn, Becky rubbed her hands over the foal's neck. His head rose slightly at her touch. His coat was drying, revealing a light color. Not white, nor palomino, gray, with subtle spots appearing with each hour

"Dappled," she whispered. "You're Warrior's grandson."

31

She whispered in his ear, "There's no one like you, not in this whole world and your mommy and daddy are going to make sure you grow up to be like your grandfather. Brave and fierce.

"And I'll help, whenever I can."

CHAPTER 5
DUMPED

Skylar clutched her small daypack and looked out the airplane's window. Mountains were all she could see, snow still topped some of them. It looked cold and barren.

This was going to be the worst summer ever.

A thin cable led to ear pods where she could hear her tunes. They were the only things her parents let her take from her home in Oakland, California. After that little problem at school, her laptop and cell phone were confiscated. She hadn't done anything, at least not successfully. If Freddie hadn't been a rat, nobody would have suspected her. Some friend he'd turned out to be.

The meeting with the principal, the assistant principal, a lawyer, and a sheriff's deputy was tense. She was told there'd be a month's suspension from school, right at the end of the term, and she was lucky that was all the punishment she'd receive. She'd have to take all of her tests in the fall, maybe even get set behind a year.

Her mom and dad overreacted, grounding her, no TV, no cell phone, no contact with her friends, locking her out of the family computer, even the TV's Wi-Fi.

"You almost destroyed government property," her mother railed at her and it did no good when Skylar argued the school district isn't "the government" and nothing was destroyed because she'd been caught. "I didn't hack into anything, didn't find anything," she shouted back.

Next, her parents announced they were going to Australia for six weeks, a vacation. And she was not going to come with them, part of the punishment.

Which was fine, the last thing she wanted was to be anywhere near them anyway. Maybe for the rest of her life.

Then the hammer came down. No, she couldn't stay home alone, no she couldn't be "watched" by her older sister who despised her. She was being dumped — DUMPED — in the middle of nowhere, on some dingy, dirty farm, with an uncle and aunt she hardly knew. For two months. Two months! A lifetime.

She'd been told to remove her fake nose ring, scrub off the temporary tattoos on her arms, wash out the highlights to reveal her natural dishwater blond hair color, and pack "casually." Jeans and t-shirts.

"You don't get your cell phone back, you can't take your laptop either," her mother said. "You'll be in the middle of nowhere and they won't have computers either!"

Hayseed city. Old people driving old, rickety hayseed trucks. Live in a hayseed farmhouse. *They'll probably make me wear cowboy boots. Bet they expect me to plow a field or feed slobbery, stinking pigs. Chores. Make me do chores. Who knows?* she thought over and over.

Where was Wyoming anyway?

The plane was approaching Jackson Hole Airport, she removed the ear pods to put in her daypack. Inside was a graphic comic book her parents allowed her to take. She smiled. Sandwiched between its pages was a gift from a fellow hacker. She might not use it, might never even look at it. She was satisfied she'd left home with *something* her parents didn't know about.

"I'm not looking forward to this," Joe Ruiz grumbled to his wife. "A teenager ... for several weeks. What are we going to do with her? I got the Double B to take care of, stake out our leases on the other side of the river *and* the conference center to get finished."

Almost fifty years old, Joe Ruiz was the Double B's foreman. He had worked for Phillip's grandfather, now he worked for the grandson. A Basque, his parents from the "Old Country," he was tall with graying hair.

"Oh, my, you have the tasks of Hercules, don't you," Lacaria laughed. "Listen to you complain! I guess I don't have a thing to do, lie around in bed eating chocolate-covered cherries."

Lacaria was a small woman with arms made strong by working on the ranch alongside her husband. Her dark hair was cut short, requiring little care or maintenance.

She was the indispensable manager of the Double B, handling correspondence and inquiries, arranging meetings, and ensuring visiting scientists and other guests were taken care of.

Joe took his wife's hand. "I deserved that. I'm sorry."

They passed groups of tourists entering or exiting the low-slung

35

building, on their way to Yellowstone National Park, or leaving to go home.

He thumbed his cell phone for the recent picture of his niece. The photo shocked him. A pouty sneer under purple and green hair highlights, eyes disappearing into black makeup.

"Is her nose pierced?"

Joe's sister and her husband were going on a "once in a lifetime" two-month trip to Australia they couldn't pass it up, but Skylar couldn't come with them, no reason given, and would it be a terrible imposition for their daughter to stay with them? And yes, our older daughter would be home from college but she didn't want to be responsible for Skylar and the two don't get along well anyway, so *please*?

Lacaria assured them, yes, of course, they'll be thrilled to have her for the summer!

If Joe had answered the call he would have said yes, but not immediately. He would have asked why the girl "couldn't come with them," and maybe even why the sisters didn't get along.

Too late now, they were at the baggage claim, waiting for the announcement her flight was deboarding.

Skylar was the last passenger off the plane.

"See?" Lacaria punched her husband's arm playfully. "No piercings."

Skylar saw a couple waving at her. Uncle Joe and Aunt Lacaria and resisted the urge to turn around and disappear into the crowd.

"Hi, Uncle Joe," she tried to create a smile, barely managing it.

"Hey, Skylar, glad you made it. How was your flight?" Joe asked.

"OK, kind of boring," was the vague answer.

"Are you hungry?" Lacaria asked. "We can get lunch here or wait until we get to the Double B. It's a little over an hour drive."

"No, I'm OK, got snacks on the plane. I've gotta get my suitcase." She headed over to the baggage claim.

A few minutes later, her suitcase rolling behind her, she followed them into the parking lot. They led her towards a large, black SUV, a luxury model.

Not a hayseed truck.

Lacaria glanced at her watch. "We'll be back in plenty of time for my podcast."

"A podcast?" Skylar asked. Her interest was piqued.

"Yes, at least once a week, maybe more if there's something going on our members need to hear about. Today I'll be streaming a video from Dr. J, she's in Iceland right now."

"Iceland?"

"She and Carl, our biologist, have been traveling to different countries, researching wild horse herds, taking blood samples."

"How many people listen to your podcast?"

"We have about ten thousand members, and thousands more listen to them. I'm kind of new to this, for years I was the ranch's 'chief cook and bottle washer.'"

Joe gave a short laugh. "Don't let her fool you. She keeps us in line, takes care of the banking. Miserly."

"I'm frugal," she protested. "You won't believe what these guys want to spend money on, if it were up to them, we'd be broke in no time flat."

"She's great at this high-tech stuff," Joe added. "She even hooks me in on it. I'm a regular ol' cowboy, better off out on the range."

Looking more closely at Uncle Joe, Skylar wasn't so certain. His shirt looked new, his jeans clean, he wore sneakers, not cowboy boots. Hair closely cropped and face clean-shaven. His brown eyes sparkled as he talked.

And Aunt Lacaria? A podcast? She wore a sleeveless summer dress with sandals, not at all like a hayseed farmer's wife.

Both wore sunglasses, the latest styles.

"So," Skylar muttered, "you have Wi-Fi or something?"

"We upgraded about two years ago," Lacaria answered. "Had to with everything we're doing, and planning to do. Lots of computers, laboratory, the studio. Scientists are always coming in and out for meetings."

"The ranch?" the teenager wondered out loud. *Computers? Scientists?*

"It's not so much a ranch anymore, we converted it into a research center," Joe explained. "Mostly about wild horses, the mustangs. You'll meet Phillip, the owner."

The SUV's phone interface chimed. Skylar craned her neck from the backseat to see the screen. A young woman's face appeared.

Lacaria answered. "Hi Becky."

"Hey, you two, heading back?" the woman asked.

"Leaving Jackson right now."

"Got something to show you." Lacaria tilted the phone so Skylar could see.

The camera panned to a stall, showing a horse lying on a thick bed of straw.

"Autumn?" Joe and Lacaria said at the same time.

"Yeah, and her bouncing baby boy." Another camera angle showed a gangly foal, barely able to stand up. They heard laughter in the background. "OK, he's not bouncing, yet, he will be soon."

"A dappled gray," Joe whispered. "Warrior."

Lacaria reached over to squeeze her husband's arm. "Like his grandpa."

Joe shook his head, chuckling. "Autumn. That little horse."

Lacaria looked back at Skylar and smiled. "We have a stop to make before we go home. We're going to say hello to an old friend."

CHAPTER 6
ICELAND

Dr. Faith Jergens looked through the long-range lens of her video camera, double-checking the settings before clicking on the record button.

"We've been watching these horses for almost an hour. They are in remarkably good shape," she said for the benefit of the recording.

Fifteen horses were gathered in a cluster, some standing, others lying in the thick fen. They were an assortment of browns, tans, and whites, some with blonde manes and tails. Smaller than their American cousins, most stood at thirteen or fourteen hands. The stallion of his family was only slightly larger, and was dark brown. He watched the humans warily, showing no signs of alerting his mares to move away.

Despite the sun's warmth, a persistent cold wind kept the temperature to the high forties, normal for this time of year. Dr. J pulled her thick sweater around her a little closer and swept her hair back from her face. She was a tall woman, almost fifty years old, imposing, commanding respect with good reason as one of the world's foremost experts on wild horses and equine genetics.

Carl MacKendrick sidestepped the wetlands near the road, carrying several plastic bags of different plants.

"These horses have a different diet from about every other herd we've seen," he told Dr. J. "Except perhaps the herds in Mongolia." He stacked the bags in a small cooler and snapped the lid shut.

Anna, their guide in this country near the Arctic Circle, emerged from the vehicle. "I logged the GPS of our location for you," she told Dr. J. Anna was a graduate student, thrilled to be assigned escort duty to the American scientists.

Carl leaned against the small electric vehicle parked on the road overlooking a field. "Your government takes good care of the environment—and these animals."

"We're proud of our *hestar*," Anna beamed, using the Icelandic word for horses. "We think they're one of our most important national treasures. Two summers ago, I went to the United States, Nevada, and was appalled at what I saw. Wild horses corralled, penned together in horrible conditions. Some were hurt, others malnourished. The smell was awful."

"We're doing what we can to stop it," Dr. J said, turning off her camera, then began to pack her equipment away. She exchanged glances with Carl. "But it's an uphill fight."

"You're leaving soon?" Anna asked.

"Two days. We'll send these samples to the lab today," Carl nodded to the container. "We Expressed-mailed the vials of blood last week, hopefully they'll have the results by the time we get back to the states."

Carl was the Principal Biologist for the Double B, a job that suited him much more than his previous employment ever could. He liked the travel, studying the different ecologies, their plants, and climates wild horses thrive in, or are challenged by.

Still, he missed his wife, Tess, and the small farm they called home in western Wyoming. He also missed his daughter Becky, visits with her were few and far between now that she was in college. He was looking forward to spending a few days this summer with his family. Quiet times, some camping, fishing on the river, those were his plans.

"Where will you be going next?"

"Alaska, by the end of summer," Dr. J answered. "Some of the horse herds there might be as isolated as Iceland's. A biologist is doing some interesting work, we've been reading his studies."

A few hours later at their hotel in Reykjavík, Dr. J set up her laptop for a podcast with Lacaria at the Double B. Connections tested, notes gathered, the geneticist was efficient and thorough.

Carl smiled.

"What's so funny?" she asked

"I was remembering that meeting with you and Al Ebbers in my office when I was district manager for the BLM."

"Not my finest moment."

"Nor mine. Nor his. It was a horrible idea getting both of you in the same room, trying to find some agreement on managing wild horses. You talked about saving them, when all he wanted was to kill every last wild horse in the state."

"It was the last time I saw him alive." The realization made her pause. "Only a few days later he was killed."

And my life changed.

Waiting for the connection to verify, Dr. J poured herself some tea in the lobby. She sat down at a small table, remembering the meeting with old man Ebbers.

"You're only interested in your special feral horses, you don't care about the others." His cruel words hit home, made her defend herself and her work. Was he right? Was she so determined to prove her theories about the origins of wild horses in North America while ignoring the entire gene pool? Should those few unique herds be her focus?

Dr. J was a tall, attractive woman with close-cropped black hair, she was always immaculately dressed. Besides her profession, she was also an ambassador for her Shoshone Tribe.

The name she went by, Dr. J, was an affectionate euphemism used by friends, and with snark by foes. She had plenty of both.

A full professor at the University of Colorado, her office bustled with activity, students and associates, submitting papers, ideas. Her research was impeccable, peer reviewed. Her books on equine genetics were well-received, but there were still naysayers, critics who did not share her theories, her visions.

It was always a struggle getting money, grants, attention from the media. A few weeks after Al Ebbers died, she looked up from her desk to see Phillip Ebbers, looking awkward with a sheaf of papers stuffed in a file folder.

"I own the Double B Ranch now," he told her. "And I have money. Lots of money. Do you want to come work with me?"

The memory made her smile because that one question was the answer to her prayers. It also led her to the journey she was on now, forcing herself to admit the truth.

Old Al was right.

By focusing on the atypical, the typical was being ignored.

A chime on the laptop reminded them the podcast was beginning.

"Dr. Faith Jergens, coming to you from Iceland where biologist Carl MacKendrick and I have continued our research for our Horse Genome Project."

Carl's image appeared on the split screen next to Dr. J's.

"Greetings from almost the top of the world," he smiled.

"Before we talk about Iceland, you were in Arizona last month, tell us what you saw there."

"I saw the Salt River mustangs. Those horses immerse their heads totally in the water to get to cress and other aquatic flora. Local observers call it snorkeling. It's incredible, watching horses' heads disappear for several seconds, before pulling the sweet, nutritious plants to eat. Younglings are taught to do the same."

"An evolutionary adaptation."

"We wonder how many other horses in other parts of our country have learned, on their own, to survive in unique ways. If the United States government has its way, we'll never know. All wild mustangs will be gone in a decade, maybe less."

"I want to remind our podcast members and visitors we've been to Mongolia, Japan, France, Germany, Spain, England, and Sweden. We've collected DNA samples from more than two hundred thousand horses, and teaching others how to collect and analyze. We're building a vast database to connect them in a way never available before, looking at their evolution, different skeletal structures, even propensities for disease or other problems."

"We know you're interested in the Icelandic ponies," Carl added, clicking on a series of pictures showing the horses on fields, near streams, and the team collecting various specimens.

"This country is an ideal setting, the animals here are some of the most genetically pure equines in the world, kept isolated from other horses for a thousand years. Despite this isolation, recent testing by Cornell University scientists shows the horses are remarkably diverse in their genetics."

Dr. J nodded in agreement. "For decades, the United States government has pushed the idea the mustangs in our country are not native, brought here by Columbus and other Europeans beginning in the 16th century. Not native, an invasive species, and should be wiped out, eradicated, slaughtered.

"But Icelandic horses are not native either, brought by Vikings a thousand years ago. Icelanders do not consider their horses an invasive species. If, and only if, you believe our wild horses were brought to the North American Continent five hundred years later, I would offer:

"What difference does a few centuries make?"

CHAPTER 7
SILVER MOON

Silver Moon had a great deal to contend with this morning.

First, the vicious wind the previous night blew dirt and dried-up bushes everywhere. He shook his head and swished his tail, trying to dislodge twigs and seeds.

Second, here was Juno coming to nag him about something. She was his second mare, he loved her, but she could be ponderous, difficult, and insistent.

"Have you seen Autumn?"

He shuffled slightly before turning around. "No. Did she have her baby?" he asked.

"I left her near the big rocks down there," Juno tossed her head towards the canyon. "She was hurting real bad, she told me not to worry. The next time I looked for her, she was gone. I thought she'd come back up here, like she has the last few mornings."

He shook his head, then bent down to nibble some flowers. He wasn't worried, he was accustomed to the comings and goings of his mares when they gave birth, sometimes being gone for a few days before they introduced the new arrival to the family. It was certainly not unusual they did not want him around, and that was fine with him. A stallion doesn't have to know everything his mares are doing.

He sauntered over to the trail. There might be humans in the canyon, walking or riding their contraptions. How many times did he warn his mares to not wander down into the depths, for fear they would meet those humans, be chased, or even harmed?

Silver Moon held an intense distrust and dislike for humans, he would never forget watching his family chased by a round thing in the sky, by whooping and hollering humans. Horrible sounds of horses being hurt, loud sounds, "cracks" in the air before they lay still, bleeding, and broken.

His own panic-stricken father, looking for his mares, his colts and fillies, disappearing from sight in the maelstrom of hundreds of horses.

Silver Moon was there when his mother died, kneeling down next to her, comforting as best he could as he saw the light disappear from her eyes.

He crossed the river the next night to escape the memories, find safety for two mares who followed him. Juno was one of them, she showed courage and a strong heart. A few days later he reclaimed Autumn, his first love. Nine mares, seven sons and daughters, three born this Spring, were his family.

Five years old, Silver Moon was one of the fiercest stallions among the several families in the high meadows. He was an immense horse, what the humans would describe as 18 hands high, with a striking full mane spilling over his head and neck.

Despite his hatred for humans, and eagerness to create as much distance as he could between him and them, he was one of the most photographed horses among the wild mustangs in the country, perhaps even in the world.

Looking down into the canyon, he tried to pick up Autumn's scent, the air was calm. Returning to the meadow and his family, he decided there was no reason for concern.

A mud bath by the waterfall would be nice.

Two new foals were getting breakfast from their mothers. Another was testing its legs, dancing and jumping in the high grass. Autumn would be back soon enough, joining them, with her baby.

He was about to trot over to the lake for that mud bath when something caught his eye across the meadow.

"Uh oh, here comes trouble."

Nan Whittier swung the high-powered telescope around to where the other photographers pointed. Tripods and long lenses were already set up on the knoll north of the high meadows, a good distance from Silver Moon and his family.

She immediately saw what they were referring to. Galloping towards Silver Moon was Liam, one of his lieutenants.

"He's acting strange. What's he up to?" Nan asked. She turned her video camera on.

"Weird, not like him at all. He's always been content with his place," another photographer pointed out. "Some of the mares in nearby families are getting old enough to leave, set up housekeeping with another stallion."

Nan shook her head. "Liam is a smaller horse. Surely he's not going to challenge Silver Moon for *his* mares?"

Seconds later her question was answered.

Silver Moon raced across the meadow. He smelled the odor of Liam's challenge on the wind. His own hormones coursed through every muscle, fury exploding in his hooves.

The two horses met in an explosion of dirt. Liam screamed, thinking this would intimidate the larger horse.

It didn't.

Silver Moon responded with a louder, more prolonged scream before lifting himself up on his back legs, hooves slashing down onto Liam's neck, delivering a brutal cut.

Liam shook his head, then backed up. Was he ceding this fight so early?

Silver Moon also backed up, wary. The two stallions stood ten feet apart, snorting, their bodies heaving with deep breaths. "What's got into you?" he asked.

Liam stomped the ground. "I'm ready to head up a family. You haven't been paying attention."

Silver Moon was confused. "Many of my aunts and cousins left my father's family when I was a colt, I watched them leave, find their own stallions, their own herds. All you have to do is wait, others will join you." He tossed his head. "Perhaps some of my daughters will."

"You are young. You do not know the ways of things. Your fillies are not yet old enough to leave, maybe your mares want to come with me."

"You can't have them. Not today." Silver Moon decided he was finished talking. He charged Liam and knocked him to the ground.

Liam struggled to get up, legs and hooves flailing dangerously. He staggered back up, teeth gnashing. He tried to bite Silver Moon's neck, and almost kicked him in the head!

The white stallion reared, kicking his front legs into Liam's chest. The blow could have been deadly but Silver Moon turned his hooves away as they landed against the other horse. Liam gasped and turned to his right, his eyes wide and filled with pain. He stood huffing for several seconds to catch his breath.

"It's time you leave." Silver Moon was also panting heavily.

Liam gave up.

"I will come back. Someday."

Silver Moon watched his new rival gallop away. He was exhilarated, engorged in pride and victory. The next thought tempered any thought of celebrating. He realized Liam told the truth. Silver Moon needed to add a few mares of his own to offset the times when his daughters would leave.

Did he have to fight for them, each and every one, maybe get hurt, have to hurt somebody else?

He needed to rethink this stallion business.

Something else to ponder as he returned to his mares, more interested in a recent bloom of some sweet flowers than the fight.

Still no Autumn. The worry came back.

The photographers chatted, excited by the antics of the two stallions.

"My heart almost stopped," one laughed. "When Liam went down,

I thought Silver Moon would stomp him hard."

"I wonder why he didn't. He had the advantage."

"Silver Moon's a young horse, maybe he's a lover, not a fighter."

"He's going to have to learn to fight eventually."

Nan turned to the others. "Did anybody see Autumn?"

They all shook their head. "I'm sure her foal's been born by now, she was looking quite pregnant the last time we were here."

Nan hoped so. "I bet next time we're back, she'll be nursing the little one. And Silver Moon won't let us get within a mile of her."

She packed up her camera to leave. Some of the photographers stayed, hoping to get more action shots. "I could stay out here for the next twenty years doing this," one remarked to laughter and nods all around.

That made her pause. She wondered if they knew the reality, that in twenty years there wouldn't be any wild horses left to photograph, they'd all be gone, wiped out by a government all too willing to accommodate the livestock industry. Did they know the "numbers" and what they meant?

Cattle and sheep ranchers pay less than a dollar and forty cents a month for each animal to graze on public lands. The United States government spends more than seven thousand dollars a horse to capture, trap, corral, or kill a mustang.

What will they do when the government gets its way, all of the mustangs gone? What will they take pictures of then, what will they do?

What will I do?

CHAPTER 8
LIES

Tab's mother welcomed him with her usual effusive words of praise, sympathy, and encouragement before perfunctorily telling him she was leaving the next morning for a three-week cruise of the Bahamas with friends, which might or might not include a new boyfriend.

"If I'd known you didn't have a job, you could have joined us, I'm sure the ship's sold out," she told him.

"I'm OK," he assured her. "I need time to rest, make some plans." However, an all-expense paid-for-by-mom vacation would have been nice.

Now, alone these past few days, her apartment was stifling. Large pieces of furniture, too many knickknacks, the hardwood floors noisy to walk on. Slits of windows afforded views of Central Park. He wasn't interested in parks, hiking, running, or outdoor activity of any kind.

There was one good thing: Without her listening to all of his conversations, he was alone to hear or read every rejection in his search for another job. Even in New York City, the poisonous vapors following him from D.C. were penetrating the walls of every law firm. From emails to phone calls, the answers followed the same script: "No, we're not taking resumes at this time;" "No, we have no openings;" "You need at least ten years' experience." (Which, of course, Tab didn't).

Tab spent this morning of unemployment looking through various files on his laptop. Most were briefs of a few cases, some signed contracts, nothing to help him score at least an interview.

Except, perhaps, one. A big ranch owner from Wyoming called the firm two years ago. Al Ebbers was his name, he had big plans to expand, and needed a good D.C. law firm to "get her done," as he told them via various follow-up phone calls. Something about a land trade with the government.

Two of the partners planned a trip to meet him, get a better idea of what he needed. They were promised a good time, hunting, fishing, relaxing in a ranch house. They saw pictures, the "house" was opulent, a real gentleman's lodge.

Before anything happened came the news Al was dead, their services no longer required. It was a minor blow to the firm, there were other clients to woo, legal lives went on.

Scrolling through the sparse documents, the pictures, and his notes, Tab found himself wondering if there might be a possibility there.

Wyoming? He searched for a map, noted Cheyenne was the capital, then found the town where the Ebbers ranch was on the other side of the state. Here was the old man's obituary, and several articles. One jumped out at him.

The head of a big livestock association, Jack Brinkle, was quoted in the Wyoming Big Mountain Daily. *"This is a tragic loss," Brinkle said. "Al Ebbers was a third-generation cattleman, one of the best there was, knew his ranch. Can't say enough good things about him."* Brinkle went on to say he was concerned about the Double B's future. *"I know his grandson is the only heir, we're not hearing good things about what he's planning to do. Seems he's inviting a bunch of eco-terrorists in, and if he does, this young man don't know what he's getting into."*

Tab searched for the name *Jack Brinkle*, confirming the guy was still president of the group, then searched for the Double B Ranch. Several results came up, including an article from a Denver newspaper.

Historic Wyoming Ranch Makes
New Plans, Raises Eyebrows

The article went on to say the ranch was in the process of being analyzed as a sanctuary for wild horses and a habitat for endangered species.

"We're only in the preliminary stage," stated Phillip Ebbers, who inherited the ranch from his grandfather. "We're involving a wide range of experts, including Dr. Faith Jergens, one of the leading scientists on equine genetics. Plans are being made to build a conference center to host symposiums and conferences. I'm excited about the future of the Double B."

Tab made some notes on a pad, and sat back.

It was after noon in Wyoming, he thought. He found the name of Brinkle's group, The Greater Tetons and Western States Cattlemen's Association, and a phone number.

He knew making this call was a long shot. He was running out of options.

Mind made up, bucking up his courage, he quickly dialed the

number; a man answered.

"My name's Tab Taggart calling from Washington D.C." He used his full name, and figured the location, [even though it was a lie] would impress a country local yokel. "Is Mr. Brinkle in?"

"Yes, he is, hold a minute, please," came the crisp reply.

Brinkle came on the line, a hesitant "Yes" in a gravelly voice.

"Tab Taggart here, I'm calling from Washington, D.C. My law firm is following up on some files we have about Mr. Al Ebbers and the Double B Ranch. We'd met with him before his untimely passing concerning some land issues. We're cleaning house, so to speak, wondering if we should archive his folder. Your name came up as a good person to contact."

[Almost all of the above was a lie.]

"Oh, yes, Al mentioned hiring a big lawyer-lobbyist firm to represent him." Brinkle now sounded relaxed, on common ground. "I didn't know he'd got so far."

"We were actually getting ready to go to Wyoming," Tab assured him [which was the truth]. "I was really looking forward to meeting him." [That was a lie.]

Brinkle chuckled. "Al loved showing off his ranch to tenderfoots."

Tab had no idea what a tenderfoot was.

"Well, I don't want to bother you, take up your time, we're doing some due diligence before we send those files over to our archives. Once they're there, in my experience, it takes a lot of time to find them again." The inference was it would also take a lot of money.

"No, you're not bothering me at all. So, you're a lawyer, then?"

"Yes, sir."

"You know, it might be a good thing you called today. We have lots of questions about what the government's doing, and we don't like what's going on with Al's ranch, either. Maybe we could use some advice. I take it you're up on grazing leases and whatnot, since you were working with Al, right?"

"Of course. You bet."

[Another lie.]

"Ever been to Wyoming, son?"

"Yes, I have friends who used to live in Cheyenne. They owned a cabin outside Jackson."

[Yet another lie; unlike the others, this one could never be checked.]

"Listen," the sound of a chair squeaking, "if you have time, can you get away from your cushy law firm, maybe come on out here in a few days? I don't like those Internet camera meetings, I'm old-school, need to meet a man face-to-face. I know how this works, we'll send you a plane ticket to Jackson, put you up in a nice hotel. We'll talk, see if there's a good fit. Plan on being here five or six days."

Tab swallowed hard. This was too good to be true. He steadied himself. "I'm looking at my calendar now, I'm about to leave for New York [he was already there, Brinkle didn't know that.] I suppose I can fly out from there?"

"Wonderful, perfect. I'll have my assistant text you the ticket and where you'll be staying. He'll also send you some information on what we're about, what we're needin' to do. Lots to see, lots to talk about."

The call ended. Adrenaline coursed through Tab's body. He gave the air a double-fisted celebratory wave and forced himself to breathe.

A long shot. And pay dirt.

Steady, Tab, he told himself. This was only a meeting, a job interview. He would have to finesse the details about how he was no longer with the law firm, but there was time to come up with a plausible story.

Jack Brinkle tapped his fingers on his desk. He could tell Taggart was young, maybe a little green. Good. He could be impressed, molded into the kind of lawyer Jack needed for these times.

He fixed his eyes on the scenery outside the large window opposite his desk. The Grand Tetons a hundred miles distant, outlined against a blue sky. He loved those mountains, loved Wyoming, loved being a cattleman.

He had seen a lot of changes in his seventy years, and the ones in the last few years troubled him. A lot of the land was being bought by people who didn't appreciate how the state's livestock industry made it productive, despite harsh winters, and scorching winds of summer. They wanted to "conserve" and "protect" which meant men like Jack Brinkle weren't wanted, or needed.

What particularly rankled Jack, however, was the Double B. For three generations it was a cattle ranch, pure and simple. He'd watched Al's grandson grow up, figured the boy was cut from the same cloth. He should have continued the traditions. But no, the boy was intent on turning it into some harebrained scheme to "conserve" and "protect."

Jack tried to set up meetings with Phillip, bring him into the cattleman's association, take him under his wing. He was rebuffed each time. Too busy, he'd been told, out of town, he'd been told. Perhaps next year, he'd been told.

Nobody—*nobody*—ever said "no" to Jack. His jaw clenched at the thought.

He looked for ways to shut the Double B down, even asking his long-time lawyers in Cheyenne to look into it. Maybe a hot shot lawyer from back East was what they needed. Fresh eyes, some experience with federal laws. A go-getter, not afraid to cut some corners, throw dirt in some eyes, even ram it down their throats.

This Tab Taggart might be the one to do it. He'd find out in a couple of days.

CHAPTER 9
HORSE COUNTRY

"We're keeping the lights down for Autumn," Becky told Joe in a low voice. "She hasn't woken up from the anesthesia."

Autumn was lying on a thick bed of straw, legs folded underneath, her nose close to the floor. Becky knelt near the horse's mouth, making sure the mare was breathing regularly.

Next, she moved to the small figure near the mare and smiled.

"Look what Autumn did."

Joe knelt down, moving his hands across the foal's back. "Almost a miracle."

Skylar blinked her eyes, struck by the pungent odor of the barn. She peeked out from behind Lacaria.

"A baby horse," Skylar whispered.

Her aunt brought the girl around to get a better look. The foal lay on the straw, his head was down and it wobbled back and forth.

Sitting only inches away was a red dog.

"That's Corky," Becky waved to him. "I think he's appointed himself the foal's nana, hasn't left his side."

"Is he OK? His head is so large." Skylar bent down to get a closer look.

Joe laughed. "Perfectly normal."

"It's one of the reasons why horses sometimes have a little problem giving birth," Becky added. "Autumn needed more than a little, she needed a lot of help." She explained what Dr. Shultz had done, the procedure, and the worry. "A lot of stress in this barn, let me tell you."

"The pictures you sent didn't do him justice." Joe continued to stroke the foal. "Have you thought of a name, yet?"

Becky shook her head.

"Something regal, heroic," Lacaria suggested. "How about Alexander?"

Becky laughed. "I like it. Alexander the Great."

Joe said, "He's gorgeous, like his grandpa."

"Who's his grandpa?" Skylar asked.

"Warrior, one of the most amazing wild horses in this part of the country," Joe answered. "Of course, his daddy isn't a slouch, either."

Lacaria bent down to stroke Autumn's muzzle. "Neither is his beautiful mama. You always surprise us, don't you, Autumn."

"Can I touch him?" Skylar pointed to the foal.

Becky opened the gate. "Better yet, you can feed him."

Skylar gasped, looking back at Lacaria, who laughed. "Go ahead. You're smack dab in the middle of horse country. No better way to get introduced to the chores around here."

Becky grabbed the jug of formula from a shelf and handed it to Skylar. "He's only a few hours old and needs to be taught how to nurse," she instructed Skylar. "Guide it into his mouth, gently, we need to make sure he knows how to suckle. Tilt the jug a little."

Together they inserted the nipple into the foal's mouth. After a couple of tries, he began to suck on it, gradually at first, then greedily.

"He's taking it!" Skylar was thrilled. If this was a chore, she loved it. "How often do you feed him?"

"About every hour or two for the next few days. Hopefully, we'll have Autumn on her feet. She'll start to lactate and he can nurse off of her. We'll have to wait and see."

Lacaria reached down to stroke Autumn's neck. "Doesn't she need to wake up soon?"

Becky nodded. "I hope she'll rouse herself later today. I'll check her lungs, and if I hear any congestion, we'll try to wake her up, get her on her feet." She pointed to the bales of straw stacked up against the wall. "We'll move them around on either side of her, cushioning her in case she falls down."

"I'll come back after I drive Lacaria and Skylar home," Joe said. "Looks like you need some rest."

Becky agreed. "It's been a hectic morning."

"You need to go out in the field," Becky told Dot. "You've been a faithful nursemaid, couldn't have done any of this without you." She smiled, watching the older mare saunter outside.

Corky, on the other hand, would not be dislodged from his post near the foal.

She appreciated Joe's offer to return after lunch. Why didn't Phillip? Why wasn't he here? Sure, he said he'd come back before evening, hours away. Why was Joe the one to see how tired she was? Why hadn't Phillip?

She sank down into the straw next to Autumn. She needed to put these silly school girl thoughts away. Phillip loved her. She loved him. Later they'd have a nice, long talk.

It was time to check the horse's heart and lungs again with her scope. She bent her head to listen.

The drive from the MacKendrick's farm to the Double B was short.

Skylar rolled down her window to get a better view of the green fields bordered by well-maintained fencing. A glimmer of water was in the distance. "You have lakes?"

Lacaria nodded. "We have several on the ranch, for irrigation and wildlife."

The truck turned into a wide, circular courtyard. On the far side was a two-story house made of stone and gleaming timbers. The house was immense, with two wings on either side of a high, double-door entry. The girl gaped in surprise. This was not an old, rickety farmer's shack. This rivaled anything she might see in some of the more posh neighborhoods in Los Angeles.

Three all-terrain vehicles were parked near a garage.

"You have ATVs?" Skylar pointed to them. "You don't, uhm, ride the range with horses?"

Joe laughed. "Not these days. ATVs are cheaper, go places horses can't go."

"We still have a few horses," Lacaria added. "Just for pleasure, not for working."

The inside of the house was even more impressive. The living room was the center room with a twenty-foot ceiling. Leather-bound chairs and sofas, and solid wood tables, filled the room in a haphazard manner. Rugs of various sizes dotted the floor. Dozens of western paintings in ornate frames were prominent features. The windows on the far side were almost as high, rising from the floor, capped off by an arch of pine and glass. Mountains to the north provided a sweeping view.

A redwood deck jutted from the outside of the living room, with many lounge chairs and benches. Further on was a building under construction. Workmen were entering or leaving, carrying boxes and supplies.

A young man stepped in from the deck door. Lacaria made the introduction, Phillip extended his hand.

"Happy to meet you," he smiled. "Hope you like being here this summer, don't get bored. I'm sure it's a lot different than L.A."

Skylar saw several boxes in a corner of the living room and recognized the logos.

"Those are drones!"

"We have several, different sizes. This one's new, got it last week," Phillip said, hefting a large box from the top to open it. Inside was a large drone with ten propellers. "We'll be using this for some high-tech surveying. Have you ever operated one?"

The teen shook her head. "I've seen videos, they're fascinating."

"We'll be taking this out in the next day or two, you can come with us if you want."

Skylar nodded vigorously.

Phillip turned back to Lacaria. "Did you see Autumn and her foal? I'll go back later tonight, we're taking turns watching them."

"Joe will help, too," Lacaria laughed. "You should have seen the look on his face."

They all turned as one when Joe called from the staircase. "Skylar's suitcase is in her room. I'll make us some sandwiches."

Skylar hadn't given a thought to where she would be sleeping. Her aunt motioned her to the top of the staircase.

"We have eight bedrooms up here, four on each side. One is reserved for Dr. J, our resident chief scientist. She lives in Boulder, stays here when visiting, holding meetings, or appearing on our podcast in person."

Another finger pointed further down the hall. "That's Phillip's room, and the others are for guests."

They moved to the other side of the vast upstairs area.

"Thought we'd put you here, we have four guest bedrooms on this side so you can switch if you want."

She opened the door to the corner suite. Skylar's eyes grew large. This was four times the size of her bedroom at home. Several paintings of landscapes, some with horses and dogs, graced the walls. Large windows afforded views of the west and north, sun beams crowding onto the hardwood floor. There was a queen-sized bed, two large chests of drawers, several chairs, a desk, and glory be! a computer with two large monitors.

She dared not ask if she could use it, surely her parents told Joe and Lacaria she wasn't allowed.

Her aunt's next words dispelled that notion.

"If you need help," she pointed at the taboo equipment, "let us know. The Wi-Fi password is in the drawer."

An open door on the other side indicated a bathroom. Her own bathroom? She stepped on gleaming tiles and moved her hand over the vanity. A double-sized walk-in shower would be all hers, too.

"Your uncle and I have our own quarters on the other side of the kitchen, you're welcome to visit us anytime. We're pretty informal around here.

"I'll let you unpack," Lacaria was leaving the room. "Joe will have lunch ready in a few minutes, I bet you're hungry."

Alone, Skylar ran to the bed and jumped on it.

A baby horse. ATVs. Drones. Her own room, fancier than anything she could have imagined. A computer with Wi-Fi.

Worst summer ever? Not even.

"See? All that worry for nothing," Lacaria told her husband later in their apartment. "I think she's nice. Smart, too, she knows when to ask questions and listens to the answers."

"You're right. I guess I was thinking about all those teenagers we see on the Internet, on TV. Mouthy, cursing, yelling, dressing weird."

"Your sister and her husband have done a nice job raising her."

Joe stretched out on the couch. "She seems to like it here. No way she'll get into any trouble," he chuckled. "Smack dab in the middle of horse country."

CHAPTER 10
DREAMS

Autumn grunted. Or, she thought she grunted. She wasn't sure.

She remembered the pain, overwhelming to the point where she could hardly think clearly. All she wanted to do was to get rid of the hurt, go back to a place and time when she was happy.

Her mind gave her a dream, but was it a dream?

A harsh, angry human. Bad food. Bad water. Left alone, in the desert. Almost killed. Saved by her Silver Moon, then taken away by another human, Becky. This human loved her, took care of her, and gave Autumn the greatest miracle she ever received: a choice.

The dream swirled. She's standing close to Silver Moon, so close they were almost one. The feel of his body next to hers, warm, loving, as he reached over to nudge her neck, nickering softly.

Nights and days. Days and nights. Galloping through lush grass, jumping over logs and rocks. Smelling flowers and trees, even the air paraded its own odor, sweet and enticing.

Exhilarating to the sound of their hooves pounding the earth, a sound like no other. Faster, faster, faster, strength she never knew she had, coursing through her legs. Flinging her head up in a display of defiance.

"See me, know me. I am Autumn, beloved of the mighty stallion Silver Moon, and together we own this land."

This! This is what it felt like to be wild and free.

The dream swirled again. Something was making her push, hard. Push push push. A wet sound, seemed like there was something urgent, a swirl of human hands. Then, calm. She was aware enough to know there were humans nearby, looking at her with worry.

The dream faded. Autumn felt hands, bringing love. Gentle, affectionate, a soothing voice.

Autumn opened her eyes.

"There you are, my beautiful girl." A whisper. Becky's face came into view.

Autumn tried to move her head. Becky put a gentle hand on her muzzle. "Take it easy. You've been through a lot."

The pain was gone. Her thoughts were jumbled, barely remembering her journey to Becky.

Another sensation hit her. She smelled the odor of her baby "His name is Alexander," Becky told her.

She heard the gruffing of familiar horses. Autumn answered back. "Hello, Dot and Max."

"I'm here, too." Corky padded in and sat down next to Becky.

It was enough to satisfy her, at least for now. Tomorrow would be another day, and time for the world to tell her what to do next.

She closed her eyes.

CHAPTER 11
LILY GULCH

Bang! And another bang! Metal corral panels flew from the lowboy trailer onto the ground. For good measure, and because it helped satisfy his anger, Harold Franklin flung another piece from the trailer into the dirt.

He paused for a moment to look around. Harold was on his own, his teammate calling in sick. He was in a remote area known as Lily Gulch, far away from any town, farm, or ranch.

The contractor-issued truck had barely made it here on the rough, rocky road, worsening his mood. Patches of deep sand almost bogged it down and the truck bounced and rattled in protest when Harold gunned the motor to escape any possibility of stalling out.

He hefted the last of the metal fencing from the trailer, and jumped down to begin putting them together. It was an arduous task fitting the heavy pieces together with long linchpins, one after the other, to form a large square.

Two hours later, sweating and still in a foul mood, he stopped to eat his lunch, a ham sandwich and chips. Sitting in the cab of the truck with the air conditioning on full blast, he realized his anger was becoming a problem. Sometimes the tirades were barely in check, almost lashing out at his bosses. He couldn't catch a break, no matter how hard he tried or how hard he worked.

His run of bad luck began two years before when Al Ebbers hired him to dig a reservoir on his high meadow. Everything went really wrong, really fast. How could he know the biggest thunderstorm of the century would bring down a mountain, flooding Silver Moon Canyon, destroying everything in its path?

Harold escaped blame, and possible legal problems, simply because Ebbers kept his word, nobody knew what he was doing, or who he was. Then Ebbers went and got himself killed, stiffing Harold of the other five thousand dollars owed to him. What made matters worse, his brother said he owed him for a piece of junk backhoe he'd borrowed, and lost in the flood.

For a year, Harold drifted from New Mexico to Arizona, working any job he could find, staying out of Wyoming, until last year he got this job rounding up wild horses in Utah and Colorado.

Harold bought a horse for a hundred bucks, rode well enough to get the job done. Even shot an injured horse or two, putting them out of their misery. He was getting a good reputation, too, a promotion, easy money, working outdoors.

One afternoon, finishing a roundup of eighty horses, his horse stalled and threw him off, breaking his left arm.

Eight weeks later, he sold the horse for fifty dollars, didn't care what happened to him, thought he could return to his old job, but was told, sorry, no more roundups for you (the inference was he didn't know how to ride a horse.) He could, however, set up bait traps. It was less money, hardly any travel, still a paycheck, and he was back in Wyoming. That made him nervous.

It would have to do until he found another job. He'd start looking in a few weeks.

Lunch eaten, he set to the task of lugging ten bales of fresh, sweet hay to the far side of the corral, which was the trap. The hay was the "bait."

The premise was simple. Wild horses could smell hay from miles away, and approach the trap. Some might be cautious, would not even enter, others would be hungry for the treat they would normally not have in their natural diet.

Harold, and hopefully with his co-worker, would add to the hay and watch on a bluff nearby day after day. When there were fifteen or twenty (hopefully more) horses, they would hurry down to close the gate, and call the livestock hauler in to load them up.

The gate was the last connection. The piece was heavy. With a mighty effort, he man-handled it into the hinges.

Several minutes—and many grunts—later, Harold got the last pin in and stepped around to inspect the corral, testing each section to make sure they were upright and solid in the ground.

He returned to the truck to get the long rod that would be inserted on the edge of the gate and hammered into the ground to ensure it stayed open.

The truck was empty, no rod. He looked on the trailer, still no rod.

He must have missed it when he loaded the truck at the shop.

The gate needed to stay open or the horses couldn't get in the trap. He decided a large rock would do the trick. He found one the size of a football to prop up. Yes, that would hold until he returned the next morning with the rod.

He pulled out his cell phone to upload the GPS coordinates of the trap to the bureau's website. He grimaced when he realized he hadn't uploaded the locations of the other fifty traps he'd set these past few weeks. Leaning against the truck, he batched them onto the form, and clicked the upload button. Hopefully his supervisor wouldn't catch his forgetfulness. Besides, he knew everybody forgot from time to time, no big deal.

Job done, he started the truck, and drove away.

Shielded by large boulders, Juno stood on a bluff, watching the strange goings-on below her.

She was leery of the sounds the man brought with him, but the smell of the fresh hay was enticing.

Maybe she'd go down to the bottom of the gulch tomorrow.

The human gone, she left the bluff to join her family in the verdant meadow.

CHAPTER 12
THE COFFEE WRANGLER

Tab searched the Internet for information and government documents—federal, state, or local—concerning grazing leases, fees, controversies, and complaints, and there were *a lot* of controversies and complaints, mostly from environmental groups. All of which he found superbly boring.

True to his word, Brinkle's assistant texted plane tickets as well as rental car and hotel confirmations. He texted his mom to let her know he was going out of town (no specifics, and she didn't reply).

He packed his best, most expensive suit, dress shoes, sneakers, and a short-sleeved shirt and khakis.

He flew from New York City to Denver, then caught a small commuter to Jackson Hole Airport, where his car waited. It was an economy. He passed several luxury vehicles, considered changing the reservation on his own credit card, before deciding an upgrade would not be a "good look."

Bags loaded, he entered his destination in the GPS system, and drove out of the Jackson Hole parking area.

Wyoming, he soon discovered, was unlike any state along the eastern seaboard.

He was accustomed to huge cities digging into the ground with high buildings, thick asphalt, the ever-present noise of traffic and construction, and millions of people on a single square block.

He passed a few small towns, sparse buildings, some people walking about.

Fields of who-knew-what-was-being-grown were on either side of the highway, even these seemed small and condensed, almost as though they were waiting to be taken over by tall pine trees.

Groups of cows, some pure black or brown, others white, stood on the other side of fences. He remembered reading about specific breeds and he imagined if he got this job, he would have to learn what they were, something else he would have to pretend interest in.

Large houses, some two-story, marred the landscape. Many looked new. Ranchettes for the wealthy, a few acres, and the obligatory horse or three, and yes, there they were, grazing on tall grass, swishing long tails back and forth.

Every few miles he saw yellow signs warning of wildlife crossings. A fierce wind began to rock his car, forcing him to grip his steering wheel to stay on the road. Dust and tumbleweeds chased each other across the road

The outside temperature was cool, the sky clear and sunny, not oppressively hot and humid like New York City or D.C. were this time of year.

Two hours later, he found his hotel. The sound of drills and hammers assailed him. He asked the office clerk, an older woman whose nametag said "Rachel," about the construction.

"Adding on," she answered, "doubling our rooms. Getting ready for the opening of the big conference center down the road, the Double B. Going to bring lots of business to our little town."

The room was suitable in tones of light brown and beige. A faux painting of a cattle drive with horses and appropriately-dressed cowhands dominated one wall.

He quickly unpacked, hung his suit up and smoothed out any wrinkles. Would he be over-dressed for Brinkle? he wondered. His meeting with the rancher was in the morning, giving him plenty of time to stress over what he considered an important detail.

Downstairs, he asked Rachel for recommendations on where to eat.

"If you're looking for fancy sit-down, the Riata's pretty good. If you want something like sandwiches, The Coffee Wrangler's open until six," was the answer. "It's down the road, you can see the sign from here."

Tab nodded his thanks, deciding a sandwich would be good, he could check out the "fancy" restaurant tomorrow. As he walked away, he looked around. High mountains dominated the eastern vista. A river was somewhere to the west.

He saw the sign to The Coffee Wrangler below another: *Organic Grocery Store* near an outdoor patio. A few people sat at wooden tables, eating and chatting. He went inside to order.

Several rustic tables with matching rustic chairs were scattered about. The place smelled like fresh brewed coffee, spices, and the tantalizing aroma of fresh bread.

Two large television screens were on to sporting events, a safe choice.

The walls drew his attention. They were covered with photos of horses, all in frames, some large, some small. Horses grazing, close-ups of horses. Many of the photos featured adult horses with their young, or young horses cavorting and playing.

It seemed to Tab every color a horse could possibly be was represented. Black, white, brown, red. Black and white. Brown and gray. Dark manes and tails, white manes and tails.

A door from the kitchen opened and a young woman stepped out, balancing two trays of food.

Plates were jostled as he almost ran into her. He held out a hand to help her support them.

She smiled up at him. "Thank you! Almost a disaster for me to clean up."

"No," he stammered. "My fault, I should have looked where I was going." And then he did look—at her.

Long, red hair, startling blue eyes. A blanket of freckles across her nose. She smiled again and it threw him off, his thoughts out somewhere looking for a way back into his head.

She was dressed in a dark blue blouse and jeans, loosely comfortable and nicely molded around her figure. Her nametag said "Becky." Unconsciously, he looked down at her shoes, surprised to see sandals.

She followed his gaze and rewarded him with another smile. "Caught you. Betcha you were looking for my cowboy boots. You're not from around here, are you?" A light tease.

"You're right, and you can probably tell from my accent, too." He teased her right back. *What am I doing?*

"Ha! New York, I bet. A real tenderfoot." She stepped away to deliver the plates to her customers, and returned to him. "You can sit wherever you want, inside or out. What do you want to drink?"

He looked inside, most of the tables were empty. He opted for inside near a large window; menus were in a stand. "I'll take some water," he said. He watched Becky go to the counter and fill a glass with ice and water.

"So, New York, what can I get you?"

"I'll take a ham on rye," he answered. "And I didn't say I was from New York."

"You're right. Where you from?"

He smiled coyly. "New York."

They laughed together and Tab liked the sound of both of them sharing a joke. *I don't know this girl,* he chided himself, *but maybe I want to.*

"I'm Tab Taggart." He extended a hand to shake.

"Becky MacKendrick."

A few minutes later she returned to him with his sandwich. He contrived several questions to ask. The first one was easy.

"Does the wind always blow this bad around here?"

She nodded. "Oh yeah, today isn't bad, but some days? You can't see out the windows. We have our standard bit of advice, before you paint your house ask your neighbor what color he wants his."

He laughed. That *was* funny.

"What do people do around here—when the wind isn't blowing?"

She looked him over. He hadn't changed and was still wearing a white shirt, black slacks, and casual leather shoes.

"I'm guessing you're not into mountain biking?"

He shook his head.

"Fly fishing?"

Another headshake.

"How about rock climbing, hiking?"

"Looks like I'll have lots of time to work." He was about to tell her he was an attorney, when a voice from the counter interrupted their conversation.

"Becks, are you about ready to leave? Your father called, don't forget to pick up baby formula from Dr. Shultz."

"I'll leave right now, Mom."

Tab heard the exchange. He realized he hadn't looked for a wedding ring. A baby? His hopes sank.

"You have *a baby*?"

"Yup, the four-legged kind, about this high," she held up a hand to her hips, "and eats like a horse, because he is."

"Ah," a relieved sigh. Tab waved at the photos on the walls. "I take it horses are a big thing around here."

"Oh, you have no idea. We're proud of our wild horse herds, people come from all over the world to see them.

"I gotta run. Meg, the other waitress, will take care of you."

Now he not only needed to get the job, he *wanted* to.

Wyoming, he decided, might not be so bad after all.

But he'd have to look up the meaning of the word "tenderfoot." He guessed it wasn't particularly complimentary.

CHAPTER 13
GUILT

Joe eased himself down into the straw. "Let's take a good look at you, shall we?" he whispered to Alexander.

The foal flicked his ears as if he knew what was being said. "You have kind of a big name for such a little guy, I bet you're going to grow into it."

"Dr. Shultz said we might allow Autumn to go outside, maybe stretch her legs a little if she wants. On a lead, of course, don't want her to get frisky. But," Tess chuckled, "not sure she's up to 'frisky' yet."

"She's been through a lot, hasn't she," Joe turned his attention to the palomino who was standing patiently near her wall of straw. She nickered as he stroked her neck. "When will she be able to nurse the little guy?"

"Hopefully in a day or two, I think her nipples are swelling, a good sign."

"When's his next feeding?"

"Before you came in, I fed him, so give it another two hours. Maybe. He might tell you he wants a bottle before that. He's a pushy child." She turned to go, telling him she'd be in the house if he needed anything.

Alone with the foal, he clicked his tongue. Alexander stood up, legs still wobbly. He stared at Joe with large, doleful eyes.

"You don't know it, your mommy and daddy are two of the most famous horses in the world—and your grandpa? His name is Warrior."

Is. Present tense. Joe always used the present tense when talking about Warrior. He could never bring himself to refer to the great stallion of Desert Oak Basin in the past tense.

Warrior is still alive, he told himself. *I know it.*

Joe wasn't there when Warrior and his family were taken, hadn't seen the carnage and death first-hand.

Back then he was still a ranch foreman, a cattleman, for one of the largest outfits in Wyoming. Working for Al Ebbers, a name meaning status, wealth, and generations of Wyoming ranchers.

It also meant he went along with, *believed* the ranchers' creed: Nothing could threaten their livelihood, their existence, their rights to use the land any way they wanted. Leases, government lands, were fenced for a reason, to let their livestock graze on whatever scrub plants they could find, every year, all year long in some places. And to keep everyone else, everything else, out.

Al lived the creed all his life, and when Joe went to work for him, Joe did, too.

Joe was good at his job, grew up around livestock, sheep in Utah, cattle on Colorado's Uncompahgre. He was a quiet and capable cowboy.

Al's wife was sick, cancer. A few months later she was dead. Joe was called to the office. Al's son, Bryan, was a teenager, the two men needed a woman around.

"Your wife, she can come to work here, too. I'm going to need somebody to take care of the place, keep up the house, cook for us."

A couple of rooms were being added adjacent to the big ranch house. "This way you'll be close to the ranch, close to me."

Deal done, Joe and Lacaria moved in three months later.

Joe supervised ranch hands during high seasons, making sure the cattle were grazed, fattened, and ready for auction in the fall.

Before he realized it, he was a cattleman. And his loyalty to Al Ebbers ran deep.

So much so when his boss told him to move a fence line on a grazing allotment a few hundred feet, because "nobody will notice it."

So much so when his boss told him to adjust a setting on an irrigation line to deliver more water than he was legally allowed, because "nobody will miss it."

So much so when his boss and other ranchers talked about shooting wild horses because "nobody will care," Joe understood, and agreed.

Wild horses. The term was snorted in derision by Al. "They're invasive, like weeds, need to be put down, taken out."

Deals with the devil—the United States Government—were struck. Wild horses were eating all of the grass, leaving cows to starve. The American consumer was told beef prices would skyrocket. And they believed it.

Year after year, thousands of wild horses were captured. The livestock industry smirked, if bleeding heart horse lovers wanted to save them, they could, buy them from the holding pens. "Adopt a Wild Horse" became a PR campaign.

Many people who adopt horses don't know they're expensive to keep. Year after year, there were many failures, few successes.

Then Desert Oak Basin happened.

The day Joe came face to face with the truth.

The day guilt and regret began to consume his soul.

Joe was a cattleman, no reason to be there, no reason to watch. Cattlemen didn't bother to watch wild horses rounded up.

But others were there. Phillip saw it all. When he came home, he confronted Al, furious his grandfather was part of the slaughters, even ordering them.

"You've betrayed me for the last time," Al hurled those words at his grandson, telling him to get out. Hours later, Al was dead.

A few days passed. Joe decided to watch Dr. J's video, uncut, unedited, find out for himself what Phillip had seen.

Mustangs running at breakneck speed, trying to get away from the helicopter in the air and wranglers on the ground. The horses were chased into the corrals, packed together, swirling in confusion and fear. They jumped on one another, trying to see their families. They weren't exhausted; their panic gave them adrenaline—and fury.

At least a hundred mares were in the corrals set up for them, churning the dirt, screaming for their colts, fillies, and stallions. More than a dozen stallions were herded into the wrong holding pen, the much smaller one set up for the younger horses. Several of the little ones were trapped with them.

Hooves smashed the metal rails. Two of the stallions were able to topple it, leaving the tiny babies on their own, trying to get to their mothers. Five of them were crushed to death in the melee.

A stallion tried to get into the pen where the mares were, his legs caught in the gaps. He went down, both front legs broken. Agonizing screams filled the air until a wrangler shot him in the head.

The colts and fillies were frantic to get away from the stallions' hooves, back into the open. One of them wriggled free on her stomach, and scooted under the rail. A leg bone protruded from the skin. Another shot from a rifle and she lay still.

The mares spun around in confusion, several trying to jump over the rails, none having the strength or height. They fell back into the dirt with heavy thuds.

Two of the stallions managed to topple over the rails. A solid black mustang galloped away with a wrangler in pursuit.

The other, a pinto, stumbled a short distance before falling. He tried to get back up, fell again, his head flopping unnaturally. His neck was broken. Again and again, he tried, and failed, to stand up.

"I can't watch anymore." Joe recognized Becky's voice in the video. Crack. Another rifle shot.

The camera zoomed in on one horse: Warrior, one of the most well-known mustangs, a large dappled gray with a black mane and tail.

Warrior reared up on his hind legs, again and again.

"He's looking for his mares." Another, voice, Dr. J's, shouting above the melee. "His family."

More than a dozen mares, acting as one, toppled the gate and escaped down the chute. One of them fell into the hurricane fencing and rolled into it. Legs flailing, she tried to get back up but was caught between two metal poles. She fell again, this time impaled. A gut-wrenching scream split the air.

The helicopter appeared, descending straight down, then hovered.

A single shot rang out from the dome.

Blood sprayed up and over for several feet in all directions. The mare's body went limp.

An hour later, the horses who survived were loaded into trailers and taken away.

Warrior was one of them.

The video ended. Joe lost all sense of time, his mind going back and forth between the man he was and the man he wanted to be.

Phillip was taking the Double B in an entirely new direction, no longer a ranch, no longer focused on cattle. He wanted Joe to share his vision.

Joe loved Phillip like a son. Could he get over his guilt after seeing the horror of Desert Oak Basin?

He decided the only way he could, the only way to earn redemption, was to find as many of those horses as he could. He began to search the Internet for horse sanctuaries, the holding corrals, and even the killing pens where he discovered most of the wild horses ended up. It was sickening information.

With Phillip's support, and Double B money, over the next few months Joe found more than a hundred of the horses from the basin roundup.

Some were taken by prisons for training, a practice begun many years ago and was rife with controversy. Horses abused, horses dying of infections; disease seemed common in the prison yards.

Several were adopted by "good homes" but Joe found those good homes were not always the case. Horses could still be abused, mistreated, and eventually sold to slaughter houses for horsemeat.

If Joe doubted the intent of anyone adopting a horse, or its care, he bought it and arranged transport to one of the sanctuaries. Sometimes he only needed a few dollars for a horse, rarely more than fifty.

Phillip began the process to get the ranch approved as a wild horse sanctuary.

But one horse eluded the search.

Warrior.

He did not find him in any of the corrals, the killing pens, no record of any adoption.

He vanished like smoke after a fire.

Warrior's pictures, taken over the years when he was free and wild, were taped to walls and computer screens. So many false alarms. No, this horse was a mare. No, that horse has a gray mane. No, too small. Or too young. Or too old. Or was taken from the range before, or since.

It would have been easy to give up. The guilt Joe felt wouldn't let him.

Alexander was tired of standing and wobbled back to Joe. He fell with a grunt near his lap. Joe's resolve grew once again. He put his face down to the foal's muzzle and hugged his neck.

"I'm going to find your grandpa, baby boy. You deserve it. I don't, but you do."

CHAPTER 14
THE COLD TRAIL

Skylar scrolled through folders of videos and photo galleries, pausing from time to time to open one.

She was learning to brace herself for what showed up on her screen more often than not: horses getting chased into holding pens, some trampled to death, and several shot by men with pistols or rifles. Dozens of horses crammed into livestock trailers, crammed again into holding pens. Dust and blood everywhere.

The Double B was a new world, meeting these people who were so passionate about what they were doing with their lives.

I've actually never met many people at all. The thought made her grimace. Her world of video games and Internet "friends" hadn't prepared her for this. But, what could?

The front door opened, Skylar craned her neck to see Joe come into the living room.

"I'm in here, Uncle Joe," she waved.

"Where's everybody?"

"Aunt Lacaria and Phillip went to Pinedale. Not sure where Dr. J is."

She pointed to her computer screen. "I've been looking at these pictures, the videos, for a couple of days now. Can't get them out of my head."

Joe shuffled into a chair. "I'm the same way."

"I'm confused. All of these pictures on the wall, here," she pointed to the large corkboard above a table. "This is the same horse, right? Different angles, maybe when it was younger, older?"

"Warrior."

"Alexander's grandpa! Where is he?"

"We don't know. He was taken two years ago. He fought for his family, some of them escaped. He didn't. Ever since then I've been looking."

"How?"

The question made him blink. Indeed, *how*?

"The first few months there were a lot of sightings. We knew he'd been shipped to a holding facility in Nevada, I went there first. He was gone.

"Maybe he'd ended up in a prison compound, prisoners break the mustangs for saddle riding. Wasn't there, either. Not sure how many kill pens I went to. Oklahoma, Texas, Pennsylvania."

"Kill pens?"

"They stuff all kinds of livestock in those, horses, bulls, donkeys, goats. Old animals, animals no longer wanted for whatever reason. Hurt, sick. People can buy 'em for a few bucks, no questions asked, a lot go to slaughter houses in Mexico." He paused. "The meat goes to pet food, some people eat horse flesh, considered a delicacy in some parts of the world."

"And you think Warrior is gone? Dead?" She let the words drift between them.

Joe shook his head. "I can't accept that. But there have been no sightings for almost a year now."

"The trail's gone cold."

"Yeah. The trail's gone cold."

"You think he's still out there? Somewhere?"

"I hope so. I want to believe."

Skylar indicated the computer's screen. "How about we put him out there again, social media, emails, cross-post with a lot of other postings, get some fresh eyes on this, more people." She leaned back, staring at Warrior's pictures. "Flash them twenty, thirty times a day. I can research the best key words besides the obvious ones. Code in some algorithms."

Joe laughed. "Whoa, you're speaking a different language. Remember you're talking to an old cowboy here."

"Sorry, got taken away. I'll talk to Lacaria when she gets back, explain what I want to do." She had a far-away look on her face. "We'll call it *Operation Warrior: Bring Him Home.*"

She glanced at Joe. "We'll blaze a new trail. Across the World Wide Web."

For the first time in months, the ol' cowboy discovered some new hope.

CHAPTER 15
LUCKY

"The United States Government has created a medieval kind of feudal system."

That was the first sentence Dr. Faith Jergens spoke to Carl MacKendrick when they met more than a decade before.

They sat next to each other, an unfortunate pairing, at a conference in Seattle. He knew her reputation, a famous scientist, college professor, a leading voice for wildlife, especially wild horses. Always referred to as Dr. J.

Associates told him he was "lucky" to sit next to her even though he was warned she had a nasty reputation for drawing bureaucrats like him into an argument.

Despite his misgivings, he asked what she meant. "Cattlemen have come to believe they own millions of acres of public lands because they have a lease. Now, you and I know what a lease is, it's a piece of paper saying somebody can use something."

"Right," Carl agreed. "But they don't own it."

"They act like they do. They fence it. "

"Fences are necessary to keep animals in their allotments," he argued.

She continued. "They set up camping trailers."

He interrupted her again. "For seasonal workers."

"That somehow stay in place year-around. And, *Mr. MacKendrick,*" the formal usage of his name meant she was warming to her subject, "the leases are inherited, generation after generation, not available on the open market for bidding. These leases are even marketed as land actually owned by ranchers when they are selling their property."

"Look at almost any advertising almost anywhere," Dr. J pointed out. "The way they're worded would leave an uninformed person to think a ranch is larger than it is. For example, the property is a thousand acres, then they add 'another five hundred acres' rangeland or 'grazing rights.' The ad doesn't mention a lease, it's misleading."

He had seen some ads like that, but he never gave them much thought.

"Land that is not really owned, and is never taken away either. A 'wink wink' system of the 'haves' versus the 'have nots,' don't you think?"

Dr. J left their table. She had given him something to think about and her backward glance told him she knew it.

Carl MacKendrick graduated from a New Hampshire college and immediately went to work for the U.S. government's Bureau of Land

Management. They needed biologists, he was told, to monitor public lands, take samples, look for areas degraded by overuse. He liked the idea of working out in the field, traveling around the eastern seaboard, trekking through old-growth forests, and meeting fellow scientists.

When a job opened in Wyoming, he was reluctant to apply. He thought the state was mostly windy, mostly dry, and mostly flat. He knew Yellowstone National Park was in Wyoming, and not much more than that.

He quickly realized Wyoming *is more*. Besides mountains, the state also has high-altitude deserts, canyons, rivers, and lakes. Fierce winters deliver several feet of snow to some parts, while others seem to be in perpetual stages of drought.

The Wind River Mountains held mystery, the deserts teemed with life he did not know existed. He appreciated the fact there are no traffic jams, sunsets are world-class, unimaginable in the crowded over-grown eastern states.

He met Tess, a farmer's daughter and fell hopelessly in love with her. They got married, Becky was born two years later. Settling in as a family was good, making plans, days filled with happy challenges, long nights together watching their daughter, and each other, grow.

Tess opened an organic grocery store at the crossroads; her parents died close together, leaving this world after fifty years of a loving marriage, and leaving their only daughter their small farm and large house.

Carl's work was good. Most mornings he headed out with a survey crew to stake and mark lands rich with plants and animals he'd only seen in books.

Carl specialized in finding ecosystems at risk from development, disease, and the insidious new threat, climate change.

The bureau was good to him, with several promotions and nice pay raises. He was named district manager and before he knew it, paperwork covered his desk, and his life. Politics and the on-growing controversies of public land management consumed his time.

Hunters versus mountain bikers.

Energy companies versus environmentalists.

Community leaders versus old-time residents.

Cattlemen and wild horse advocates were the most difficult to deal with. The two fought bitterly over public lands. Public lands? It was a joke they actually belonged to the "public." The majority of Americans lived east of the Missouri River with no knowledge and little interest about what was happening in the western states.

Over the decades, cattlemen had become experts at taking advantage of the public's ignorance.

For a little more than a few dollars per head, cattle and sheep are grazed on public lands for several months, "parked" as it were, a cheap way to feed those animals grass and whatever else they could eat before they are herded into feed lots and ultimately, the meat markets.

Wild horses, the livestock industry decided, were a threat to cheap forage, and needed to be removed, eliminated, by whatever means necessary.

Dr. J did everything she could to stand in their way. Books, articles, featured as a guest speaker at conferences and meetings, she was one of the leading advocates for the mustangs.

The next few years presented him with many opportunities to spar with Dr. J. Often her points would make him grind his teeth, forcing him to watch his temper.

She was one of the reasons he hated his bureau job.

Now, sitting next to her on the airplane leaving Iceland, he was amazed at the remarkable turns in his life.

Indeed, he *had* been lucky to have met her all those years before.

The intercom announced they were approaching Salt Lake City. There would be a short layover before catching the commuter to Jackson.

Dr. J asked, "Is Becky back from college?"

"She texted me the night she got in." His phone chimed, a text from Tess.

"You and Dr. J will not believe what happened in our barn. See you soon. Becks sends loves!"

They looked at each other. "Good news or bad?" Dr. J asked.

Carl shook his head. "With those two, could be either."

CHAPTER 16
A DILEMMA

Autumn nuzzled Dr. Shultz's shoulder and sniffled.

"I know what you want, you can't have it," he chuckled. "Oat cakes are off-limits for you. You're a wildling now, and we got to watch your tummy."

The palomino looked away. "Don't pout. You're a grown lady, not a little brat."

She watched Alexander standing and wobble about. His legs soon gave out and he lay back down again. Autumn looked back at the veterinarian as if to ask, "Is this normal?"

He laughed. "He's still a bit weak, but he'll keep you busy sooner than you want. Stand still while I look at you." He patted her back and bent down to look at her nipples. "You're coming along nicely." He was pleased. Autumn was one of the more unusual patients he'd ever had. Abandoned two years ago, almost killed by a mountain lion, rescued by Becky, choosing to lead a wild life, beloved by Silver Moon.

Unusual, but loved by all, including Dr. Shultz. He needed to make a hard decision, and he didn't want to make it alone. "What can I do? What should I do?" he whispered.

Dr. Shultz was the county's only large animal veterinarian. When he graduated from college more than forty years ago, he went to work for the "old time" clinic in Pinedale, learning his chosen profession on the ground, in the barns, in corrals, wherever the animals were. Long nights in freezing temperatures, long days in sweltering heat. Helping mares, cows, and ewes give birth, tending to wounds the critters would get who knew how, diagnosing diseases, and giving the horrible news to owners when nothing could be done.

Putting an animal down was the worst part of the job.

Through the open barn window, he looked at a nearby hill where a sole cottonwood grew. Slash, Becky's prized, championship horse, was buried there. Telling her there was nothing he could do for her best friend, her future, was one of the hardest things he'd ever done.

Autumn snorted again, pawing at the barn floor.

Autumn. The little horse that changed lives. She was still changing them, returning to this barn, knowing she would get help, knowing her baby would be saved.

He knew most people would scoff at the idea a horse could be that smart. Dr. Shultz needed no convincing. Animals are clever, and their emotions show up in the most unexpected ways.

"Look who's back!" Becky exclaimed, leading the way for her father and Dr. J.

"This barn is Central Station, so many coming and going," Dr. Shultz smiled, shaking their hands.

"I am having a difficult time believing what I'm seeing." Dr. J shook her head.

"You should have been here the morning she showed up," Becky laughed. "Mom was sure we were all dreaming."

"Autumn and son are both doing well, considering what they've been through," Dr. Shultz assured them. "I took blood samples of both and the lab says they're clean, although Autumn has an iron deficiency. I've got her on supplements. And yes," he continued with a look at Dr. J. "I have several vials of blood from Alexander to send to your lab."

She nodded her appreciation. As a known descendant of Warrior and Silver Moon, Alexander's DNA was valuable.

"I'll never get his grandfather's, or Silver Moon's DNA, this will be the next best thing," she said.

"Speaking of the stallion, has he been by yet?" Carl asked.

Becky shook her head. "Not yet, we're on red alert all the time. I'm sure it will be any day now. Or, any hour."

"Do you think we can let them out of the barn soon?" she asked the vet.

"Let's wait until tomorrow. One more day. I still want them watched." He clapped Carl on the shoulder. "Now you're home, we have one more volunteer."

Carl pulled his luggage from the truck. Dr. J would be going on to the Double B to stay for a few days before heading to her home in Boulder.

Dr. Shultz put his medical bag in his own truck then hailed both of them.

"I'm glad you're home, especially now." He frowned with worry. "I have a dilemma and I don't know what to do. Autumn is my patient, and I have a duty to her. She will probably return to the wild?"

It was a question neither Carl nor Dr. J could answer.

He continued. "When she does, what happens? She and Silver Moon will mate again. Becky pointed out there didn't seem to be any issue with Sandy last year, but she was small, compared to Alexander."

"And if she has another foal as large, or larger?" Dr. J thought she knew where he was going. "You want to give her a fertility drug."

Carl's head snapped up. "Seriously? That's what you're thinking?"

"It's temporary, a year or two at the most, the newer drug might last longer. It also gives her a chance, a way to heal from this birth."

Such a little horse.

"We can't talk to Becky about this." A statement, not a question.

"No, we don't get her involved," Dr. J agreed. "We might be breaking a hundred rules."

"But," Carl reminded them, "no laws."

There was silence for several seconds, a minute, maybe two.

"What are the consequences?" Carl asked. "The government is decisive: No wild horses can be kept as 'pets' or domestics without being captured first, branded, and going through the arduous and time-consuming process of being available for adoption.

"Autumn, however, has chosen to be wild," the veterinarian took up the argument. "But because she returned to Becky, does this mean she is domesticated again? As her owner, Becky can dictate any kind of treatment for the mare, including fertility treatments."

"And if Autumn returns to her wild life? How would anybody know she's been injected, or which drug?" Dr. J bit her lower lip. "Just the three of us."

Carl nodded. "And we won't talk. None of us want to go to jail."

They laughed, breaking the tension.

"I won't tell you when, and I won't tell you what kind of treatment I'll give her," Dr. Shultz said. "I'll try to make sure we won't go to jail, either."

CHAPTER 17
ROCK ART

Shadows from the clouds skipped across the canyon walls. A trio of eagles soared in the sky, tossing high-pitched screams to each other.

Skylar held field glasses against her eyes, focusing on the rocks above her.

"I can make out several figures," the teen said, "some thin, others exaggerated with large circles around them. Squiggly figures might be snakes or lizards. There's a clear image of a scorpion. And a sheep with horns."

She swung the glasses to the edge of the rock where the head of an animal was painted red. Its mouth was spitting jagged rays in all directions.

"Is that smoke?" she asked. "Or blood?"

"We don't know, you can interpret it any way you want," Joe replied.

"I always thought it was yelling out a warning to keep us out of this canyon." Lacaria smiled. "It's haunted, you know."

The night before, Joe had suggested they take their niece out for a field trip to the canyon. "See the rock art, something she's never seen before. Take some pictures to send to her parents. We'll take the ATVs in the morning before it gets too hot." Skylar was thrilled.

The next morning, she was instructed on the rudiments of ATV operation. Joe led the way on his ATV, Lacaria drove hers behind Skylar's. They made their way slowly along a dirt road before parking at the mouth of the canyon for the short hike to see the rock art.

As they walked, Lacaria recited the *Legend of Silver Moon Canyon*: "One night the monster horse will rise up from his grave and murder all of the people who have abused or killed horses. And there's the Silver Moon." He pointed to the orb in the center of the rock. Its silver patina shimmered in the sun.

"I don't know about the canyon's monster horse," Joe chuckled. "But I know I never want to be in the middle of it during a flash flood. Been there, done that."

The memory of rescuing Becky, seeing her lying on the flat rock high above the water, not moving, clenched his stomach. Unimaginable relief when he lowered Phillip to reach her, seeing she was still alive, using all of his strength to get her, and him, from certain death before the ledge fractured and tumbled out of view. That had been two years ago, but Joe would never forget how close he had come to losing both of them.

Skylar interrupted his thoughts. "How did anybody get up there? It's fifty feet above the canyon floor."

"There was probably a way, a rock path, leading to a ledge right below it," Joe explained. "See all of the rocks here at the bottom?" He pointed to the broken jumble of rocks, large slabs of sandstone lying beneath the petrographs. "These broke off hundreds, maybe thousands of years ago.

"Imagine painting these. You're a Native American, climbing up there with something like paint and a stick, or a brush, and your imagination."

"I wish we could get closer," Skylar mused.

"In a way, it's good we can't," Lacaria explained. "They've been preserved, saved. People do some pretty awful things to rock art, chip them away, destroy them with spray paint. Because they can, they think they should."

"Yeah, I can see people doing that kind of thing," Skylar said, a sudden quiet in her voice.

"There you are, in time for lunch." Lacaria came out of the kitchen to give Becky a big hug. "Phillip will be glad you're here. I was afraid we wouldn't see much of you these next few days with the new arrival. "

"Alexander's going to be a handful once he figures out what his legs are for," Becky said. "I wanted to come over and see how the conference center is looking."

Over Christmas break the building was a wooden skeleton of framing. Six months later, all of the walls were up, windows and doors installed. "I can't believe it's nearly finished. You've all got to be thrilled."

Lacaria motioned to the dining room table, covered with wires, cables, and equipment. "It will be nice for the house to be used as a house again. It's good you're home, I know Phillip will be glad having you around."

Becky found Phillip in his office, showing Skylar his "Big Book of Petrographs." She was sitting on the other side of the large desk, seeming to show interest.

"Thought I heard your voice." He glanced up, then down again. "How're Autumn and Alexander?"

"They're doing great. Out in the field, getting some sunshine." *Why did the air in the room feel so awkward?*

"Showing Skylar the Big Book?" Becky asked, sitting down next to him.

The "Big Book" wasn't really a book in a normal sense, but a loosely-held collection of hundreds of photographs, some large, some small, all of petrographs from around the American Southwest. Tabs divided them into categories by state (Utah, Nevada, Arizona, Colorado, New Mexico, and Wyoming). The pictures were also cross-referenced by dates ranging from five thousand years ago to the more modern 1800s, as well as possible identities of various Native Americans peoples. Numerous notes stuck out of the pages, giving it a less-than-organized appearance.

"I got to drive an ATV to Silver Moon Canyon!" Skylar was still exuberant from this new experience. "Now I'm learning all about petrographs."

"I got some pictures from an archaeologist in New Mexico." Phillip handed them to Becky.

"Are these new?"

He nodded his head. "Some. She's using some new 3D software."

"What does it do?"

"It gives depth and even color to the rock art, a tool we didn't have ten, fifteen years ago. It's controversial, some people say it distorts the petrographs. I think we should be open to anything. Especially here, as we try to prove horses are native, not invasive."

"Because these petrographs are hundreds, thousands of years old, you're looking for horses in them, correct?" Skylar asked.

Phillip sat back in his chair and let out a big sigh. "Yes, it's a daunting task, for a couple of reasons.

"First, any images of horses on rock art have been discounted as 'recent,' after 1500 CE, for example. They haven't been given any attention, rarely photographed, and not protected.

"Second, there's an idea horses, if they *were* here before Columbus, should have been drawn, etched, on rock a lot. A whole lot, some say, if they were important."

Becky said proudly, "But Phillip has written numerous articles that First Nations peoples, Native Americans, used dogs to carry supplies, went on hunting trips. In South America, llamas and alpacas were domesticated. These animals were important to them, but are rarely depicted as well. His theories have received a lot of attention."

Phillip's smile told her he appreciated her words. For a moment, Becky thought, it was like before. Warm, loving.

Then he looked away and once more, there was that chill in the air.

Skylar leafed through several of the plates, shaking her head. "You're right. I see lots of goats and snakes, a few birds. What about bears?"

"And mountain lions," Phillip added. "They show up from time to time, not in the numbers one might expect.

"I always caution we have found only a tiny fraction of the petrographs in the Southwest United States." Phillip held up his hands. "We have no idea how many are out there, it seems every year dozens, hundreds more are found. It's a race to get to them, document them, try to protect them against the elements but also vandalism.

"Here's my favorite petrograph, the Serranía de la Lindosa panel in Colombia. The largest mural of rock art in the world." He slid a picture over to her.

"A horse!" the girl exclaimed.

"Painted on a rock a thousand, maybe two thousand years after horses supposedly became extinct." He showed her a map. "This is how far glaciers came south in the last Ice Age."

"They don't reach Central America, not even close."

"It's possible the Ice Age did not contribute at all to their decline."

Skylar got it. "If they became extinct, what about fossils?" She continued to leaf through the pictures as she asked questions. "Wouldn't there be fossils of horses if they were here? "

"Good question. We find fossils of animals that lived hundreds of thousands of years ago, millions of years. It takes special circumstances for fossilization to occur, the animal has to die in the right place, for example, perhaps next to a lake or a river. Then, almost immediately covered, like a mudslide. However, we find skeletons, sometimes intact, of Ice Age animals such as mammoths or giant sloths. They're not fossilized, they are preserved because they have been in a deep cave."

"Or the LaBrea tar pits!" Skylar exclaimed. "My parents took me to see them a few years ago. What about horse skeletons?"

Phillip shook his head. "This might be the most troubling aspect of our work. It's been drilled in our heads for decades modern-day horses didn't live here, horse skeletons found anywhere such as kill sites, where Native Americans harvested large numbers of buffalo or other animals, were discarded, ignored.

"Last year I was at a conference of scientists, talking with a respected archaeologist. I told him what I was doing, my research, and I brought up the lack of horse skeletons. He looked me straight in the eye and said, 'For years, whenever we were digging a kill site, a thousand-year-old pueblo, or an ancient camping area, and we found horse skeletons, we tossed them away, thinking they were of no consequence, modern.' His next words chilled me," Phillip remembered.

"He said, 'Maybe we shouldn't have done that.'"

"So, all of it is lost."

Phillip's story reminded Becky how little time they spent together these last few months, or how rarely they talked. Yes, she was in college, but they talked or texted each other almost every day, he even visited her on campus several times.

When did that stop?

Am I being ignored? Am I imagining this? Becky wondered, watching Phillip and Skylar passing photographs back and forth. Lacaria told her Phillip would be glad to see her. Turned out, she thought sadly, he didn't seem glad, not at all.

Phillip watched Becky leave, a pang of regret. He knew he'd have to talk to her sooner or later, but preferred later. Was he wrong in distancing himself from her? He wanted only what was best for her, and her words over Christmas break, made him think about her future, and his. Did he have a place in her life? Was it fair to expect he did?

Yes, he decided, he would talk to her in the next day or two, get it over with.

His heart hurt even more when he thought about life without his

Cowgirl.

CHAPTER 18
A BAD MEETING

"How was Iceland?" Ronnie Corman, BLM District Manager, folded her arms and rested them on her desk. Her smile was friendly, matching her question.

"Wonderful," Carl answered. "A little stormy. Beautiful country, wouldn't mind going there again."

"The people are wonderful," Dr. J agreed. "We made a lot of friends. And, saw a lot of wild horses, how they're taken care of."

"Easy to do when you have a hundred of them. Not thousands." Ronnie's smile was not as cordial. The scoff in her voice was unmistakable, her feigned friendliness gone.

She was a short woman in her late forties, with long, curly auburn hair and brown eyes. Promoted after Carl's resignation two years before, Ronnie was a career government employee, working her way up in posts from Alaska to New Mexico before landing in Wyoming.

She was known as a micromanager, with a sharp, biting temper lashed out at anybody who disagreed with her.

Carl looked around. For several years, this was his office. Although he'd been here a few times since, it still felt odd.

"You've added some artwork," he commented. Large, framed photographs of cowboys and cattle drives, backed by mountainous landscapes, were on every wall.

The message was blatant: Ronnie Corman was on the side of the livestock industry.

Ronnie nodded. "These were sent to me by some of the ranchers in the area. Seemed a waste not to use them.

"I only have a few minutes." She got down to business. "I want to bring you up to speed on your horse sanctuary request."

Dr. J noticed she didn't use the word "approval." The look on Carl's face said he'd noticed it as well.

"Is there a problem?"

"Maybe, on several fronts. As you know, we went through the public scoping process, getting comments. Some of the residents, are concerned about a number of issues." She shuffled some papers over to Carl.

"They're worried about traffic, if there are a lot of visitors to the sanctuaries, to see the horses."

"Other sanctuaries don't report problems, we have statements from them in our application."

"It's not the only issue. Some comments are about water, horses drink a lot."

Dr. J laughed. "No more than cows."

"We eat cows, they're a consumer product." Ronnie's retort was sharp.

"Which leads us to the most substantial complaint. Your sanctuary would be a different use than what it's been for almost a century and a half. There're rumblings you may need to go to the county, get a land use variance, before you proceed. The Double B was a livestock ranch, you're trying to make it something else."

Carl sat back. That got his attention. "Horses are considered livestock. Even if we don't eat them."

"Livestock are breedable. They propagate, have offspring. These horses don't and can't. Stallions are castrated, the mares are given fertility treatments to make sure they don't go into heat. You know that. So, by some definition, they cannot be considered 'livestock' anymore."

"You're splitting some pretty thin hairs," Dr. J protested. "I don't know anybody, anywhere who has made this kind of argument."

"It's being made here and I can't ignore it."

"You're rejecting our application?" Carl's face was red with anger.

"Not yet, I've kicked this up to Washington, haven't heard back from them. I encourage you to start the process with the county."

"Wyoming already has several of these sanctuaries, maybe we don't need any more."

Dr. J couldn't believe what she was hearing. "What about the horses we've found, they're in holding pens in Nevada. We're ready to get them here."

"Not my concern." Ronnie stood up, the meeting was over.

"She's going to turn us down?" Phillip was incredulous.

Carl held out his hands. "She's listening to the wrong people. We're going to have to figure out how to fight them."

They were back at the Double B, sitting on the deck.

Dr. J agreed. "We'll review the documents from other sanctuaries, see if they have this problem, and how they countered it."

Phillip stood up, hands on hips, and began to pace. "This is unbelievable. After everything we've done."

"We have a lot of enemies, Phillip." Dr. J pursed her lips. "We're going to have to up our PR game."

Phillip gave a short laugh. "Turn into my grandfather, you mean, invite bigwigs over to hunt and fish here, wine and dine them. How about roast a pig on an open pit, or a whole cow?"

"I don't think we have to go that far." Carl shrugged. "Maybe some bagels and croissants, a veggie tray, in-season fruits."

Dr. J and Phillip looked at him, then burst out laughing.

"I'm sorry," Phillip said. "I lost my temper."

"Understandable, I'm angry, too." Dr. J nodded. "But I think we're going to have to change our tactics. Maybe we need to hire a good lawyer."

"Anybody in mind?" Phillip asked.

"Maybe. Let's wait and see what happens before we make any calls. Ronnie might come to her senses, or get overruled by Washington. Or, not."

CHAPTER 19
WHAT TOOK YOU SO LONG?

"I got to get serious about this," Silver Moon told Juno. "Autumn has been gone too long."

"She's probably enjoying being alone. Do you want me to help you look?" She glanced back at Peggy Sue, who was nudging at her mother's belly, ready for another breakfast.

"No, stay and help watch the young ones." He sauntered past her towards the canyon.

Sandy started to follow, but her father told her, "Stay with Juno, be here if your mother comes back. Maybe she's across the other meadow."

A few minutes later he stood at the bottom of the canyon.

No Autumn, and no sign she has given birth. He nosed the air, trying to find some scent.

Ah, he caught a trace, near the rocks. It was clear she might be deeper in the canyon, relieved he did not sense any mountain lions.

Almost an hour later Silver Moon stood on the flat ground near the river. "Why would she come here?" he asked himself, stomping the ground and snorting. He knew the answer. And he was furious.

Becky was giving Autumn fresh hay, feeding it to her by hand. "Don't want you to overdo it, now, do we," the girl said, smiling.

Alexander finished his first morning bottle. "I love doing this," Skylar said, taking the nipple from the foal's mouth. "Your farm, the Double B, sure are different. I go outside and there's smog and noise. I went outside last night and saw the Milky Way for the first time in my life."

"I guess we're making a country girl out of you?" Becky smiled.

Corky was sitting on the bench. He jumped down to touch Autumn's nose.

"I didn't know horses like dogs and dogs like horses." Skylar bent down to ruffle Corky's fur.

"Most do. Horses are even gentle with small puppies, careful to step around them."

Phillip came in from the field, taking off work gloves. "The fencing looks good. Are you ready to let them go outside?"

Becky nodded. "Yes! Fresh air will do both of them good."

Phillip held the wide door open. Autumn flared her ears and looked at Becky.

"You go on, now, take your baby with you. It'll do your muscles some good."

Autumn snorted, then turned and walked out.

Alexander finished with his bottle, followed his mother.

"Maybe he'll start suckling now, too," Phillip wondered. "Give us a break from feeding him every two hours. It will also be better for him."

Dot and Max were in the other field. Becky thought it wise to keep the older horses separated from the foal for the time being. Alexander jumped and hopped around his mother in exuberant happiness.

"He has some pent-up energy, doesn't he?" Becky laughed. She followed them, staying close behind Alexander as he took his first steps outside the barn.

A breeze ruffled Autumn's mane and carried her scent towards Silver Moon Canyon.

Dot sauntered to the fence line. "Autumn! You're looking good."

Autumn called back, "I still want to sleep—a lot. Seems like even eating exhausts me."

"We saw what they did to you," Dot nodded to Max.

"Yes, it was awful. Disgusting, actually." Max bared his teeth. "Frankly, I never want to see anything like that again."

Dot nudged his neck. "She doesn't need to hear this right now. She's fine, and look at her little boy. He's so full of joy."

Max shrugged in the way that horses do, shaking his head. "Gets me tired looking at him. I'm going to stand in the shade."

"I see he hasn't changed much," Autumn laughed.

"Oh, he's old. He thinks he's seen it all, nothing new, grumpy all the time, but don't let him fool you. He was watching over Alexander through the night, didn't sleep one wink. We've never had a baby, you know. He was trying to be protective."

Dot left to join Max under the trees.

Silver Moon knew humans would see him on this road, but he didn't care. He passed some of them on their contraptions, they pointed and he heard their loud exclamations. A loose horse, no bridle or saddle, large and pure white. They did not know this was Silver Moon, the mustang.

He was at a full gallop now. *Hurry, hurry, hurry, I know where you are.*

Autumn's scent was powerful, he was close. There! He saw the fence line. Head down, he barreled towards it.

Phillip heard Silver Moon before he saw him, the unmistakable sound of hooves on the ground, a big and heavy horse. "Becky!" he shouted to her. She was with Autumn and Alexander, a distance away in the field. "Get back here, now. Silver Moon is coming! Run!"

She got to the barn just as the stallion seemed to explode across the road.

"Autumn!" Silver Moon shouted to his mare, anger in his voice. He shook phlegm from his nostrils and mouth, reared up on his hind legs, putting on a show of possessiveness. "You are mine, not theirs."

She raised her head, then with measured calm walked to the fence line.

"If you calm down and look, you'd see why I'm here," her head indicated Alexander, shaking in fear. "Get rid of your anger. I have only one question for you. What took you so long?"

Silver Moon was about to rear up again, but stopped midway, which was comical and made Autumn laugh.

"What do you mean, what took me so long?"

"I've been here many days," Autumn chided. "I was in a bad way, and I knew it. I did the only thing I could, came here for help."

She called for Alexander. "Come meet your daddy, even though he's quite the ninny."

Silver Moon watched the foal step uncertainly to his mother. He leaned against her to keep from falling. "A son? You gave me a son."

"I gave *us* a son. His name is Alexander."

"A good name. He reminds me of my father. Same color. We'll see how he grows into it."

"Yes, we will."

"When are you coming home?" The stallion was mollified, but only a little

"Soon, I'm sure. Our baby needs to be a little steadier on his legs. The humans will see to it."

"You know I hate them, I don't trust them. The humans."

"I know, and I know why. I don't trust most of them either. These humans," she looked back at the barn, "I trust."

"They look silly standing there looking at us."

Indeed, Becky, Phillip, and Skylar stood shoulder to shoulder at a window from the safety of the barn. Corky sat on the window sill, his mouth open with his goofy smile.

Autumn laughed. "They do, don't they. I think they're afraid of you."

He liked the idea humans were afraid of him. It gave him confidence and pride.

"You've even scared poor old Dot and Max over there," Autumn pointed out. Indeed, the pair shied away as far as they could into a corner, standing stock-still the way frightened horses do.

"They're *human* horses," Silver Moon scoffed. "Not our kind."

"I was a human horse, once," his mare reminded him.

His eyes softened. "Your human didn't care about you."

He remembered when she was led out of the square contraption in the middle of the desert, left alone. Day after day, night after night, he watched her from a distance, wanting, yearning to meet her. They did only because Autumn was attacked by a mountain lion. Saved by his quick, brave actions.

"Go on back to our family," Autumn instructed. "Let all know I am well, and we have a son."

Silver Moon reached across the fence to nuzzle Autumn's neck. He could never explain how much comfort this simple act always gave him, more than with his other mares.

"You chose me, over all others, over the humans," he whispered. "You are my first, you will always be my first."

There were sighs of relief watching Silver Moon gallop away, presumably back to his mountain meadow. They hadn't realized they'd been holding a collective breath.

"Is it my imagination, or is he bigger? A *lot* bigger?" Phillip ran a hand through his hair."

"Definitely more muscular in the chest," Becky agreed. "And he might be a half hand taller. Not sure you'd be wanting to get close to him now, especially if you found yourself between him and Autumn."

"You and those horses have the most incredible relationship, Cowgirl." He almost put his arm around her, held back, hoping Becky didn't notice.

"Why did he leave?" Skylar distracted them. "He could have jumped the fence easily, right?"

"Horses aren't eager to jump obstacles unless they have to," Becky explained. "And Silver Moon is a large horse, a lot of bulk to push over a fence. I'm guessing Autumn talked him out of it."

Skylar frowned. "Horses talk?"

"You saw them together. Something was going on."

Phillip and Becky moved away from the window leaving Skylar to watch Autumn and Alexander, who resumed practicing his jumps and hops.

Skylar petted Corky, who was still watching Autumn and Alexander.

"Horses talk," Skylar said to him. "Do all animals talk?"

She giggled at his toothy grin. "Do dogs talk?"

CHAPTER 20
FREE RADICALS

Dr. J was in a bad mood.

The sour taste in her mouth from the meeting with the BLM manager would not go away. Ronnie was shifty, sly, clearly could not be trusted, and made no secret of it. She would need to be watched, and hopefully would trip up somehow, hang herself with her own rope.

Those were dark thoughts, Dr. J chided herself for them.

Settled in a large over-stuffed chair, she leaned her head back, closed her eyes, willing herself to a calm place, finding her center of peace.

The door opened, Skylar peered in.

"I'm sorry, I didn't know anybody was here," the girl said. She began to back out.

"It's all right, I'm about ready to leave."

Skylar stepped in. "I didn't know about this room. The house is so big, I'm still exploring."

Dr. J chuckled. "Phillip's grandfather didn't know when to stop with his additions. This space under the stairs" she waved a hand, "wasn't used much until we converted it into a library."

"Sure are a lot of books." Skylar approached the shelf.

"Mostly technical, nonfiction, science related, might not be of much interest to you."

"We hiked the canyon to see the rock art. Never thought I'd be interested in that, but," she shrugged, "now I am. And, horses."

"Watch out, you'll get hooked on *Equus*."

"I love Alexander, watching him play and frisk about."

"Glad you're having a good summer."

Skylar picked up a book from a small table. "*The Horse: The Free Radicals of the World*," she read. "By Dr. Faith Jergens. That's you!"

"My latest. I got a lot of good reviews on it, and some criticism, too. The title, using free radicals, some didn't like it."

"Why?" Skylar sat in the opposite chair.

"A free radical is normally not a good thing, in the body can cause mutations, cancers. I used it to show how horses have been used—and misused—over the millennia, as farm animals, in wars, sports. They remain loyal to us, but down deep is their yearning to be free. Radical, defiant."

"Phillip talked about the last Ice Age, theories about horse extinction. What about early man? I've read they were the real cause, hunting, killing all of them?"

"I used to support those theories. Now I have my doubts. The woolly mammoth, lived at the same time, went extinct about the same time. They obviously couldn't have survived in hot climates, which is what they were faced with as the ice shield regressed to the north. Steep mountain terrain might have been difficult for them.

"Horses would adapt, migrate, evolve, and possibly did. Horses can be found on every continent except Antarctica. Today they survive in mountains, deserts, cold climates, hot climates, no reason they didn't thousands of years ago."

Dr. J leaned forward. "Another argument is the gestation period for both animals. How long it takes for a baby to grow in mom's tummy. A mammoth's gestation period was most likely two years, like today's elephants. A horse? Eight or nine months. That makes a big difference in populations.

"Look at it from today's perspective. More than a hundred years ago, there were at least one million horses in southwest America, possibly two million. It's taken modern weapons, and technology, to reduce that number to less than eighty thousand. How many horses were in all of the Americas ten, twelve thousand years ago? And early man killed every last one of them? I'm not so sure."

Skylar's look brightened. She understood. "And they wouldn't be the only guys hunting them, right? There were saber tooth tigers and cave bears and all sorts of things, and they were hunting them for thousands of years before man came here."

Dr. J nodded, impressed with the girl's thinking. "Exactly. I wish some of my college students caught on as easily as you."

Skylar blushed with the compliment. "You're all working on the same thing, in different ways. Phillip is an archaeologist, looking at rock art and skeletons. You're looking at DNA. I'm beginning to understand." Skylar smiled. "I think."

She got up to peruse the other books on the shelves, tracing the titles with her fingers.

"If you see something interesting, take it," she was told.

Towards the end of one shelf, she found one book with a different title than the rest.

Dr. J got up to leave. "I'm guessing your summer isn't going exactly like you imagined."

"Oh, yeah. I thought I was going to be stuck in some hayseed farm. Not science camp."

Dr. J laughed.

Skylar sat down to read.

Dr. J took no notice of the book the teenager chose.

CHAPTER 21
FRESH HAY

The wind assailed the horses most of the morning and showed no sign of relenting into the afternoon.

Wind always makes animals testy, blowing dust in their eyes and nostrils, fouling water, and generally making life a little harder.

Sheani told the others she was going into the gulch. "Maybe the wind won't be so bad at the bottom."

"But there's no water there," one of the other mares said. "And hardly any grass."

"I smelled something sweet yesterday," Juno said.

Sheani looked interested. "Let's go check it out." She paused only a second. "Should we ask the others to come with us? Maybe Silver Moon?

"Tomorrow, we can always ask them tomorrow."

The two mares, with little Peggy Sue following, walked across the meadow and down the hill. No one else followed.

At the bottom, near an open spot, they saw something unusual. The mares stepped around the enclosure, cautious, unsure, but the sweet smell of fresh hay overpowered their caution.

They found the opening on the other side. Ears flaring, they shuffled and snorted.

Peggy Sue, energetic and high-spirited, didn't care about her mother's hesitancy, and sprinted through the opening. She wasn't interested in the hay, her mother was giving her plenty to eat, but she had the natural curiosity of any youngster.

Her daughter gave her no choice, she followed Peggy Sue in, and found the mounds of hay. Sheani joined them, filling their bellies before they got thirsty and took the trail back up to the meadow's lake.

Clank. Clank. Clank. The gate closed a little more, a few inches at a time.

CHAPTER 22
BIG ELK

Tab prepared a litany of questions for Becky to show his interest and that he'd paid attention to her the day before. Women liked that.

His appointment with Jack Brinkle was at 9 a.m.; GPS told him the cattleman's office was only twenty minutes away. There was time to stop by The Coffee Wrangler, see Becky again, and hopefully talk to her more.

To "razzle dazzle" the locals, he was dressed to impress in his best suit, with a dark blue tie, and shiny black shoes. He walked across the outside patio, satisfied more than a few heads were turned at his good looks and expensive clothes.

The place was busy. Several mountain bikes were stacked near the outside patio, people of various ages, dressed in various colors of stretchy garb sat on benches, most scrolling through their phones.

Inside was a cacophony of sounds, laughter, some serious

conversations.

He sat down and scanned the room, no Becky.

An older woman approached, ready to take his order. She was attractive, with thick black hair. Her nametag read "Tess."

He ordered black coffee to go, his voice clipped, perfunctory. He wanted to ask if Becky was available. Maybe he shouldn't be so obvious.

"Tess" got the hint her customer wasn't in a mood for idle chatter and returned with the large container.

"If you bring this next time," she pointed to the cup, "your coffee is half off."

Tab shrugged, mumbled, "Thanks" and headed for the door. He saw Becky on the patio.

There she is he thought, happy to see her. He waved to get her attention.

One of her eyebrows shot up.

"You look like a city slicker," she said, her eyes traveling from Tab's face down to his shoes.

"Big meeting with a client." He leaned against the split rail fence. He liked the way she was looking at him.

"You didn't tell me what you're doing here."

"I'm a lawyer," he answered. "Thinking about taking on a client in the area." A slight lie, it would be up to this particular client to take *him* on. "In fact," he glanced at his watch. "I have to leave or I'll be late."

"Maybe later, this afternoon, I can swing by here and we can talk some more."

She shook her head and waved a hand around. "My mom owns this, and the grocery store, so I help sometimes in the morning. I work at the veterinary clinic near Pinedale most days. "

"You're an assistant? To a veterinarian?" Might explain that *baby horse*, he thought.

"In college, studying to be a veterinarian. I spend my summers getting the hours I need to show experience."

She waved goodbye to him before he could ask when they might meet again.

He watched her go. College student. Veterinarian. She was smart. Did he blow it, assuming she was "only" an assistant? Hopefully, he would have the chance to make it up to her.

Fifteen minutes later, Tab pulled into the parking lot of the Western States Cattlemen Association. It was not a large area, the center dominated by a larger-than-life metal sculpture of an elk with an impressive, multi-pronged rack. On the other side of the walkway were two other figures, a mountain lion and a bear, appropriately snarling and intimidating, carved from huge slabs of wood.

Could they get more stereotypical? Tab wondered. *Probably not.*

Inside, the main office was a small room with two desks and a few tables. The walls sported several western-themed paintings. More stereotypes, of course.

A younger man was at one of the desks and stood up when Tab entered.

"I'm here to see Mr. Brinkle," Tab said, extending a hand. Being friendly to office staff always scored points.

"Mr. Taggart, yes, I'm Larry. Jack's expecting you."

Tab was led down a short hallway to a half-opened door. Larry rapped, then opened it. "Mr. Taggart's here."

Tab entered one of the largest offices he'd ever seen. Law offices in D.C. were often impressive, filled with brass and black glass. Jack Brinkle's office rivaled those.

The gleaming wood floor matched the wall panels. On one end was a low table with leather-upholstered sofas and matching chairs.

Large floor-to-ceiling windows dominated two sides, with views of distant mountain ranges to the east and north. The other two walls held more western paintings, cowboys on horses surrounded by cattle, shooting at unknown varmints or enemies. Tab guessed all were originals.

Jack stood up from behind his desk and smiled broadly.

"Glad you could come out here so fast."

Jack was a big man, taller than Tab, with wide shoulders. He was bald, with a graying beard and moustache, giving him an appearance that might be perfect for any western movie.

Another stereotype.

Jack's desk was an astonishing piece of furniture. It seemed cut from one solid plank of wood, immense in size, easily ten feet by twelve feet. Behind it was a matching credenza with a display of three computer monitors.

He noticed Tab's look of admiration at the desk. He swept a hand across it. "Cut from one of those big redwoods in California, more than a hundred years ago. Cost me a pretty penny, don't mind telling you, when it came up for auction." He laughed. "You couldn't get something like this nowadays, no sir, it's one of a kind."

Tab nodded in appreciation.

"Couldn't help noticing the elk sculpture you have in the front." Tab continued the small talk. "Impressive."

"Artist in Colorado did it for us. Cost us almost half a million," Jack bragged. "And cost us almost as much getting it up here and put in place."

Spending big money on desks and rusty metal. *If they have that kind of money*, Tab thought, *I'll be able to charge them twice the normal hourly rate.*

Tab was escorted into a meeting room and quickly introduced. A large rectangular table dominated the center surrounded by a dozen chairs. Half of them were already occupied by men about the same age as Jack. Larry, the younger man from the office, sat at the head with a laptop.

An explanation was given, two members would attend via the Internet.

Small talk. "Smells like rain." "Hope so, my irrigation system's jammed up." "Did you see the price of corn this morning? It better get a lot higher before fall."

Jack pointed to a chair for Tab. "Let me know if you want coffee or anything to drink, we'll be bringing in lunch later."

Tab settled in for his first meeting of The Greater Tetons and Western States Cattlemen's Association.

CHAPTER 23
BEARINGS

Tess watched the exchange between her daughter and the customer with some interest.

"Who's the guy?" Tess asked Becky.

"Some lawyer from back east, passing through, talking to clients. Tab something, don't remember his last name."

"Seems like kind of a jerk," Tess said, craning her neck to see what kind of car he was driving. An economy, the plates of a rental company on the front.

"You know how these guys are, trying to impress the local rubes," Becky shrugged. Her tone was nonchalant, maybe *too* nonchalant.

This "lawyer from back east" showed more interest in Becky than she in him, and her keen mother's intuition was on alert. Was there something going on, something she'd missed? Becky was home from college only a few days, and there'd been the hectic emergency and worry over Autumn and her foal to contend with.

None of your business, Tess told herself watching Becky leave. *None of your business.*

Still.

Tess returned to her small office at the back of the building. She reached for a stack of papers on her desk. Most were orders from various supply companies for the restaurant, a few bills to pay by the end of the month. Business was good, she could cover her expenses easily, and make a profit.

She relaxed in her office chair for several minutes. A shelf above the desk held a few trophies, horsemanship awards from county fairs, wins from her barrel racing days more than twenty years ago.

When you're young, all days are simpler, easier. *What would my life be like now, if I'd done something else? Anything else?* she asked herself, not for the first time. It was good to ask these questions, from time to time, mark her bearings, plant her feet in the soft ground of her life.

Marrying Carl, the bookish biologist from back east, having her daughter, were the best things that could have happened to her.

Opening up her organic grocery store was also a good thing, more than fifteen years ago. The Coffee Wrangler wasn't a whim, either. She did her research, asked questions, went over budget sheets a hundred times before adding on to the store. It was an instant hit, helped by the surge in mountain biking and, of course, passion about wild horses.

She returned to the stack of papers.

Still.

That word hung over her shoulders. She realized Phillip hadn't been around much since Becky was home. Usually he'd be at the house, maybe for dinner, the two would go riding horses or catch a movie. True, he was busy with the conference center, and yes, he had been there when Alexander was born.

Still.

That word again.

Was something going on between Becky and Phillip?

CHAPTER 24
STORIES

Alexander was doing a happy little zig-zag dance across the field, finding sunbeams stretching from tree to tree.

Autumn flicked her tail back and forth impatiently. Like all mothers, she did not like him getting so far away from her and finally called him back. It was time for his second breakfast. It gave her pleasure to feed him, a mother's need to be needed by her son.

Watching Autumn and her little boy was a welcome diversion for Dot. Gentle and affectionate, Dot would have made a great mother.

"His legs are getting stronger," she told Max, who was chewing on some oats.

"Mmmph," he mouthed, faking interest because he loved Dot and was not about to ignore her enthusiasm for the foal.

A few minutes later Alexander left his mother and lay down in a patch of tall grass. Free from those duties, Autumn ambled over to the fence separating the two fields. She would have liked to be with the other horses, but the gate between them remained closed.

Corky scooted under the fence to Autumn's side

"It's going to be hot today," she told the dog, looking up at a cloudless sky. "I think we'll spend most of the day inside. Take advantage of it before we go back to our family."

"What do you do out there?" Corky tossed his head towards the hills. "Is there a barn you stay in?"

"No, there are high cliffs where I can find shade between the rocks. I also take mud baths near the waterfall. Keeps me cool much of the day."

"Doesn't sound sanitary," Max snuffled.

"I think it sounds lovely," Dot countered. "We saw your stallion, Autumn. He's quite imposing."

"Frightening," Max interrupted. "He almost scared me to death. Big beast."

Autumn bent her head to touch one of her front legs. She was not about to let Max see her laughing. Composed, she nodded.

"He's gentle with me and the other mares."

"Other mares?"

"There are several of us, plus his daughters—one of them is our girl, Sandy—and four foals. Oh, and his lieutenants. They keep an eye on things, too."

"Quite the family."

"Yes, not nearly as large as some we've come across with many more mares. Their stallions are older, of course."

Dot asked, "Do you get along with those other families?"

"Sort of. Maybe there are words, some dust flying. Frankly, I'm not sure what's supposed to be happening. Remember, I'm new to that world."

"I remember, dear," Dot assured her. "When you first came to us you told me about the horrible place you were in before, bad food and water, nobody caring about you."

"The two of you helped me so much, I don't think I ever thanked you. Things happened so quickly. I got caught in that flood, I nearly drowned. Silver Moon saved me. Then Becky let me go with him."

"Corky told us all about it, or at least his version," Max said. "Not sure it was entirely accurate."

Corky sniffed, insulted. "I always tell the truth."

"What happened after?" Dot wanted to know.

"It was wonderful. Silver Moon brought me into a meadow, and there were two mares, Juno and Sheani. They made me feel right at home, showed me all the best grasses and what to avoid. I think pine trees taste bad, Juno loves them. We galloped and jumped, something I'd never done before, having fun." Autumn laughed. "I discovered my legs can run!

"I met other animals, too. Raccoons and skunks—you don't want to go near them, they're pretty nasty. Coyotes keep their distance and at night we hear wolves far away.

"Mountain lions. We have those, too."

Max looked around at Autumn's back leg. "I remember your meeting with one of those."

"One of them comes around from time to time, keeping Silver Moon and the lieutenants on their hooves, let me tell you."

"What about the winter, it gets so cold," Dot asked. "Snow, frozen water."

"We break the ice to get water," Autumn said matter-of-fact. "There are deep clefts where we can get out of the snow, bunch together for warmth.

"It's not an easy life, I will grant you, but understand, being with Silver Moon is everything for me. I love him more than I thought I could ever love somebody." She glanced at Alexander, who was still slumbering. "If I didn't have my stallion, I wouldn't have my children."

Dot touched Autumn's nose. "I understand. Thank you for telling us your stories. In some ways I envy you. But I still worry."

"Silver Moon will always protect me, always protect all of our mares. He will never let anything happen to any of us."

CHAPTER 25
A GOOD MOOD

Jack liked showing people around, introducing them to Wyoming his way, with his point of view. Impress them, introduce them to other people, make them think he was the big wheel. It always put him in a good mood.

The young lawyer, Tab Taggart, was interesting. Slick and smooth, not telling him everything. The day before, Jack did some checking, told some contacts in D.C. to ask around.

They told him Tab didn't have a job at some law firm, he'd been fired days ago. Jack figured the young man was hungry, maybe desperate. He didn't tell the other board members, some of them might not understand the advantages this knowledge might someday give him.

He left his office to drive the short distance to his home. He sat for a few minutes in the driveway before going in, craning his neck to see the roof at this angle. It needed replacing, wished he could afford a metal roof. Wished he could afford a lot of things.

He ground his teeth thinking about Al. They were almost the same age, went to school together, but they were never friends, the prestige, and money, of the Double B conferred status that Jack could never have.

Al seemed to pay cash for everything. Adding on to the ranch house? No problem. New trucks and cars? No problem. The best bulls for his cows? No problem. Putting on the best parties for a hundred guests or more? The list of his extravagances seemed endless.

Jack knew it was irrational to be jealous of Al. His wife died young, he lost his son in a car accident, leaving him to raise his grandson, alone.

But Al never seemed to let any of it get him down. Kept spending money, having a good time, rolling with the punches.

Lettie, Jack's wife, opened the front door. "You coming in? Supper's getting cold," she yelled at him.

He smiled and waved. She was his third wife, and the costs of two divorces behind him still hurt in the bank account. Five kids, all grown now, moved away, rarely seen. Once or twice a year a passel of grandkids showed up. Most were teenagers living in big cities, he wondered how often he'd see them.

Pursing his lips, he got out of the truck. Thinking about the bad roof, envy of a dead man, divorces, kids, and grandkids, put him in a bad mood.

CHAPTER 26
HORSEBACK RIDING

Horses shuffled to the door of their stables, nodding their heads in anticipation. They watched as blankets, saddles, bridles, and reins were carried out. Phillip led Chaco, Teddie, Marshall, and Durango into the yard.

The early morning air was cool, a few clouds from the west floated over a blue sky. A distant meadowlark sang his tune.

Lacaria, Becky, and Skylar came out of the house, all dressed in jeans and short-sleeved shirts.

"Found some boots." Skylar indicated the footwear. "I guess you don't ride horses in sneakers."

"Some do, let's get you started right," Phillip said, handing her a helmet. "Including this."

Blankets were placed on each horse, saddles hefted with a rigging of straps and clasps were next. Skylar watched with interest. Lacaria and Becky were as efficient and thorough as Phillip, making sure the saddles were tight and secure.

Bridles were next. "We use hackamores here," Phillip explained to the teenager as he clipped a set of reins on his horse. "We don't use bits."

"What's the difference?"

"Metal bits are jammed in the horse's mouth, used to control turns and stops. Hurts them. We don't think it's necessary."

He patted the Durango's neck. "I think they appreciate it."

The night before the suggestion to go horseback riding seemed like a good idea. Now, however, seeing how large these animals were, Skylar wondered if she should have agreed. Curling up on the deck with a good book might have been a better idea.

"Let's get you mounted," Lacaria said. "This is Chaco, he's the oldest horse, gives a gentle ride."

A wooden box was brought for Skylar to step up on. She inserted her foot in the stirrup, and was astride Chaco a second later. She felt a thrill, gripping the saddle's pommel. She hadn't been given the reins yet.

"Keep your back and shoulders straight," Becky instructed. "Turn your legs and knees inward, to hug Chaco's sides. This is kind of hard, I know, especially when you're beginning. If you don't, you'll be sore and hurt all over tomorrow."

Phillip laughed. "You'll still be."

Lacaria gave him a punch in the shoulder. "Don't scare the girl."

Becky continued. "Keep the toes of your boots higher than your heels. Let's walk around the yard."

Becky made a clicking noise and Chaco followed her, Skylar trying to remember everything she'd been told. They did several wide circles.

"Keep your toes up. Here are the reins. Tell Chaco to start walking by squeezing his sides with your legs. He knows what to do."

Skylar clutched the reins in a tight grip.

"Ease up on the reins, relax," Becky said.

Skylar took a deep breath. When she was ready, she squeezed the horse's sides and sure enough, the horse began a slow walk.

"Pull the reins to the left or right, wherever you want to go."

Lacaria mounted Marshall, then reminded Skylar to keep her back straight, her knees bent.

"You're doing good," Lacaria praised her. "You're a natural."

Skylar grinned. Watching several videos online about how to ride a horse, what to do, what not to do, was different than the real thing. *Horses are big!*

She reached down and patted Chaco's neck. "This is fun. You can see so much from up here. Can you take my picture?" she asked Lacaria. "My friends will never believe I did this."

Satisfied the girl wasn't going to fall off, Becky went over to Teddie and with one fluid motion, almost a blur, mounted him and directed the horse to the road.

Phillip watched, mesmerized as always, at how Becky rode a horse, effortless, like she was one with the animal. Despite that, he wished Becky wasn't here, with them, with him, this day. He was still avoiding her.

Last night, after agreeing to teach Skylar how to ride a horse, Lacaria called Becky to invite her along. "You could use a break, what with taking care of Autumn and Alexander. You need to get out, fresh air will do you some good."

Phillip couldn't protest, how could he?

"Autumn and Alexander are doing well, we're thinking about

releasing them tomorrow," Becky mentioned as they rode

"They'll be gone?" Skylar shook her head, worry in her voice. "Will they be all right? Safe? Have lots to eat?"

"Autumn's a wild horse, we have to let them go back home."

"Doesn't see fair," the teenager shook her head. "I just got to know them."

A lake appeared around a bend. Large shrubs hugged the edges of the water. Trees, cottonwoods, and tall pines, provided a shady forest.

"This is our largest lake. It will be our sanctuary, once we get permission," Phillip said.

"Why do you need permission?" Skylar frowned.

"The United States government says it owns wild horses, and you need to get its OK to do anything with them. Lots of rules, to make sure the horses are taken care of. And, to make sure nobody's bringing in a stallion to breed the mares."

"No stallions?"

"The mustang stallions are gelded, they can't breed."

"You mean none of the mares can have babies."

Becky pulled her horse up closer. "The government doesn't want any more wild horses, even in a sanctuary. Dad says there might be problems getting your final approval?"

"The local BLM manager's giving us a hard time. Dr. J thinks we'll have to hire an attorney. She has somebody in mind."

Becky thought, Tab's an attorney, new to the area. She realized he hadn't given her a lot of information about why he was here. The Double B might have to hire an attorney. An odd coincidence?

"I need to get some water samples out of the lake, check for any bacteria. You all ride back when you want. Sun's getting high."

"I'll come with you," Becky said, and before he could protest, she prompted her horse to a gallop.

Phillip caught up to Becky.

"I'm not stupid," she turned on him. "I know you didn't want me to come with you today. If you had, *you* would have called me last night, not Lacaria."

He swallowed. She was right.

"What did I do to you, Phillip, what did I say to you? You've been cold, hardly talking to me. This past semester in college, I don't think you called me twice, and you didn't come up to visit like you used to, either. What did I do to deserve this?"

"Do we have to talk now?" Phillip held up a hand. "Maybe back at the ranch."

"No. We're alone here, and we're never alone there."

Phillip chewed his lower lip, gave up trying to avoid this conversation. "It's something you said over the holidays, been thinking about it."

Becky frowned. "No idea what you're talking about."

"We were at your house, the day after New Year's. After dinner. We sat around talking. Your dad said he'd read an article, a lot of veterinary students were switching to small animal classes, didn't want to be a large animal vet. He asked if you'd want to change your major."

"And I said, no."

Phillip tilted his head. "Not exactly. You said you could understand why a small animal clinic would be great to have. The idea of being called out in the middle of a freezing winter's night to stick your arms into a cow to turn a calf wasn't that appealing."

"And everybody laughed. You did, too."

"But you went on, said you're lucky Dr. Shultz was going to retire and you might take over his practice."

"Yeah?"

"You used the word *might*, Becky."

"I'm not taking it for granted."

"You went on, said hopefully the Double B would give you enough work, some of the cattle ranchers might not be keen to hire you because of your association with the sanctuary—and me."

"No, I didn't say that, at least not that way." Becky shook her head. "I'm proud of what you're doing here, I want to be a part of it. You know I do."

Clearing his throat, Phillip continued. "Think about it, Becky. My grandpa wanted me to be the ranch's veterinarian, you know I wasn't cut out for that. I hated my classes, and I came to hate him for making me do something I didn't want. Am I making you do something you don't want?"

She started to say something, but he went on.

"Becks, I can't hold you back. You're brilliant. You can write your own ticket to any college, any job in the country. Heck, in the world. The Double B doesn't have to be your life."

She shook her head. "Until I met you, I was in a dark place, thinking about leaving the farm, moving away. But after the flood, letting Autumn go, I knew what I wanted to do. It was my idea to become a veterinarian. Phillip, you saved me, you saved my *life*."

"Are you here," he waved a hand around, "because you feel obligated to me? Just because I saved your life, doesn't mean I have to *be* your life."

The two stared at each other for a few moments, both of them realizing what they were saying to each other.

Becky looked directly at him, seeking his eyes "This is my home. My family. I thought you were my family. You've been stewing about this for months? Without talking to me about it? I love you. Isn't that enough?"

"I don't know anymore." Phillip looked down. "You aren't my first girlfriend."

Those words stung. Becky turned on him, furious. "Why would you say something like that?"

"Maybe you need to explore, date other guys."

That did it. Becky turned her horse's head, she needed to get away.

"I guess I shouldn't have expected anything from you. You're flawed, Phillip, I'm not sure you *can* love. Your grandfather never showed you how, did he? The two of you ended up hating each other.

"Joe and Lacaria? They raised you, they love you, have you ever told them, once, you love them? They're your father and mother in all ways that matter, you wouldn't know it to see how you treat them."

"That's not true. You've gone too far."

"Me, gone too far? Have you been looking for an excuse to break up with me, is that it?

"You're telling me to explore. Other men? Fall in love with somebody else? Well, Mr. Ebbers, maybe I already have."

Becky urged her horse into a gallop and with a kick of dust, she was gone, leaving Phillip alone, furious, and confused.

To question his relationship with Joe and Lacaria?

Unforgiveable.

And her parting shot, maybe she's already exploring? Falling in love with somebody else?

What did she mean?

IN THE DARK NIGHT

CHAPTER 27
THE LAY OF THE LAND

Jack picked up Tab at his hotel early. The young lawyer was told they would be going over some rough roads. "Let's go see my backyard," the rancher said with a laugh.

Two rifles hung in a rack behind them above the truck's backseat. Jack noticed Tab looking at them.

"For plinking around," he explained, "shooting at the odd can. Or, varmints that we see. Coyotes mostly."

Passing The Coffee Wrangler, Tab wondered if Becky was there.

"What'd you think of our guys?" Jack asked as he turned onto the state highway, referring to the association's board.

"They know the issues," Tab complimented. "I learned a lot."

Even though much of the previous day's meeting was boring, Tab found interest in some issues. A review of his notes last night helped him realize most of the discussion, and complaints, boiled down to two issues:

All of the ranchers were disappointed and frustrated with two entities:

The public for not understanding where food comes from and the challenges farmers and ranchers face;

And their distrust and even hatred of the government.

"They don't understand we have as many years of failure as we do of success. Hard winters and scorching summers, they make or break us," one of the board members said, all agreed.

"These are our lands, been using them for generations."

"When we lose a calf or cow, that's thousands of dollars we'll never get," another said. "Money has to be made up from somewhere. Grocery stores are the middleman, and they're not exactly nice to us, either."

"Too slow making decisions."

"You should see the forms we have to fill out to keep our grazing leases."

"They like to surprise us with these environmental decisions," Jack scorned. "Wolves are protected, owls are protected, this year they're telling us to set aside lands for sage grouse. Sage grouse!" There was laughter around the table.

"And don't get us started on those feral horses. They've removed four hundred off the land, should be twice that. And what is going on with the Double B, that gang over there? When Al Ebbers was killed things changed." Jack's voice trailed off. There were headshakes all around.

Tab had wanted to ask more, but the meeting broke for lunch and the rest of the day's meeting was dominated with budget issues.

Today, however, Tab would have lots of opportunities to pepper

Jack with questions.

"We're going on some backroads, show you the other ranches, a few farms," Jack was saying.

The land was hilly, backed up against the Wind River Range. Jack pointed out fields of wheat and alfalfa. "We don't have a real long growing season here, long-term crops don't do so well, there are a few greenhouses for vegetables. Cows and sheep, those are our mainstays."

Several turns and twists in the road, Tab realized he would get completely lost in this maze. Another turn and a huge two-story stone house loomed into view.

"This is the Double B. Al's place, now owned by his heir and grandson." A harsh emphasis on the word, *heir,* nearly spat out. "Our very own tree hugger." Jack gave a short laugh. Did Tab discern a note of bitterness?

Tab counted five nice, newer trucks with the Double B logo on the doors parked around the house. Several men unloaded boxes from a delivery van in the driveway.

"The guy with the long hair. Phillip," Jack pointed out.

Tab saw a tall man about his age, wearing shorts showing well-toned legs. Tab asked about the large building behind the house.

"Their new conference center, almost done. They're promising to bring lots of money into the area." Another short laugh. "A scam, as far as I can see. Tried all I could to make it hard for them, protested to the county, the state, muddied up their permits. Managed to run up their costs a good chunk. Forced 'em to put in an elevator, a cool hundred grand by itself."

Tab remembered the hotel clerk's answer to his question. Yes, the town was counting on the conference center even while Jack and the other cattlemen tried to stop it.

Jack sped up past the Double B to cross the state highway and the bridge over the river. Minutes later, they came to a closed gate; Jack instructed Tab to get out, dislodge the chain around a pole, open it "all the way," close it after the truck went through, making sure the chain was dropped back down over the pole.

The road was rocky, Jack maneuvered his truck around stands of stubby scrub oak, and crested a hill. Several prairie dog mounds pockmarked the land, the little brown animals poking their heads up or running to and fro. High above in the blue sky, several hawks circled, looking for an easy meal.

It didn't take long for Tab to realize Jack's "backyard" was the wide expanse of mesas, desert meadows, ravines, hills, and cows.

Lots of cows. Droopy eyes, snotty snouts, and mouths chewing cud in a lazy, nonchalant manner. There were also a number of calves.

The animals were on either side of the dirt road in small groups as far as Tab's eye could see. Jack informed him they were Black Angus, and they were, indeed, solid black.

"How many head do you have?" He was eager to show he had some of the "lingo" down.

"Here on this lease, about two hundred, but I have four other leases with another hundred," was Jack's answer. "I have fifty cows and steers, and a couple of bulls, back at the ranch."

"Why aren't they all out on the range?"

"The bulls are for mating, artificial insemination of course, make some extra money that way, selling the semen. But we don't want them out here with the cows and their calves," Jack gave out a short laugh. "They're ornery. The others, for eatin', me and my wife. I often get a few orders for beef on the hoof, take 'em down to slaughter and then the butcher. Make pretty good money, tides us over until the auctions this fall."

"Do you sell all of them at auction?"

Jack shook his head. "Depends on the market, how much beef prices are going for. We keep the heifers for next year's grazing and fattening, maybe a few of the older cows who've produced well for us. We keep data sheets on all of them, their ages, how many calves they've had. We take the science seriously. My dad ranched these parts for fifty years, he'd hardly recognize the way we handle these animals now."

Tab did some quick math. In part of his "research" in New York he learned the going rate for livestock at market. By his reckoning, he might be staring at nearly a half million dollars or more in these cows' faces.

Jack steered his truck around a sharp bend, another hill climbed, and he brought the truck to an abrupt stop.

"Right there," he pointed, "is the biggest problem we face."

Down the slope, a hundred feet away in a wide basin, stood a dozen horses.

The two men got out. Jack led the way to a better vantage point.

"This is what's left of the Desert Oak herd, the ones that got away. There's the lead stallion." Jack pointed to a roan horse who was taking an interest in the men. The horse shook his head and reared up, then stomped the ground with his hooves, scattering dirt and rocks.

Tab wondered if they should walk away, back to the safety of the truck. "Is he threatening us?"

"Nah, letting us know he doesn't like us here." The herd held an assortment of browns, grays, whites. Pintos, roans and bays. Foals scampered about, twirled around, stayed close to their mothers.

Jack continued. "The horse people, photographers and such, give them names, call them families. They even have social media pages for them, genealogy charts, it's sickening. Makes no difference to us."

"What do you mean?"

"These horses, they don't belong here, they're invasive. Weren't here until four hundred years ago, so you can't call them native, no sirreee. They're stupid, don't produce a thing, have no value."

"You said something about sage grouse yesterday? I'm not sure I understand."

"There are these environmentalists that want to 'restore the land' back to what it was a thousand years ago or something," Jack answered derisively. "Re-introducing species we spent the last hundred years blowing to bits. Like the sage grouse. Stupid prairie chickens don't do a dang thing for this land. They're trying to tell us it's no big deal, they'll bring in a few dozen of them to see how they do, pilot programs. But," he tapped his forehead, "they think we're a bunch of dumb cattlemen. We know what they're up to. I got an idea or two to mess the Double B's plans up, got to find the right way to do it.

"This is grazing land for our cows. That's where they want to put those chickens. Now, those chickens are endangered species, so it means the land will be restricted, too. No roads, no recreation like dirt bikes, no 'interrupting' their precious little chicken lives. Our grazing leases suspended, so no cows. The horses? Oh, they'll be allowed to stay. Because prime chicken habitat is also, wait for it, prime horse habitat, too."

Tab saw where Jack was leading. "They're trying to do an end run around your leases, save the horses."

"No more gathers, no trapping, leave the horses alone to breed like the weeds they are."

They watched for a few minutes, the stallion lost interest in the men and returned to his mares.

"Next year, these are going to be gathered, all of them gone."

"What happens to them?"

Jack shrugged. "Sent to the slaughter house. And good riddance."

"Now that you're getting the lay of the land, so to speak, we'll have to start talking about your future with us. You'll have to take the Wyoming bar exam, but that shouldn't be too hard with your Big College Education, right?"

Tab blinked, startled. Pass the Wyoming Bar? He hadn't thought that far ahead. Maybe he was just here on a lark, a fun time somebody else was paying for, a job interview, sure, but did he want the job?

Moving to Wyoming. Finding a place to live. Setting up an office. He visualized his name on a sign. "Tab Taggart, Esq., Attorney at Law."

And what influence did a certain red-haired, blue-eyed young woman have on his decision?

He knew one thing for certain, he would never return to D.C., work for another big law firm, stuck in a cubicle for years, maybe the rest of his life.

He nodded at Jack. "I'll find out when the next rotation of Bar exams is—"

Jack interrupted him. "Already did. Next month in Laramie. Just sign up with your bona fides. In the meantime, you can act as our consultant."

He fished out a slip of paper from his shirt pocket. "How does this amount settle with you?"

Tab unfolded the piece of paper and read it, trying to keep a poker face, and most likely failing. He cleared his throat, swallowed. "This looks fine. I'll start on Monday."

"Son," Jack said, waving his hands to the landscape, "you've already started."

CHAPTER 28
COWBOY BOOTS

"Where can I buy a pair of cowboy boots?" Tab smiled at Becky as she placed his cold drink on the table.

"Gotta be the Red Ranch Barn. It's about fifteen minutes away, not far." She laughed. "Are we making a cowboy out of you?"

"Maybe. I might be moving to Wyoming. Things are looking good. You're working here today?" Mid-afternoon, The Coffee Wrangler wasn't very busy.

Becky nodded. "Our vet went to Jackson to meet with the state agriculture board." She rolled her eyes. "Paperwork is the least favorite part of being a large animal veterinarian."

Tab leaned back. "Large animal?"

"Small animal vets take care of dogs, cats, puppies, kittens. Large animal vets take care of cows, horses, hogs, sheep, goats."

"What kind of paperwork is needed? Government stuff?"

"Proof of vaccinations and blood testing, mostly, we also making sure brand inspections are up to date. County fairs are coming up later this summer, there's always lots to do, making sure animals are healthy and don't have any disease."

"I had no idea," Tab said, and he was sincere. He really didn't have any idea.

A group of customers came in and sat on the other side of the room.

"Better get to work."

Tab tilted his head. "Do you think you'd have time to go with me to look at those cowboy boots? What did you call me when we first met? Oh, yeah, a tenderfoot. You're right. I have no idea what I'm doing. I'll drive."

Becky paused. Tab was older than her, nice looking, but there was Phillip.

No, she remembered, there is no Phillip.

She made a decision.

"Sure. I'm off in half an hour."

Becky sat in the passenger seat as close to the door as she could get, her arms folded tightly against her chest. She chided herself, *Why am I so nervous? Why did I say yes? We're going to look at boots, for crying out loud. This isn't a date. Is it?*

Tab steered the car onto the road. Asking Becky to help him pick out boots was an impulse, certainly not like any other first date he'd ask a girl out to. In D.C. it might be asking her to coffee, or a club. Of course, this wasn't really a date. But, he'd asked. She'd accepted.

Glancing over at her, he figured he could do worse in this little sojourn to the middle of nowhere.

"How's your baby horse?"

Becky's face broke into a wide smile. "Perfect. He's a frisky little guy. We've named him Alexander. He and his mama are both able to go outside in the field, and that's helping their attitudes—a lot."

"Horses have attitudes?"

"They're smart, have feelings, emotions that run the gamut from being very loving to being very stubborn. Every horse is different."

"You have a ranch, then?"

"No, my parents have a small farm, only a few acres. We have two fields of alfalfa that we harvest one or two times a year. And horses, we've always owned horses."

They pulled into Pinedale and Becky pointed the way to the Red Ranch Barn. True to its name, it looked like a barn, and it was painted red.

They passed shelves of shirts and blue jeans. "Maybe I'll get some shirts, a couple pair of pants." Tab leafed through the selections. "I didn't get a chance to pack much."

The footwear section was large, holding hundreds of different varieties on shelves and in racks. The men's cowboy boots were a dizzying array of colors and patterns.

"You look like you're a deer in the headlights," Becky chuckled. It was true. Tab gaped at the selections in front of him.

A salesman approached. Becky suggested a pair of "dress casual," nice looking, black with a nice pattern, not for riding or work, for inside. "Meetings and such," she smiled up at Tab.

He smiled back. It was almost as though she already knew him, and he liked this feeling.

He picked out an expensive pair of black and white diamond boots. "Now I can fit in," he laughed.

He added a couple of shirts and a pair of blue jeans, paying for all with a credit card. They returned to the car. Becky asked him to drop her off at The Coffee Wrangler.

"How about a proper thank you for helping me today? Have dinner with me tomorrow night. I hear that restaurant, the Riata, is pretty good."

Becky turned her head away to look out the window. Dinner? With this man?

Why not? She'd already told Phillip she was "exploring," so why not make good on it? *He doesn't care anymore, I'm free to do what I want.*

"I'd like that, thanks."

After leaving Becky, Tab went to his hotel. A brilliant idea hit him. As he passed the counter, he asked the clerk if there was a local florist.

"Pinedale, a gift shop, and they also have flowers."

"We need to discuss Autumn and Alexander," Carl said to his wife and daughter. They were enjoying a cool evening outside.

Becky looked down. She'd been quiet through dinner.

"Does Dr. Shultz think it's OK to take them back to Silver Moon?" Tess asked. "He was here this afternoon, didn't stay long. I didn't get a chance to talk to him."

Carl pursed his lips. He knew why the veterinarian had been here, hadn't stayed long, but he was sworn to secrecy, and that included his wife and daughter. "He texted me before he left. He sees no reason to delay it."

Becky leaned back, closing her eyes. "No reason," she whispered. "Except it's so dangerous for a wild horse, out there." Skylar's questions came back to her, questions for which there were few answers.

Hard winters, hard summers, hard men who might be the worst danger mustangs face.

Tess reached over to hold her daughter's hand. "I know how difficult this is for you. We were there the first time you let her go."

"Seems like I'm always saying goodbye to that horse." Becky looked up. "Tomorrow?"

Carl nodded. "Early, before dawn just before first light. Beat all of the wildlife photographers. I'd rather nobody else knows and I sure don't want our pictures showing up on the Internet, releasing two horses up on that meadow. We'll trailer them up, it'll be faster that way. Dr. J volunteered to go up too, find Silver Moon and his family."

"Good plan." So, it was decided. This would be the last night Becky would have with Autumn and Alexander. *I'm losing so much. What else will I lose?*

CHAPTER 29
MOSAIC

Aarón Blanco stepped out of his stone-and-mortar casa. His cat, Napoleon, jumped on a nearby rock, waiting for a scratch behind the ear. He wasn't disappointed.

Aarón lingered with the cat for several minutes, enjoying this early morning routine. "You are spoiled, amigo."

The cat purred, rolled over on the rock, then curled up for his nap. Satisfied the cat was settled, Aarón stepped around the corner, knowing what he would find.

"Hola, my friend." Mosaic, the black and white stallion, stood on the hill behind the casa. "You've been waiting patiently for me, haven't you. It is still dark, the sun has not yet come up. What are we going to do today?"

The horse sauntered down the hill to the narrow trail leading to the towering rocks overlooking the mountain meadows.

He turned, inviting Aarón to join him, which the man did.

For more than five years, Aarón and the horse were friends of a sort. When he first appeared one misty morning, Aarón thought he was a ghost, an apparition from one of his grandmother's superstitious stories. No, the horse was real, skittish, not trusting the man.

Perhaps he was from the reservation's wild horse sanctuary, many miles and several valleys away. Aarón knew all of those male horses are gelded, castrated. This one wasn't.

Perhaps the stallion was from across the river, a likely explanation. The horse showed no interest in returning, nor did he show any interest in leaving to seek out his own family, fight for mares, sire foals.

Aarón saw him often, drinking from the creek, traveling back and forth over nearby hills, never coming close to the casa, sometimes seeming to want the old man's attention, for some reason. The striking black and white pattern on the horse gave him the obvious name: Mosaic.

Mosaic would often disappear for a day or two before wandering back home, looking none the worse for wear. Mostly he seemed content to keep a good distance, watching Aarón go about his business on his small farm.

He was especially curious when Aarón got into his old truck and drive away down the dirt road, the mustang rearing up and kicking dust and debris into the air. From anger? Concern? Who knew what was going through Mosaic's mind. Always, the horse would be at the roadside when Aarón returned.

Was it wrong to encourage Mosaic to stay nearby? Aarón knew

better than to give the horse treats such as fruits or oats, the stomach of wild horses cannot tolerate such a diet, but on harsh winter days, he filled a bucket with water from his well and placed it a hundred feet from his door. Mosaic wouldn't have to break ice from the stream to drink.

When snow began to fall, he also moved his truck out of its lean-to, figuring the stallion might like the shelter from the storms.

Perhaps it *was* wrong, perhaps Aarón should have reported Mosaic to "the authorities," watch him captured, forced into a trailer, disappear to a fate surely worse than death.

He carried a cell phone and while reception was terrible in his casa, it wasn't down the road closer to town. Yes, he could have called. One year led to another. And another. And another. The call was never made.

There was one person Aarón confided in. The only person he trusted with this secret about the wild mustang, the one person who would never betray his trust, the one person who loved Mosaic almost as much as he did.

Now the old man followed Mosaic, keeping his customary, respectful distance, learning over the years not to crowd the horse.

The towering rocks were a short distance.

Right at dawn, Mosaic and the old man reached the narrow opening between the rocks. It was shady here, the light never penetrated; they both knew they were concealed as they looked down on the mountain meadow, and watched what was happening.

CHAPTER 30
REUNION

"Come on, beautiful girl, you're leaving us." Becky tried not to let her emotions get in the way, but was failing by the minute. Tears stung her eyes. This was a tough morning.

Becky led Autumn into the horse trailer by a thin rope around her neck, she easily entered the horse trailer. Alexander was eager to join his mother, but hesitated. Carl picked him up over the step.

"Saying goodbye to her is harder than it was two years ago," Becky told her mother.

Tess remembered watching her daughter standing in the mud and debris from the flood, remove Autumn's lead rope, giving her the choice to stay, or leave with the white stallion looming over them a few feet away.

That was the day she chose Silver Moon.

Today she'd be returning to him. Tess put her arm around her daughter's shoulders. "She trusts you to do the right thing."

Carl started the truck and the two women got in. Dawn hadn't yet nudged itself over the mountains, the air was cool.

Minutes later they approached the road leading from the Double B to the switchbacks. Joe held the gate open for them. The look on his face showed his emotions were as torn as Becky's.

"Phillip and I are right behind you," Joe motioned at the Double B's truck, idling nearby. Phillip sat, stone-faced, at the wheel staring straight ahead. Becky was surprised he was there.

A half hour later, the two trucks skirted gullies and rocks as they made their way across the meadow.

Dr. J waved to them from some rocks near the cliffs. Well before dawn, she left to scout the area in her own four-wheel drive, looking for Autumn's family. She found them below the waterfall.

She pointed to Silver Moon watching intently from the top of a knoll.

"It's almost as though he knows Autumn's coming back to him," she told them.

"I think he does." Becky agreed.

Phillip and Joe joined the others to open the trailer's door.

Autumn came out first, trotting a few feet towards the herd. Alexander stepped to the door, uncertain.

"Come on, little guy," Becky coaxed.

Phillip reached in to pick him up. "There you go." He put him down gently on the ground.

Alexander sprinted after his mother, who stopped to wait.

"They're home," Tess said, reaching back to Becky's hand.

Something unexpected happened. Autumn returned to Becky, and nuzzled her shoulder.

The girl threw her arms around the horse's neck and grabbed a piece of her mane, holding on as tight as she could, as long as she could.

"I love you so much, Autumn," Becky sobbed. "I'm losing you. Again. You be a good girl. Don't get into any trouble, understand? You don't want me coming back up here and kicking your butt, got it?"

Autumn snuffled. They stood this way for several seconds, until finally the horse broke away and galloped towards Silver Moon, her little boy behind her, trying hard to keep up.

Silver Moon greeted his first mare, putting his head on her back, rubbing it several times, nibbling at her ears.

"What took you so long?" he joked.

She laughed. "Did you miss me?"

"More than you'll ever know. Let's introduce our son to the others."

He led the way down the other side to the waterfall where the herd waited.

Above, in the cleft between two tall rocks, Mosaic and the old man stood in the shadows.

Mosaic shuffled his two front legs, pawing at the ground with his hooves. He stared intently as the horses below them join the rest of the herd. He neighed when he saw the foal stumble.

"He's OK," Aarón assured Mosaic. "See? He got back up and is running to his mother."

The sun began to rise, lighting the scene below.

"This means something to you, doesn't it?" Aarón said to the horse.

"Do you want to go down and join them?"

Mosaic glanced at the old man and shook his head.

"When you do that, I am positive you know what I'm saying," Aarón chuckled, leaning against the rock. "Kinda spooky."

Mosaic backed up, turned away, and walked down the rocky slope to the trail leading to their home.

Aarón stayed a few minutes longer, hoping to find some clue, an idea, of why the horse insisted on leading him there that morning.

The people got in their trucks and left the meadow the way they had come.

It seemed all was well with Silver Moon and his family. The mares drank water, pulled at grass and wild flowers, the foals began a game of hunt and chase.

Peaceful. Loving. Nothing to see here.

Was there?

Before she returned to her truck, Dr. J's eyes traveled up the waterfall, to the dark shadows of the rocks.

Her sixth sense pricked at her. Was somebody there? Was somebody, *something*, watching them?

She was sure there was, and she was sure she knew who.

CHAPTER 31
ROSES

Phillip felt his insides shred to pieces as he watched Becky with Autumn. He desperately wanted to go to her, hold her, let her cry on his shoulder, whatever it might take to make her feel better.

His pride and hurt feelings wouldn't let him.

How could he have let their "talk" the previous day get so out of control? He regretted his words, telling her he didn't want to "be" her life, telling her he'd dated other women.

He'd forced her to sling her own hurtful words at him. He didn't know how to love, didn't know what a family was. She was already "exploring" other relationships. Did she have a boyfriend in college? No, Becky was not that kind of girl, sneaky or secretive. Still, what did she mean?

Fortunately, the conference center monopolized much of his attention, answering questions from the contractors, studying a myriad of inspection approvals for everything from electrical to windows seals.

Joe met him upstairs in the conference room, the offices almost finished except for the flooring. "Dr. Shultz called, he needs one of us to sign his last inspection of the cows and he has those supplements for the horses. Can you go? I want to make sure those electrical outlets are where they need to be for Lacaria's studio." Joe laughed. "Lacaria is fit to be tied, she won't allow one piece of her equipment in this building until it's all cleaned up."

Phillip tried not to cringe. The vet clinic? Maybe Becky wouldn't be there.

It was a short drive to the clinic. Walking in, he was hit with the pleasant aroma of flowers, and immediately saw the source. An immense bouquet of assorted roses, three dozen, reds, whites, yellows dominated the counter.

Dr. Shultz heard the clinic door open.

"Ah, Phillip," he pointed and winked at the flowers. "Nice of you to have these sent. Becky was pretty torn up when she got here this morning. She's at lunch, hasn't seen them, yet." The vet winked again and went into his office.

Phillip didn't know what to say, his tongue couldn't form any words. *I didn't send these flowers.* He touched one of the roses, saw a card sticking out from the vase. Making sure the door to the office was closed, he read it.

Becky, thanks so much for your help with the boots.
They are so comfortable, don't know why
I never got a pair before!
Looking forward to dinner tonight.
- Your Tenderfoot, Tab

Tab? Who's Tab? Phillip frowned, reading the note again. Boots? Dinner? He felt his face get red. This was who she was "exploring" her life with, some guy with a dumb name? *How long has this been going on?* He hastily returned the card to its holder as the office door opened.

Phillip took the forms from the vet. Mumbling thanks, he couldn't get out of the clinic fast enough. He didn't want to be here when Becky returned.

"Wow, a lot of flowers!" Becky exclaimed. "What's the occasion?"

"Somebody wanted to let you know he's thinking about you," Dr. Shultz answered with a sly grin before returning to his office.

Her heart skipped a beat. Phillip? Phillip sent her flowers?

She read the card and her heart tumbled.

From Tab, a guy who meant little to her. Thanking her for some trivial help.

Not from Phillip, watching with no emotion on his face as she let Autumn go this morning. Not offering help, nor sympathy, nor giving any indication he wanted to take back his hurtful words, make up to her, or at least try to.

She put the card in her pocket. She didn't want anybody to read it, ashamed the flowers weren't from Phillip.

Silly girl, she chided. *Get over it. Get over Phillip.* The thought hit her hard, and so did the tears stinging her eyes.

The phone rang. One of their clients needed help with a cow, came up lame last night.

Back to work, the distraction was welcome.

CHAPTER 32
THE HEIR

Lacaria began to open the boxes in the garage. All of the new equipment for her studio was in them, and she wanted to make sure nothing was damaged or missing. She picked up a binder and began to shuffle pages back and forth, looking for her inventory sheets.

"Can't wait to get in there, can you?" Phillip leaned against the open doorway. He meant her new studio.

"No, I can't. If I could get all of this installed and working today, I'd do it," she laughed. "I never realized how important something like this could be in my life."

He helped her open more boxes while she checked off items. Computers. Monitors. Headsets. Microphones. Cameras. A small box held software, another revealed a myriad of cables and wires.

"You've really taken to podcasting, been amazing to watch."

She sat down on a bench. "When Dr. J first showed me how to set her podcast up, I was pretty intimidated. A few hours later," she shrugged, "I seemed to know what I was doing. I also felt like I was doing something important."

"You've got a tech-wired brain," he smiled, joining her on the bench.

They sat for a few moments. Lacaria knew Phillip was worried about something.

"Joe said Becky was pretty torn up about releasing Autumn and Alexander," she started the conversation, but didn't mention Joe told her Phillip ignored Becky. "Didn't even try to console her or even talk to her," was Joe's description. "Something's going on between those two."

Phillip cleared his throat, hung his head down. "Yeah. Suppose I could have helped. Uhm, she and I, we're not getting along too good."

"She hasn't been here much, of course she was occupied with Autumn. But you haven't been *there*, either, as often as you used to," meaning the MacKendrick farm.

"Yeah." He bit a lower lip. "I've been thinking a lot about something Becky said. Maybe I'm holding her down, like Grandpa did to me."

Lacaria smiled. "I don't think Becky is the kind of woman to be 'held down.' And she'd let you know pretty quick if you even tried."

Phillip shrugged. "Is there something wrong with me? I'm tired all the time, can't seem to get enough sleep."

"You've pushed yourself hard, maybe too hard?"

"Becky said something, got me thinking. Do I know how to be in a family, do I know how to love?"

She was shocked. "Why would you ask that? We're your family, Joe and I. We know you love us."

Phillip shook his head. "I came here when I was a little kid. My mom and dad were gone. I don't remember them, I don't remember if they loved me, I don't remember if I ever cried. I do remember meeting Al. Everybody said he was my grandpa, he was going to take care of me." He grimaced. "He scared me. All I wanted to do was hide under the bed."

"We've never talked about this, have we." Her eyes softened.

"Did you know my mom and dad?"

"We watched Al groom him, getting him ready to be the heir to the Double B. Not sure he counted on him meeting Mary, them getting married so soon.

"The wedding was here. It was a big affair with people coming from Jackson to Cheyenne, ranching families with strong ties to Al.

"Joe and I weren't invited, of course, we helped with the plans from catering to decorations. I baked the wedding cake, covered with pink and purple sugar roses."

Lacaria wondered if she would be supplanted by Mary, two women in the house after all. Mary was content with letting Lacaria carry on, especially after she got pregnant.

"You were born on a blustery spring day."

Four years later, Bryan and Mary were returning from visiting Mary's family in Cody. Hit a spot of ice, the car spun out of control into a gully.

The couple was killed. Phillip, in the back seat, survived.

It was quickly decided the boy would come live with Al. The Big Man owned the Big House, the Big Ranch. Mary's family owned a furniture store, barely getting by with two other children still at home. In the years following, Joe and Lacaria often wondered about the hurried decision, if Mary's family regretted it, bullied by Al with his money and status in the state.

"You came home in the middle of the night, a little tow-headed boy, alone."

"You fixed me a peanut butter and jelly sandwich and chocolate milk." He smiled at the warm memory.

"My heart went out to you, how couldn't it? Trying to be so strong and brave. No question, Joe and I were going to love and take care of you. We couldn't have children of our own. You became our son. Joe took you camping, fishing. I made sure you were dressed in the best clothes, got good grades in school, read you bedtime stories, took your temperature when you were sick.

"We always wondered if Al saw what we did, maybe even resented it. If he did, he never said anything. By then, maybe his heart was closed. He'd lost his wife, then his son. He wanted you here, as his heir, but didn't seem to be interested in anything else where you were concerned."

Phillip's laugh was sarcastic. "Then when I grew up, I ruined it by rejecting him, the ranch."

"No, you didn't ruin anything. Al ruined it. He could have done things different, he chose not to. He should have been as proud of you as I am."

Phillip wasn't sure if his questions were answered. He put his arm around Lacaria.

"Do you ever wonder why I never call you my mother?"

"No." She shook her head. "You had a mom, I understand."

"Maybe you could get used to it? And calling Joe, 'Dad'?"

"We could, but it has to come from *your* heart."

"What if it's too late for me, for us? And," he closed his eyes, "for Becky?" He squeezed her hand.

She squeezed back. "What if it isn't?"

IN THE DARK NIGHT

CHAPTER 33
PEGGY SUE AND ALEXANDER

Peggy Sue was a black and white Pinto, with a white skull face, white mane, and white tail.

Wildlife photographers discovered her when she was born to Juno. It was remarkable she "found" her long legs within hours of birth and only a day later was seen scampering about, to and fro, from mare to mare. Pictures and videos of her flashed from social media page to social media page.

She soon became the darling of the mountain meadow.

This morning, she found a new playmate.

Alexander was shy at first, uncertain about this new place.

"I miss Dot and Max. Where's Corky?"

His mother was reassuring. "This is our home. These are your aunts and cousins." Autumn swished her tail back and forth.

"I'd rather stay with you," he whined.

Peggy Sue nudged him. "What's your name?" she asked.

"Alexander."

"Want to play?"

"Doing what?"

"I like to jump over rocks and there's a bunch of water to splash. And mud. Mud is good."

"Go on," Autumn encouraged. "I'll keep an eye on you."

Peggy Sue hopped across rocks and tufts of grass, showing the way. Alexander followed her lead. Stopped.

"What's wrong?"

Alexander stared at the white horse standing on the knoll. "I'm frightened of him. He's so big."

"That's Papa. He *has* to be big. Once you get to know him, he's not scary. Mama says he'll always protect us."

Before long, Peggy Sue and Alexander were splashing in the lake until they got hungry and returned to their mothers for another breakfast.

"He's a sturdy little fellow." Silver Moon watched his daughter and newest son prancing around the meadow.

"He might be as big as you are when he grows up," Juno agreed.

Autumn pulled a tuft of grass. "I heard what happened with Liam."

"Hmmph," the stallion responded. "Completely unnecessary challenge, I put him in his place."

"It'll happen more often, Silver Moon." Juno was his oldest mare, and the wisest. She knew how families were. "You have to be ready, always watching."

He looked at her for a few moments. She was right, but he hated the idea. "I remember how I felt when I was attacked by my father. Running away from him, leaving my mother."

"Warrior was a great stallion." Juno mumbled through a mouthful of wildflowers.

"Did you know him?" Autumn asked her, curious.

"I saw him from time to time, he stole a mare or two out of my family. He was, shall we say, greedy. Never seemed to be content with what he had."

Autumn turned to her stallion. "What happened to him?"

Silver Moon shook his head. "After my mother died, I never saw him again."

"The same thing with most of my family," Juno said. "We ran and ran, and then saw you."

"It was a bad day." Silver Moon turned and moved away. Remembering was hard, watching his mother die, unable to do anything except cross the river, try to find a safe place, a new life.

Sandy was near enough to have heard the conversation. She touched her mother's nose affectionately. "I'm glad you're back. I missed you."

Autumn nipped at Sandy's back, a loving gesture. "I'm sorry I was gone so long. Your baby brother gave me quite a time of it."

"You smell different."

Autumn knew her daughter smelled humans. "I needed some help," she said as explanation. Sandy would never understand, or appreciate, Autumn's affection for humans. She was like her father.

They watched Alexander and Peggy Sue for a time, burning off their endless supply of energy.

"You'll be having one of your own soon enough," Autumn said.

"Start your own family, away from here."

Sandy shuffled her body closer to her mother. "I hope not too far away. And, I hope, not with Liam. He's such a wuss."

"I think you'll do better than him," Autumn shook her head laughing. "No stallion will be as good as your father, of course."

Sandy glanced at Silver Moon, standing on a nearby hill overlooking the meadow.

She agreed. "Of course."

Peggy Sue and Alexander chased each other around, learning together how to play and have fun. He tripped over rocks more than once, but always righted himself. It wouldn't take him long to master his gangly legs.

Once, they got too close to one of the older mares, she snapped at them impatiently. Alexander shied away, but Peggy Sue laughed. "Our aunts don't like to be teased," she told him, "but it's still kind of fun to do it."

The two youngsters were getting tired and hungry. They found Autumn and Juno together, pulling grass and wild flowers from the ground. Soon they were tucked in between the two of them, nursing in their mothers' safety and warmth before exhaustion and full bellies forced them down into the tall grass for a long afternoon nap.

CHAPTER 34
DINNER

Why aren't I looking forward to tonight? Becky wondered for the tenth time. Phillip is a jerk and doesn't want me anymore. Why not be with somebody who likes her, makes her feel special.

She looked at herself on the back of her bedroom door. Her dress was a dark green shift topped with a flower-patterned vest, a little dressy, not formal.

She tucked a wisp of hair behind an ear, deciding not to put on some makeup.

"Looking a bit haggard, aren't I?" She reached down to pet Corky.

Sleepless nights were catching up to her. Autumn and Alexander had required many watchful hours.

The awful fight with Phillip. She'd said things she shouldn't have, he said things he meant. He broke her heart, and didn't seem to care.

Tab sent her flowers. She should be grateful, she should find some sense of happiness in his attention. She didn't, and she knew why.

Tab wasn't Phillip. And he should be.

Phillip slept little these last few nights.

He couldn't get his mind off the card attached to those roses.

Who was this Tab guy, and what kind of a guy has a name like "Tab"?

She helped him with boots? And was having dinner with him? Tonight? Where were they going? What time? What would she wear?

Again, who was this Tab guy?

Tab left his hotel room, a skip in his step. In a few minutes he'd be with Becky, and he couldn't wait.

He hoped sending her those roses would be appreciated. He'd thought long and hard about having them sent to where she worked, what kind, how many, how much to spend? Whenever he'd dated a girl before, they always seemed to like flowers, often the gesture paid off in his favor. Becky shouldn't be any different.

There was another reason to be happy. He was working out a contract with Jack, a good one, more money than he would ever make in D.C. He looked forward to telling Becky he would be moving to Wyoming, maybe she could help him scout out locations for an office? Who knows, maybe she would even give up this silly idea of her becoming a veterinarian and come work for him as his assistant? Options swirled in his imagination.

Good options. For both of them.

Becky looked for Tab in the Riata's dining room.

Most of the tables were occupied, she spotted Tab in a corner.

He waved, smiled. He *was* good looking.

Come on Becks, she whispered. *Be happy. Who knows what this will lead to?*

"You sure look nice," Tab complimented, standing to hold out a chair for her.

They made the customary small talk, she thanked him for the roses because it was the thing to do.

"Did you really like them? I called my mom to ask her if I should send them, she said women always like roses." (A lie, Tab hadn't talked to his mother since she'd left on her cruise.)

He asked more questions. How was her day? How was her job?

She told him about the lame cow, no obvious injury, quarantined in a barn stall, blood tests taken, still no results.

He seemed interested.

She ordered the special, trout amandine, he ordered a rib steak.

"Gotta admit, never tasted beef like you have here. New York, D.C., those restaurants don't have a clue."

She stared. *This man has no clue what the actual cost of that beef steak is.*

Did he wonder why she wasn't asking about him, his day, how his "interviews" were going? She wasn't even curious about his mother, where did she live?

She realized he didn't, and she realized *she* wasn't curious about him, his day, his job, his mother, or anything else about him.

Tab paid the bill. He put his arm around her as they walked outside.

"Beautiful evening. Would you like to come back to my hotel, how about a nightcap?"

A nightcap? She looked up at him. "Not sure what you mean."

"I have a bottle of wine chilling on some ice." His grip on her shoulder tightened. "I have something to celebrate, I'll tell you all about it."

"Oh, uhm." They walked across the parking lot. "I should be getting home, Dr. Shultz wants me in the office early."

His grin seemed to be have turned into a leer.

Phillip decided to take a little drive, get his mind off of things. Things like Becky.

He ended up near the Riata. He couldn't have known where this Tab guy was taking her for dinner.

He craned his neck to see the parking lot in front of the restaurant. His heart skipped a beat when he saw her car. It skipped another beat when she saw Becky and a tall man coming out the door.

What were the chances?

Becky stepped away from Tab, putting some distance between them.

"Thank you for the flowers, thank you for dinner, I've gotta be getting home."

"And you'll get home, come up with me to my room." Tab reached out to grab one of her arms.

"Come on, dinner was great, I sent you flowers. Most girls like to get flowers."

Before Tab could touch her again, he felt a hand on his shoulder.

"What?" Tab was pushed away, he turned to face his attacker, a larger man with long, blonde hair.

"Who are you?" His tone was indignant.

"Right now, somebody who's telling you to get out of here, leave, now, before I do something I will regret. Not *might* regret, *will* regret."

"I know who you are now. You're that Phillip Ebbers guy. This is none of your business. The lady and I are talking."

Becky stood, arms folded, a shocked look on her face.

"It is my business and it's clear you weren't just talking." Phillip stepped closer to Tab, who backed away.

"Fine, I'm leaving, don't want any trouble, not from anybody around here, got it?" Tab held up his hands, then walked towards the hotel, giving a backward glance every few feet.

"Are you OK?" Phillip asked.

"You didn't have to get involved," she said through gritted teeth.

"I did, and I'm not sorry."

"Not sorry. You say and do whatever you want, and you're never sorry." She shook her head. "Well, I'm sorry, for a lot of things, and a lot of them are about you. You broke up with me, remember?"

She wasn't finished telling men off. Tab was several feet away when Becky shouted to him, "And, I'm not most girls!"

She didn't know if he heard her or not, but Becky felt good yelling at him.

Phillip watched her walk away. At least now he knew who that Tab guy was, but was left with another question: *How did he know who Phillip was?*

Becky slammed the kitchen door behind her and ran into the living room.

Carl and Tess were finishing some apple pie.

"Me or you?" Carl mumbled between bites.

"Me. I think. Maybe." Tess found Becky on the couch, hugging a pillow.

"I don't know what to do."

Biting her lower lip to keep from crying, Becky told her mother about the fight with Phillip, the things both of them said to each other.

She also told her about Tab.

"I don't know why I agreed to go out to dinner with him. I'm not interested in him, don't even find him that attractive. Well," she paused, "maybe a little. I like the flirting, the way he looks at me, laughs at my jokes, listens to me."

"Sounds like all of that comes with a price." Tess put her arms around her daughter. "Some men are like that. Remember when I said he was a jerk? That's what I meant, he's that kind of man."

Phillip isn't, Becky thought. She put her head on Tess's shoulder. "I'm so tired right now, all I want to do is sleep and forget about everyone and everything. Disappear."

Tess closed her eyes. This was the Becky from two years ago, when she'd lost her champion horse. Shutting me out, refusing to talk, refusing to see a future.

Oh, please, don't go back there, please.

CHAPTER 35
STAMPEDE!

"Do you hate cows?" Skylar asked. Several groups of the animals, many with calves, stood on either side of the dirt road, curiously staring at them or languidly walking along a fence line.

She was in the back seat of the truck. Phillip drove and Joe was in the passenger seat.

Phillip chuckled and shook his head. "No, I'm an American. Love hamburgers. Truth is, cattlemen have over-extended their welcome on public lands. Overgrazed is an understatement, cows foul waterways, ponds, lakes. A hundred years ago, ranches were large, certainly large enough for cows, the demand for beef grew after World War I. Feeding cows is expensive. So public lands were opened up to them, to feed off prairie or desert grasses or plants. It's not particularly efficient."

Joe added, "The cows are out here all summer. They don't gain weight, add fat like they do in the early fall at the feedlots, several weeks before auction and the slaughter houses. The long and short of it, cows are parked on public land. And most of the beef is exported to other countries, while Americans import their beef from South America."

Phillip drove up a small hill and parked at the top, they all piled out. "I'm glad it's not windy, I think we got lucky."

He lifted a large drone from a box in the truck's bed and handed Skylar the drone's control unit. A series of beeps followed and she bent her head to look at the large monitor.

She reported, "Batteries are good and we're acquiring eighteen satellites." The day before she had read the instruction manual and viewed various videos. The control and screen were akin to her gaming setup back home. As with everything else "high tech," Skylar was a quick learner.

"How many acres are you going to survey today?" she asked.

"I'm going to try for fifty," Phillip answered, taking the control from her. "We've staked out almost a hundred plots for leks, those are sage grouse habitats centered around mounds of plants. Those would be nests for the females to lay their eggs."

Joe carried the drone to a flat area thirty feet away. He would serve as Phillip's watcher, keeping the drone in sight, and taking notes as needed.

Skylar stepped away, Phillip keyed the rotors, the drone went up. And away.

This was good, getting away from the ranch, Phillip thought. After last night, his nerves were still on edge. *My stupid nerves, that is. What was I thinking, threatening that guy "Tab?" Becky can take care of herself. She was right. I did break up with her. Why do I care?*

Phillip paid attention to the drone's progress as it zipped back and forth across the sky. His goal was to take pictures and record video of the terrain, gullies, rock outcrops, and streambeds. The drone was also equipped with infrared cameras to show vegetation of different kinds, from rabbit brush to junipers, cottonwoods to ground-hugging plants.

He would fly the drone over the leks before they left, to make sure all of the stakes and string were intact.

All of this data would be used to justify using the Double B's grazing allotments for other animals besides cattle, such as sage grouse and, of course, wild horses.

Science, not emotion, was being used to make their case to the government.

Skylar watched for several minutes. A city girl, she had never been in such a wide-open space. No buildings, no fences, miles of rocky desert.

You can see zombies coming at you, but what if zombies flew? She smiled. Flying zombies. That would be a new twist.

She decided to explore a little, walked down a ravine near the truck, then up a gentle slope. A narrow game trail beckoned, she followed it for a short distance towards a copse of shady cottonwoods.

A movement caught her eye. She squinted against the sun's haze. A bunch of cows were heading her way. Twenty or thirty of them. No, more like fifty or sixty. And moving fast. Toward her!

She looked back, realizing how far she had walked away from the truck. Terrified, she froze.

Phillip saw the cows on his screen. The drone was a half mile away. He checked his coordinates. No, the machine was definitely above the Double B lease, it hadn't strayed. *What are those cows doing on my allotment?*

He moved the toggle to bring the drone up higher.

Phillip grimaced when he saw how far out it was.

He toggled the drone to return.

The cows heard the drone, and didn't like it. The herd began to move, then trot.

"Joe, get back here," he shouted, waving.

The Basque hurried back. The wind began to blow.

"We have a lot of cows coming our way. Where's Skylar?"

Joe pointed. "She went over there. I'll go look for her."

Joe ran, shouting Skylar's name.

Skylar heard Joe calling, but he was far away. The wind was picking up.

The cows were still running towards her. She could hear them mooing and rasping. A sea of browns and whites and blacks, kicking up dirt all around them. The sound of hundreds of hooves on the ground was unlike anything she'd ever heard.

The wind buffeted her, dust stung her face, choked her throat. She turned away, knowing she could not outrun these big animals.

Hope you're happy, mom and dad, I'm going to die here. Stomped to death by stupid cows. Enjoy your hamburgers.

The thought made her laugh, making her determined not to die. Not today, not here. Flying zombies might win the game, but not cows.

"Stop!" she shouted to them.

They didn't stop; she didn't either as some sense of survival took hold in the girl's legs. She ran towards a group of rocks and boulders, instinct telling her to climb, and climb *now*. Gaining handholds, she lifted herself up, not minding the scrapes on her hands and knees. *Was she high enough?*

The dirt choked her throat as the cows stampeded below her like a mindless, living storm. She bent her head into her arms, nearly falling over.

Somehow, she held tight.

The drone safe on the ground, Phillip ran to find Joe and Skylar.

His ranch upbringing firmly in place, he smelled the cows before he saw them. Joe was waving his hands, yelling at the animals. They avoided him, stumbled, and veered away.

"Skylar?" Phillip shouted above the wind. They heard a plaintive voice.

"Uncle Joe? Phillip? Anybody?"

They ran towards the sound, and there she was, walking (barely), waving to them (faintly), her hair and clothes caked with dirt.

"Are you hurt?" Joe asked, looking for any signs of broken bones.

"My knees and hands are scraped up. I've never been so scared in my life."

She lifted one of her legs, a shoe covered in the muck from a cow patty. She clipped her words: "This. Is. Disgusting."

"Take your shoes off, toss them in the truck's bed. We'll get everything cleaned up when we're home," Phillip ordered, giving her a hand.

"Wait! Take my picture first. I'm going to send it to my parents, show them I almost got killed, and it's all their fault."

Later, over dinner, Skylar told Lacaria and Dr. J her version of facing serious injury, if not death.

"I'm telling you right now, I hate cows," her voice oozed with drama. "In fact, I never want to see another cow again in my life."

While the teenager's accounting was a little dramatic, she could have been hurt.

Joe said, "I recognized the brand, they're Jack Brinkle's cows. I'll have to go out in the next day or two and find out how they got onto our lease. Fortunately, they were on the other side of the leks, didn't damage the test area."

Even though it was late, after dinner Phillip went into his office to download the drone's video and data from the memory card. The images, coordinates, and infrared readings were routine, no surprises.

He moved the video slider to return to the beginning, when something caught his eye.

He zoomed in closer. Enlarge. Enlarge. Enlarge.

He sat back in his chair, staring at the screen. He quickly tagged the GPS coordinates.

He found Dr. J, Joe, and Lacaria on the deck, enjoying the cool night air.

"I have something to show you. I think you'll find it interesting." Phillip thumbed his phone to text Carl. "He's going to want to know about this, too."

IN THE DARK NIGHT

CHAPTER 36
BLOOD IN THE DESERT

Perhaps what happened in Lily Gulch might have been prevented *if* Harold Franklin remembered the rod, or at least placed a much larger rock to prevent the gate from closing

If when he called in sick the next day, ("I've picked up whatever's going around"), he'd mentioned the bait trap in Lily Gulch and maybe somebody could drive out there and fix the gate. But he forgot.

If Silver Moon, distracted by the unexpected challenge from his lieutenant, paid attention to his mares, and where they were going.

If the hay in the bait trap didn't smell so sweet and inviting, *if* it was stale or of a lower quality, maybe the horses wouldn't have entered it.

If a certain mountain lion hadn't been severely injured by Silver Moon years before, didn't have a grudge, and hadn't developed a taste for young prey.

Perhaps.

The mountain lion circled the rim of the gulch several times, pacing back and forth, back and forth.

He was drawn to the smell of the horses, carried by winds to his lair in the cliffs almost a mile away. He was hungry. His last kill was a young antelope, the flesh eaten days before.

Two years ago, he'd been kicked, hard, by the white stallion, interrupting his attack on the smaller palomino. Hunting, running down prey were difficult tasks. The good times being the desert's apex predator, leaping on the back of an animal, claws outstretched, jaws open to sink into a neck or throat were past him.

Rats, some ground birds, and the occasional young animal like the antelope were his diet, which meant he needed to hunt more often, and more cautiously, to lessen the chances he'd be hurt again.

There was one good thing, however. Young flesh was sweet, easier to pull off the bone, and, as long as its mother was distracted or too far away, easy to kill.

Now, above Lily Gulch, he paced back and forth, and waited.

Juno and Sheani, followed by Peggy Sue, sauntered back and forth from the gulch to the rest of the herd several times. There they drank water or pulled at wild plants.

The sweet hay kept drawing them back.

There was plenty of it, enough for ten, twelve horses, so the mares gorged their fill.

191

"This is nice," Sheani said. "I like being here with you, without the others."

Juno nodded. "I don't know why they're not coming down. I'm not going to invite them."

Peggy Sue drank from her mother's teat. She jumped about with unspent energy, cantering past the mares and outside the enclosure. Juno watched her, unconcerned. As long as she could see her daughter, she wasn't worried.

They did not hear the final "clank" of the gate as it hit the post.

The afternoon turned into early evening.

"Maybe we should head back up before dark," Juno suggested. She called to Peggy Sue, who was lying down near some rocks, taking a nap.

The little girl opened her eyes reluctantly. It was cool in the shade, the sand was soft.

The mares walked around the fencing.

"I thought the way out was right here," Sheani mumbled.

"It all looks the same," Juno agreed. "Where's the opening?"

Confused, the two horses circled again. And again.

No opening.

"I'm hungry, mama," Peggy Sue said. She got up and went to the rails.

Juno's teats responded with an ache. "I know, I'm trying to get to you."

Another circle. The mares shook their heads. It was getting dark.

"Mama! I'm hungry," Peggy Sue's voice sharpened. She stomped the ground, thinking the tantrum would bring her mother, and the milk, to her.

Juno didn't know what to do. Her baby needed supper. There was this *obstacle* between them. What could she do?

She began to panic.

"Juno," Sheani whispered, "there's something out there."

The whiff of danger, of death, hit both of the mares.

"Peggy Sue! Run up the trail to your father, now!" Juno screamed. "Get away."

The lion saw his chance minutes before the horses were alarmed. The fastest way out of the gulch was the game trail, and it was also the fastest way in.

He didn't even have to find a hiding place to crouch. The foal came right up to him, and he was immediately on her.

"Ahhh," Peggy Sue's scream filled the air. "Mama!" She screamed again as the lion's teeth sunk into her neck.

Juno saw her baby tumble down the trail to the bottom of the gulch, the mountain lion on top of the little body. The air was split with a loud gurgling sound.

"No, please, get up, run. I'm coming."

How? Juno, whale-eyed, shook her head, ran to the far side of the enclosure.

Another scream from Peggy Sue forced her into a decision.

Sheani knew what her sister mare was going to do. "Juno, don't do this, it's too high, there's not enough room for your run."

But Juno wasn't listening, saving her baby was all she knew, all she felt, her brain drumming an incessant instinct.

Peggy Sue was still screaming, the lion hadn't finished its job.

Now on the far side of the enclosure, Juno forced all of her being, all of her strength into this moment, and ran as fast as she could.

She jumped.

CHAPTER 37
FAILURE

Two trucks rolled slowly down the rocky gulch. Becky targeted the GPS location on her phone. "Got about two miles to go," she told her father, who was driving.

A Double B truck with Joe, Phillip, and Dr. J followed them.

"I looked up bait traps on the BLM website last night," Skylar said. "They don't hurt the horses, do they?"

"Not supposed to. They're an alternative to roundups," Becky replied. "Not as effective, they trap only a few mustangs at a time by luring them into the fencing with fresh hay and sometimes water. They might get five, six, maybe even a dozen horses at a time. Then the bureau's contractors show up with trailers, force them in, take them away."

"Why can't people release the horses? You know, set them free."

Carl answered. "The locations are secret, they don't reveal where they are. Sometimes they're on private land, a rancher lets them do it. They know if some of the more, well, avid mustang lovers knew where they were, the horses would be freed. The traps might be vandalized, maybe even go missing. And, it's against the law to destroy government property."

Skylar nodded. Those kinds of rules, she understood.

A turn on the road, the bait trap loomed into view.

"Oh my god," Becky whispered. *No.*

Carl stopped, the two got out to run over to the fencing.

Phillip drove his truck a little closer. His heart raced when he saw what was in front of them.

"Sheani," Dr. J cried. "And Juno, our precious Juno."

Sheani stood on the far end of the trap. She shook uncontrollably, her muzzle covered in froth.

It was a grotesque scene. Juno had clearly tried to scale the high fence, almost making it, her front legs trapped between the rails. Bones jutted out. Dried blood stained the dirt in all directions.

Her agony hadn't ended there, however.

"She crashed down on the other side." Carl bent down. "Her jaw and neck are broken, too."

How long did she lie there? How long did it take for her to die?

Skylar came up behind Becky, who tried to shield the girl from the horror. Her eyes grew wide in disbelief. "How could this happen?"

Carl, Joe, and Phillip walked around the enclosure. They saw the gate, closed.

"There's no ground rod, see?" Carl said. He took out his phone. "I'm calling the bureau's office."

"Open the gate first," Phillip ordered. "Get Sheani out of here."

There was no argument. They stepped back, held the gate open as wide as it could get. The roan mare shook her head, clearing her eyes, and ran as fast as she could to get away.

Dr. J looked around. "Where's Peggy Sue? Her foal?"

They found the bloody remains of the little girl halfway up the trail, or what was left of her, large chunks of her haunches and neck torn away.

"Mountain lion," Carl pronounced. "Probably waiting for her at the top."

"Juno was desperate to escape," Dr. J shook her head. "She saw it all happen, her baby attacked, couldn't do a thing about it."

Skylar heard what they said. "Nobody cares about these horses? Let them suffer and die like this?" She stopped several feet from Peggy Sue. "Not a whole lot bigger than Alexander."

Joe put his arm around her. "I wish I could tell you different."

"This isn't right. It isn't right." Skylar cried, repeating the words, over and over.

"Is this on the reservation?" Carl asked Phillip who shook his head.

"It's close. By a few hundred feet."

Dr. J said through gritted teeth, "A little closer and the Shoshone's wild horse bureau would come down on them like a ton of bricks. How many more times does this have to happen, how many more times do these animals have to suffer this way? And there's nothing we can do."

"We better get our story straight," Carl told them and they knew what he meant. "Let's get on the same page. Juno was the only horse in there. Right?" They all nodded. He turned to Skylar.

"I don't want you involved in this." He pointed to the truck. "Get in and keep your head down. Don't let anybody see you."

"Why? We didn't do anything," she tried to protest.

"We released Sheani, the mare. That's technically tampering with government property."

"Maybe I should lie on the floor?" Skylar understood.

"That would be good."

They were forced to wait for Ronnie for more than an hour. She stopped the bureau truck several feet away and talked on her phone for a few minutes before emerging.

"What are you doing here?" Her tone was perfunctory, demanding.

Phillip shrugged. "This is public land, right? We were driving around, a nice morning. Came on this." He swept his hand around.

Ronnie wasn't convinced. They *were* on public land and even though she didn't believe the trap was discovered by accident, she couldn't prove it.

"And Dr. J's here with you," she scoffed. "How convenient. I called the contractor, they'll be here later today to remove the trap." Ronnie stepped closer to the enclosure.

"It looks like the gate wasn't properly secured," Carl pointed to the gate. "It doesn't have the rod."

"Might have been vandalized," Ronnie shrugged. The implication was clear: maybe the Double B people took it.

Carl stepped back. "Whoever put this trap together botched it."

"That horse should have been able to leave," Dr. J joined in. "She saw Peggy Sue attacked, tried to save her."

Ronnie looked around. "Who knows what happened? And please, don't insult me with your cutesy names for these animals. It won't work."

"You've really adopted the government mission, haven't you?" Carl asked, spitting out the words. "Cozy with the cattlemen, apathetic about contractors abusing these mustangs."

Ronnie spread out her hands. "You know how it is."

"No, I don't. And I never did." He hadn't been this angry in years. "Someday, maybe soon, we're going to make sure something like this never happens again."

Ronnie laughed. "You have a cushy job now, Carl, traipsing all around the world, making a big name for yourself. But I have the law on my side, and I will enforce it." She looked round. "There's nothing here for me to do." Her next words were deliberately cruel. "A crew will be here in a while to get the rails. Leave the mare's body to the vultures. With all this blood, no horse is going to come down here for a long, long time."

On the bluff, looking over Lily Gulch and far enough away they could not be seen by the humans, Silver Moon, Autumn, and Sheani, watched the scene below.

"Stay back, Sandy," Autumn told her daughter. "I don't want you to see this." She looked into the gulch. "Nobody should."

"Juno," Silver Moon bent his head down. "And our baby."

Sheani was still trembling, it would take a long time for her to get over the trauma of the night before. "I tried to stop her, I really did."

Silver Moon touched her muzzle gently, then wrapped her neck with his own. "This isn't your fault."

"Juno followed you across the river, you saved her," Autumn remembered. "So loyal, so wise. We will miss her so much."

Alexander skipped up to the adults, stopped short, sensing their mood. Autumn looked over to him. "Losing Peggy Sue, our babies are much more precious."

"Now you know why I hate humans so much," the stallion said, bitterness and anger in his voice. "They bring nothing but death to us, to me, to *mine*."

There was nothing Autumn could say.

Late in the afternoon, Silver Moon left his family. This was a solo journey. Anger and grief could be his only companions.

Two years before he watched his mother die, comforting her with kind words, his love. It was too late to witness Juno's death, but he could at least honor her, and their baby.

He stopped first at the place where Peggy Sue was attacked. The scent of the mountain lion hit him, hard. Familiar. This was the predator who almost killed his Autumn. He rent the air with a high-pitched whine.

Juno's body lay at the end of the trail. He knew other predators, scavengers, would devour her body. Within days there would be little left of this beloved mare.

He touched the top of her head, her mane dull from death.

"I have to leave you, this last time," he told her. "I am so sorry, I will remember you always, our family will always remember you."

Juno and Peggy Sue, two more of his family killed by humans. If he had been here, could he have saved them?

There was nothing left to do, except turn away, leave this place, never return.

Leave this place.

Where could they go? Would there ever be a safe place away from these humans who wanted to see them suffer, and die?

Leave this place?

Could he do it alone, without help? It seemed impossible, a dream only for the strongest of horses. Was he that horse?

The evening breeze stirred an answer:

Yes.

CHAPTER 38
WITNESS

Lacaria forced herself to look at the pictures and videos on her screen. As they streamed from Dr. J's phone, she sat in stunned disbelief, at first not understanding what she was seeing.

The images of the dead foal, what was left of her, hit hard, forcing her mind into reality. "Peggy Sue," the caption read, "only ten weeks old, killed by a mountain lion while her mother was forced to watch."

Lacaria began her podcast.

"Instead of our regular session today, we have some terrible news out of Western Wyoming. The pictures and videos you are about to see are disturbing, not appropriate for young eyes, so please take this to heart. You are about to see the senseless, brutal way two of our mustangs, Juno and her baby Peggy Sue, were killed last night. Our own Dr. J and Carl MacKendrick took this footage a few hours ago."

The next few minutes the members of the Double B Wildlife

Science Center watched the horrors of Lily Gulch. Dr. J described the scene, anguish in her voice.

"How long did Juno lie in agony, unable to get up, while watching, listening to her baby being killed? How many hours? We'll never know. I wish I could say this is unusual, different, an extreme case," she said at one point, turning her camera to herself. "These bait traps are dangerous, deadly. One mistake, mustangs die. One overlooked detail, mustangs die. One lapse in judgment, mustangs die. And our government is doing this, without shame, without regret."

Dr. J's camera pointed to a woman identified on a caption as District Manager Ronnie Corman.

"There's nothing here," she was heard saying. "Leave the mare to the vultures. With all this blood, no horse is going to come down here for a long, long time."

Lacaria sat back. She knew this podcast would be shared and repeated across the Internet, across the country, across oceans. The message board was a scramble of sorrow and anger.

She began to keep a log of comments. A few minutes later, the Double B email box was filled with support.

"What can we do?"

"Why doesn't this stop?"

"Animal abuse is illegal, isn't it?"

There were more, filled with anti-government screeds of no value; they were ignored.

There were also several from reporters of major news outlets. Lacaria replied to those promptly, saying Dr. J would be available for interviews.

Nan Whittier put her head between her hands after watching the podcast.

I was taking pictures of Juno and Peggy Sue the other day.

Nan looked at her watch, calculating she could be in Lily Gulch within an hour.

Dozens of cars, ATVs, and four-wheel drive vehicles were parked haphazardly near the shallow end of the gulch by early afternoon, with more arriving.

Vultures circled, circled, circled.

Nan estimated there were more than fifty people, advocates, photographers, all with cameras varying from phone to professional quality.

Two bureau contractors stood in the gulch's entrance, waving to the crowd, not allowing them farther.

"This is public land," somebody shouted, with agreement from many.

One of the contractors talked into his phone, then approached the crowd, shouting to be heard.

"We're bringing out some equipment, please stand out of the way. Once we're gone, you can go wherever you want."

Another shout: "What did you do with the bodies?"

"Left them, letting nature take its course," was the answer.

The crowd slowly made a path as a large truck with a trailer came around a bend.

The metal pieces of the trap were secured, bouncing and rattling over the rough ground.

"There's still blood on them," somebody gasped.

The truck and its grisly cargo passed, and people began to walk the short distance where the trap had been.

People stood close to Juno's body. Several vultures were landing, the stench clouding the air. Pictures were taken, hundreds of images instantly uploaded to social media accounts or emailed to friends and relatives with the message:

Here to witness what has happened to these beautiful mustangs, and to honor Juno and her little daughter, Peggy Sue.

Nan got pictures of it all, the crowd, the contractors, the bodies.

The vultures hissed, getting impatient for this day's easy meal.

CHAPTER 39
TEMPORARY JOBS

Harold Franklin didn't know it, but in a way, he was responsible for Al Ebbers' death two years ago.

Hired to dig a retaining pond on the high meadow above the Double B Ranch, Harold worked for a week, using his brother's old backhoe to move rocks, rip out shrubs and trees, and scoop hard dirt to form the pond.

He wondered if what he was doing was against the law. You can't go making ponds or lakes or diverting streams the way you want, even if it's your land, can you? But the money was good, cash, half up front. A temporary job, three weeks' work for ten thousand dollars. He couldn't turn Al down.

Secrecy was the name of the game, and Harold was more than happy to keep Al's secret. He stayed in a small camper on the meadow, nobody knew he was there, went to town every few days to get supplies, then right back up the switchbacks, to start work again.

Harold called Al the morning he left to get supplies, saying he'd return the next day. Checking in. Yeah, he mentioned seeing some horses head up the trail from Silver Moon Canyon to the meadow, thought it was no big deal. Maybe they were Al's horses, was sure he'd want to know, right?

The next morning, Harold heard on the radio Al Ebbers was dead, from a tragic accident on the road above the Double B Ranch. He skidded his truck to a stop, listening, hardly believing what he was hearing.

No way could Harold return to the meadow.

He'd never get the five thousand dollars Al still owed him, either. Sure, Al told him the pond was a secret. How could Harold be certain he hadn't told anyone? No contracts, no receipts, but maybe Al wrote his name down somewhere.

Harold needed to get out of town, even Wyoming, fast.

He drifted into Colorado, then Utah, taking the odd job before seeing an advertisement for contract workers to round up wild horses. He applied, got the job, and things were going fine until he broke his arm, and, now, until Lily Gulch.

Harold was fired when he showed up for work. He wasn't surprised, somebody was going to take the blame for Lily Gulch. It seemed to Harold he always got blamed for something, and that always meant he was out of work.

He sat in his pickup for a few minutes, trying to decide what to do next. Go back home to Pinedale, stay with his mom for a while? He hated the idea. He was a thirty-three-year-old man, for crying out loud, he wasn't about to live with his mom.

Maybe head west, to Nevada. He had about five hundred dollars in his pocket, pay for some cheap motels on the way. Do a little gambling, have some fun. He deserved to have some fun, he'd never taken a real vacation before, going job to job like he always did.

He started his truck and was about to pull out of the parking lot when somebody rapped on the passenger side window. It was one of his co-workers, Luke.

"Hey, dude, really sorry about what happened," Luke said.

"These things happen," Harold shrugged. *Especially to me.*

"You know, if it wasn't for those environmentalists," Luke spat out the word, "you'd still have a job. Splashing those pictures and videos all over the Internet like those Double B folks are doing, it ain't right."

Harold shrugged again.

"Anyway, thought I'd let you know, I heard the livestock association is looking for a worker, not sure what they need, you might check with them. Jack Brinkle is the guy you want to talk to. I'll put in a good word for you."

"Thanks," Harold keyed the information into his phone. "I was thinking of heading to Nevada, some extra money won't hurt before I leave. Maybe I'll give him a call."

Luke gave Harold a "fist's up" sign of encouragement.

Harold rubbed his forehead, not certain what he wanted to do. Of course, he might not get the job, might still be going to Nevada. A new place to start over, try to find his place, a good place.

Like he'd told Luke, however, some extra money would be nice, a temporary job to hold him over. He clicked on the number.

The conversation was short.

"Luke said I should call you."

"Yeah, I'm looking for somebody to do some work, a week or two. No need to stop by the office, we'll do this in cash."

"When do you want me to get started?"

"Tomorrow, do you have a horse?"

Harold closed his eyes. Why did every job require him to have a horse?

He answered: "You bet." He'd have to borrow a horse, maybe from one of his ex-coworkers.

"I'm texting you a map." Jack told Harold what he wanted him to do.

Harold looked at the map, was surprised at Jack's orders, but said, "Sure. I can do this tomorrow."

CHAPTER 40
THE IW

All this blood.

Before hunkering down in the truck, out of view, Skylar cracked open a window, heard everything, including the government woman's parting words.

"All this blood."

Hours later, Skylar sat alone in her bedroom, lights out, curtains drawn.

Think clearly. She almost laughed at herself, a bitter sound. How could she think clearly after seeing the bodies of the mare and her baby, knowing how they died?

She opened the book she was reading, the one from the ranch's library. *The Monkey Wrench Gang.*

It was fiction, the characters hadn't damaged or blown up a dam. Written decades before Skylar was born, it was almost a primitive time, no computers, no mobile phones. She wondered what they'd do if those things had existed back in their day.

How many more times does this have to happen, how many more times do these animals have to suffer this way? And there's nothing we can do. Dr. J's words kept rotating around and around in Skylar's head.

Nothing? Skylar chewed her lower lip. Nothing?

She stood up and stared at the computer. Nothing?

Skylar entered the high-velocity gaming world when she was thirteen, and her skills drew immediate attention.

She was a natural in all ways. Quick with the controls, showing incredible coordination and foresight, she became expert at several games, but her favorite was The Caverns of Dragon Eggs. Pitted against dozens of players at a time, she soon learned the basics of the difficult terrain of this virtual world, gathering weapons and tools, and outsmarting her class. Within a year she moved up to Mage Class, the highest of the wizards.

Moving back and forth from the game to various chat rooms, she heard whispers of the Invisible Web, called the "IW" and figured it was another group of hackers, out to steal information, wreak havoc, plant viruses. Some got paid, others do it for fun.

Games have become a multi-billion-dollar business around the world. When rumors of a new game spread, interest is immediate.

All games start in various stages of beta, internal to the group creating the game, eventually moving on to include high-level computer experts who are trusted with the super-secret elements of characters, plot, the newly-created world the game is set in, and the rules.

Becoming a beta user is prestigious. What is even more prestigious is hacking into a new game, maybe look around at the coding. Or maybe to get a leg up on the competition when the game goes live. Then brag about it.

Skylar wasn't quite up to expert status yet, but she was more than interested in hacking. Which was why her foray into the school's computer system was disastrous and embarrassing. She hadn't gotten far into some of the databases, boring schedules about maintenance and summer classes, when her computer monitor displayed the "green screen of death" meaning her hack was detected and most certainly not wanted.

Within an hour her parents were called to the school. Another hour, she was suspended. And back home for the next several hours, there was a great deal of shouting, yelling, crying, and general havoc.

One good thing came out of it, at least as far as Skylar was concerned. When word got out about her failure (and before her parents shut her computer down), she received a surprising amount of support from her fellow gamers.

One email in particular got her attention: "You should have used the IW. Want to learn how?"

She replied, "Yes."

A few seconds later she received a three-page "Manual for Dummies: The IW." She read it four times, saved it to an SD card, and taped it to a page in one of her favorite graphic comic books, hoping her parents would never look there.

When she was exiled to Wyoming a month later, the SD card came with her.

She pulled the comic out of her backpack, detached the card, and twirled it around. No harm looking at it, take a deeper dive into the instructions. She could back out anytime.

Once inserted in the computer, the SD card downloaded the instructions. Skylar reviewed the pages again, making sure she understood the steps she needed to take.

Trying to hack the school's computers was silly. This time was different. The thought gave her a thrill. A Worthy Mission was in front of her, exactly like a game. She could create the weapons, the tools to save the country's wild horses, and she would be their hero.

With a few clicks, she signed onto her gaming account and grabbed her Avatar from its folder. Another thrill, positioning herself into the opening screen which flashed: *Welcome, New Apprentice.*

Skye Queen entered the Invisible Web.

CHAPTER 41
THE HACK

The instructions from the IW involved more time than Skye Queen thought they would. She was forced to answer a series of questions. There was an insistent red alert warning on her screen.

YOU HAVE THIRTY SECONDS TO ANSWER EACH QUESTION. IF A QUESTION IS REJECTED, YOU WILL RECEIVE A NOTIFICATION. YOU ARE ALLOWED ONLY THREE ATTEMPTS AT EACH ANSWER. IF YOU FAIL AT ANY OF THESE THREE ATTEMPTS, YOU WILL BE ESCORTED OUT AND NEVER ALLOWED TO RETURN.

Duly warned, Skye Queen tried not to panic. *Come on, girl, you can do this.*

She clicked **Continue**.

Step One: Who is your target?

Her answer: The United States Government.

REJECTED. TOO BROAD AND GENERAL AND EVERYBODY WANTS TO TARGET THE UNITED STATES GOVERNMENT. BE INNOVATIVE! YOU ARE ALLOWED TWO MORE ATTEMPTS.

Skye Queen scolded herself. Of course that answer would be rejected! She keyed in another answer.

The Bureau of Land Management.

The second question appeared.

Step Two: Who is your opponent?

Livestock ranchers. Wild horse contractors in Wyoming, Utah, Colorado, New Mexico, Arizona, Nevada.

Step Three: Target dates, please be specific.

(Skye Queen put in the previous four weeks.)

Step Three: What are your obstacles? (Skye Queen considered this, there seemed so many.) She made a decision.

Bureau of Land Management rules and regulations for wild horse management.

Four: Who can help? (Another one for Skye Queen to carefully answer. She knew the question was asking for resources, tools, sympathetic voices from anywhere in the world. Some people hated mustangs to the point the cruelty she saw yesterday was a big yawn. She also knew her answer needed to be broad enough to not implicate the Double B. Seconds later, she entered her choices.)

Environmentalists. Animal lovers. Wildlife photographers.

Five: Where, or whom, do you want this information disseminated? (She knew better than to say, "The Whole World.") She typed in the

215

names of several organizations, as well as the @ contact information from scores of social media accounts.

Six: What are your key words? (This was an easy one. Skye Queen's fingers flew across the keyboard.)

Mustangs, wild horses, bait traps, roundups, gathers, kill pens, animal cruelty.

(She added two more). Juno, Peggy Sue.

Her screen went blank.

Almost five minutes passed, the cursor blinking on the screen. *What did this delay mean? Did I do something wrong? Should I panic?*

A chime, and words began to appear.

THIS MESSAGE WILL SELF-DELETE IN THIRTY SECONDS. YOUR BOT IS BEING PREPARED AND YOU WILL BE GIVEN ACCESS TO YOUR TARGET DATABASE. PLEASE BE PROMPT WHEN MAKING YOUR SELECTIONS. WHEN YOU HAVE FINISHED, CLICK DONE AT THE BOTTOM OF THE SCREEN AND ALL WILL BE DISSEMINATED TO YOUR CHOSEN RECIPIENTS. GOOD LUCK WITH YOUR QUEST, SKYE QUEEN, WE HOPE YOU ARE A SATISFIED CUSTOMER.

That message did indeed disappear in thirty seconds. The pages of a database appeared on the screen.

It did not take long for her to make several discoveries. A lot of the contractors were lazy, uploading forty, fifty, sixty, even more locations at a time.

If the locations were uploaded one at a time, which she supposed was the protocol, the database would be more secure. One upload would take only a few minutes. Fifty locations, which seemed a common practice, left the portal open for an hour or more, leaving the connection vulnerable to a cyber attack. A hundred locations? Bingo! A perfect situation for a hacker. Skye Queen flagged all of them.

Several columns of headers were at the top of each page:

GPS Location

Date Setup

Employee(s) Name(s)

Horses captured

Conditions of horses (for administration use only)

Dispensation of horses (for administration use only)

Date Removed (many of the boxes were empty)

Employee(s) Name(s)

Notes: This was space for comments about weather conditions, obstacles encountered, or condition of the rails, some indicating they needed replacing.

Scrolling down, she checked the Date Removed fields and counted the empty boxes.

She glanced at the number. Her eyes widened, surprised there were so many.

Skye Queen had everything she needed. She bit her lip. Would everybody on the "receive" list know what they were looking at? Would anybody care? What would happen? What could happen?

No use waiting, all that was left was for her to click **Done.**

The screen flickered, went blank, and her monitor resumed its normal desktop mode.

Skyle Queen puffed out air from her cheeks. Her heart was racing.

She didn't know what would happen next, if anything. Perhaps, nothing?

The IW went to work.

A car in downtown Denver pulled up to the back entrance of a four-story office building. The driver, dressed in a nondescript uniform of a service worker, walked over to a large control box and opened it with a simple screwdriver.

If anyone questioned him, he would say he was with the electric company, checking on an alert the home office received. He would point to the car, a newer model with a blue and red logo on the doors. Satisfied, the questioner would shrug and say something like, "Just checking," and he would be thanked for being diligent. "You never know these days, right?"

Five orders pinged on his tablet, encrypted. He couldn't open them, didn't know what they were, and didn't care. For each one, he would receive two hundred dollars, so today he would make a thousand hundred dollars.

For ten minutes of work.

The cover off, the man attached several alligator clips to two of the cables in the box. These led to old and unused telephone systems from years gone by, left in the box because they were of no worth, and they would never be used again.

Except by the IW.

A skilled and clever hacker, playing around one day on a similar telephone line, discovered it was still active, "live" as it was called in the trade, and did not have a unique Internet Protocol address, which meant the line was unknown, unlisted. IP addresses were particularly vexing to hackers. All computers, every modem, every Wi-Fi device, every phone, every tablet has one, easily tracked by various governments and their law enforcement departments. Yes, there were ways to get around those IP addresses, time-consuming, and temporary.

But the old telephone lines? They were installed decades before the Internet was invented. Could they be used?

The man connected the cables to a portable hard drive where the orders were. One more clip, and the hard drive's light flashed green.

Undetected, the work of five hackers was transferred to unique bots in another country thousands of miles away, then transferred to another, and another, and another before finding their ultimate destinations.

Among the files was the BLM database with the secret locations of more than three hundred bait traps in several states.

CHAPTER 42
FALLOUT

**GOVERNMENT PROPERTY DAMAGED
IN SEVERAL STATES**

MILLIONS OF DOLLARS TO REPLACE, REPAIR

GOVERNMENT COMPUTERS HACKED

LOCATIONS REVEALED TO ECOTERRORISTS

HACKERS FACE TEN YEARS PRISON, HEFTY FINES

SWIFT INVESTIGATION PROMISED

Phillip read the headlines on his laptop. "Oh boy, this is serious," he mumbled. "All of the major news organizations picked this up."

Joe and Lacaria read the articles on their own tablets. "There's a theory the attention given to Lily Gulch spurred somebody to do this." Joe slid the article over to Phillip.

"Could be anybody." Phillip grimaced. "Dozens were there that day, pictures of Juno's and Peggy Sue's bodies were viewed by hundreds, maybe thousands of people."

He continued to read down the page. "Ronnie is holding a meeting in Jackson. We'll want to go."

Dr. J scanned the laptop in her room, reading the same news reports. She wondered if this hacking, the damage done to those bait traps, could in turn damage all the good work they're doing? This publicity wasn't good, painting "Ecoterrorists" with a broad brush. Splatters of that paint could land on the Double B.

How could a government agency get hacked in the first place? Doesn't it have great security? Yes, she was blaming the victim, but right now, with a headache coming on and a ton of self-doubt on her shoulders, this was the best she could do.

On the other side of the ranch house, in her own room, Skylar took a bite out of a piece of toast and perused her email before visiting fave websites for gamers and the latest news about celebrities.

She clicked on a "Rock and Pop" link taking her to MSNBC.com, read the schedule for a concert series, scrolled past some boring political news, sports of course, and was about to move to another website when something caught her eye.

Pictures of wild horses; another picture, people standing around a stack of fence rails.

She read the headline.

A liquid sickness erupted in her stomach.

She barely made it to the bathroom in time to throw up.

CHAPTER 43
LINES DRAWN

"It was good the bureau decided to hold this meeting on a Saturday," Phillip told Joe, "to get more interest and people here." They watched a local television station setting up cameras in the back. A reporter dodged around, asking questions, getting quotes.

The meeting room at the Jackson Hotel was large, with a large table at the front and chairs arranged in neat rows. More than half were already filled.

Phillip glanced at Becky sitting in front of him with her dad. She hadn't looked at him. He was still hurting from their argument, ashamed of the things he'd said, mostly kicking himself for his knee-jerk reaction to what she'd said.

"Look, the Double B Gang is here." A loud comment from someone in the back of the room made all of them turn around.

"We're a gang now?" Joe asked Dr. J.

Dr. J chuckled. "I've been called worse."

Carl turned in his seat, and said: "All of the people I figured would be here, are." He knew many of them, ranchers and business people who made their living in agriculture.

Phillip recognized a high school friend, Darrel Bowers, and raised a hand in greeting. He and his dad ran a small operation north of the mountain meadows. Darrel turned away, the look on his face telling Phillip he was not interested in friendly gestures.

Lines were drawn.

More people arrived, including the photographer, Nan Whittier. Her arrival created even more of a stir. She began to take pictures.

"I would say our side is outnumbered by about three to one," Carl chuckled. "Good odds."

Everyone "on their side" laughed.

Becky craned her neck to see who was near the wall in the back. With a jolt, she saw Tab Taggart, talking to Jack Brinkle. *What is he doing here?*

The two men were laughing, at one point Jack even put an arm around Tab's shoulder, leaning in to whisper something. Another man approached them, Tab was quickly introduced with smiles and handshakes.

His words came back to her. "Here in town meeting potential clients," was all he'd told her, and she hadn't asked for more information.

He wore a crisp suit, professional, the other cattlemen were in casual, every-day clothes. It amused her to see he was wearing his brand-new cowboy boots.

"Now I'll fit in," is what he told her when he bought them. Now she understood who he wanted to fit in with.

She felt sick and quickly turned around, hoping he hadn't seen her. *This doesn't make any sense. Does it?*

Phillip noticed the look on Becky's face and followed her glance, equally startled to see this Tab guy here, too, with Jack. *Who is he, and why haven't I found out yet?* He couldn't pursue the thought further, the meeting was called to order.

Ronnie and two of her deputies dressed in official BLM garb carrying a myriad of papers and folders came in and sat at the table. Another man, also dressed as a BLM employee, sat at the end.

"Great turnout," Ronnie smiled at the crowd. "Hope we get out of here without a lot of bruises." There was a sprinkling of laughter.

"We're here to talk about what happened at Lily Gulch." Ronnie spoke up. "As well as the serious hacking incident on our Bureau's computers. We have some new information on both—and another incident." She pointed her look directly at Phillip, who returned it with a frowned surprise.

A slideshow appeared on a screen to the right. Pictures of the bait trap at Lily Gulch were shown one by one. A closeup of the gate, without the rod. Juno, dead near the railing. The photo of the blood trail leading up to the rocks and the remains of the little foal.

"Our necropsy of the dead mare showed a broken leg and several broken bones in her shoulder area. It appeared she eventually died of a broken neck." Ronnie's voice was crisp, clinical.

The word "eventually" hung in the air for several seconds.

"The foal was probably killed by a mountain lion, the wounds and bites are consistent with such an attack.

"After talking with the contractor, it seems the gate rod was not inserted. The employee failed to return to the trap in subsequent days. The gate might have been propped open with a rock, it's possible the horses dislodged it as they entered."

As she listened, Dr. J looked around the room, trying to gauge reactions to this news. As expected, many of the ranchers' faces were dispassionate, unmoved by the pictures or the explanation.

Ronnie continued. "We are assured the employee who mismanaged the trap has been terminated."

Carl held up a hand, ignored with a curt dismissal.

"I'll take questions when we're done. Now, as far as the hacking, we consider this to be the more serious issue."

A loud, "That's right," erupted from the back of the room, several ranchers mumbled in agreement.

Ronnie brought the meeting back to her control, shuffling some papers before pointing to the man sitting at the end of the table. "This is Ike Taylor, he's our IT specialist out of Denver. I'm turning this over to him."

"Thank you, Ms. Corman." Taylor was a middle-aged man, thinning hair.

"I have almost twenty years' experience in forensic computer violations," he began. "Known to the general public as hacking. As I'm certain all of you know, the world of hacking has become more sophisticated, and wide-spread, with each passing year. When I first started out, hackers were mostly kids sitting on their mom's couch in a basement," he smiled, rewarded with several chuckles from the room.

"Now, however, hacking is a big-time business with a lot of foreign influence. People in Africa, Asia, East Europe, being paid and rewarded to hack into company computers, stealing data or holding it for ransom.

"I'm sure you've read about hospitals, cities, hotels, all victims of these violations." Heads nodded.

"Now, this one was interesting. The exact locations of hundreds of bait traps were compromised. That hack was carried out within hours of the Lily Gulch incident." He paused, letting that statement sink in. "The two were undoubtedly connected."

"There was a tremendous amount of media attention in that incident," Ike went on. "Local, regional, and national." Covers of magazines, newspapers, and screen shots of several websites were displayed on the screen: "I'm sure most of you have seen at least some of these. They would have brought some interesting players into the issue. Players such as advocates for wild horses, yes, and basic anti-government types."

A shout from the back of the room: "Ecoterrorists."

Ike shrugged. "We believe it was anti-government hackers, with foreign influences, simply because we're not convinced advocates have the kind of knowledge and expertise required for such a sophisticated operation. And, this appears to be a coordinated strategy by several hackers."

Phillip and Carl exchanged looks. "Guess we're off the hook, in an insulting kind of way," Phillip said in a low voice.

Ike proceeded to explain his theory of how the hack occurred:

1. The hackers found a vulnerability in the contractor's database interface with the government's system. Instead of GPS coordinates uploaded one by one as the traps are installed, many times the coordinates were batched together, twenty, thirty, or more, on the same day. This made it easy for the hackers to discover predictability, rather than random uploads. The contractor has been notified and henceforth there will be mandatory GPS uploads as each trap is finished.

2. Once the data was acquired, the hackers made sure it was

dispensed to interested parties. This was easy, almost all environmental, anti-government, and wild horse advocate groups have broad social media footprints. Thousands of email addresses can be easily gathered.

3. Using an unknown method, the data was then made available as a simple spreadsheet to those thousands of email addresses.

Ike paused for a moment. "We estimate more than a thousand people received this data."

Somebody in the audience whistled.

"We don't know how the data was pushed up. Very sophisticated, stripped of all identifying code, and as I said, fast. I'm still investigating, I won't give up and the bureau has authorized me to bring in a private IT team. This is generating a lot of interest.

"But the heart of this matter is the damage that was caused. Almost half of our traps were vandalized over the next few hours. It was astonishing how fast the response was. I suppose they knew once the hack was discovered they wouldn't have much time to get to them and do their thing. They used large trucks, sledge hammers, and of course, spray paint."

More pictures appeared on the screen. Gates removed and dragged away. Railings bent beyond recognition or sprayed with blues, pinks, yellows. Pieces of metal and other debris scattered about.

"Some of our traps disappeared," Ike continued. "Gone, probably to scrap yards. Who knows?"

"Yard sales," another shout, to more laughter.

Ike remained standing, then turned to Ronnie. "You have another issue to discuss?"

She nodded and asked him to display other pictures on the screen. "There have been questions about future roundups, will we still be holding them. The answer is yes, and they have become even more important. It has come to our attention in recent days a test site involving the re-introduction of sage grouse has been seriously compromised."

A picture of trampled plants and bushes appeared against a backdrop of desert scenery.

Phillip sat up, she had his attention. He mouthed to Joe: "Those are our leks."

Ronnie continued. "This is the Double B's pilot project, as many of you know, and was destroyed by … " she zoomed in, " … horses. Feral horses. Of course, we're sorry this happened, puts your plans back a year, maybe more." Her smile indicated she was not at all sorry.

Jack Brinkle raised his voice. "Double B amateurs dabbling in saving the environment." He looked pleased, his comment eliciting a round of applause and more laughter.

Carl stood up. Something caught his attention. "Can you go back to the first photo?" he asked, moving towards the front.

Ronnie complied.

Carl stood in front of the screen, tilting his head. "Maybe zoom in a little?"

Again, she complied.

There were mutterings behind him. "Waste of time." "We're through, here."

Carl pointed towards the middle. "Can't help notice, Ronnie, sure looks like the hoof prints of only one horse. And, a horse with shoes."

He turned to the crowd. "Now, most of you know what a horseshoe imprint looks like in dirt." There were a few nods. "And all of you might agree wild horses ain't in the habit of lining up to be fitted and nailed by a blacksmith." This generated a ripple of laughter. Did Jack

Brinkle laugh a little harder, longer? Carl wondered.

He turned back to Ronnie. "I agree on one thing, this is an act of vandalism, but not by mustangs, no ma'am. Somebody did this on purpose."

The BLM manager was flustered, shuffled papers around on the table. "We'll look into it," was all she said. Her face was red with embarrassment.

The meeting broke up.

Phillip and Joe told Carl they would drive to the sage grouse project and see for themselves how bad the damage was.

"Becky, Dr. J, and I are going to lunch, I'll meet you out there," Carl said.

Becky lingered in the meeting room, catching Tab's eye, a big smile on his face when he saw her.

"What are you doing here?" he asked, congenially. "Didn't know veterinarians-in-training were interested in this kind of thing."

She didn't answer, instead rounded on him. "What are *you* doing here?"

He shrugged. "Supporting my clients. I got the job, I'm the new in-house attorney for the Jack Brinkle and his livestock association. Getting a new office, hiring some staff."

The look on her face stopped him. "You're not congratulating me. How about we go to dinner tonight, talk it over?"

"You're working for the people who are responsible for killing, hurting *my* mustangs." Her voice was searing.

"Did not know they were *your* mustangs," he joked. "I mean, they're on public land, my clients run cattle on public land. And, people eat my clients' cattle. End of discussion, right?"

Now Becky was furious. "Wrong. You misled me, from the

moment we met."

He spread his hands out. "No. I didn't. It never came up, and besides, it was none of your business. You never told ME you were hooked up with these Double B people, on their side." Not a question, a fact.

"I didn't realize you thought of us as a *side*."

"You're OK with cyber attacks, terrorism, right? You think it was justified, after what happened to those horses in the trap."

"Of course not. Vandalism, no matter how it's done, is never right." Why was he forcing her to defend herself?

"The cattlemen here," he looked back to several men standing near the back wall, talking and laughing, "have a right to look after what's theirs, what they pay for." He folded his arms. "A few horses dying is no big deal. The way they breed, there'll always be more of them."

She stared at him, trying to control her breathing. *What have I done, she asked herself. Phillip and I have broken up, ended our lives together. And this guy is one of the reasons why.*

"It's best we never see each other. Ever again." She pushed open the door, not looking back.

Outside, she saw Phillip's truck leave the parking lot. She took a few steps forward, waved, maybe they could talk for a few minutes? Is there anything she could say? Would he ever talk to her again?

If he saw her, he didn't stop.

CHAPTER 44
THE WINDSTORM

An awkward silence filled the truck's cab.

"We didn't hear anything we haven't heard before." Phillip tried to sound soothing.

Joe closed his eyes and rubbed his forehead. "I know so many of those people, been around them most of my life. All I heard was a lot of hatred." He shook his head. "Some of it was directed smack dab at me. Thought they were friends."

Phillip reached out to rub Joe's shoulder. "If it helps, I think most of it was dumped on me. They want the Double B Ranch to be what it once was." He smiled. "They want good ol' Al Ebbers back, and I ain't him."

Joe nodded. "Nothing they said changed my mind about what we're doing. In fact, it made me even more stubborn about it."

Phillip steered the truck onto the state highway. "Let's get going, before the storm hits." Storm clouds, big and black, were sweeping in from the west. The wind began to blow.

He glanced at the rearview mirror. Was Becky waving to him?

No, he imagined it.

Thirty miles south of Jackson the highway was getting pummeled with dirt and tumbleweeds. Smaller cars were forced off the road; even Phillip's large double cab truck was rocking on its tires. He slowed down to barely more than a crawl.

Visibility was cut down to twenty or thirty feet, gloomy headlights of passing trucks split the wall of dirt.

"Typical Wyoming weather, different every five miles," Phillip chuckled. He struggled with the steering wheel.

"Look," Joe pointed out. A group huddled against the sting of the wind and debris a few feet off the road. Three mountain bikers, barely holding on to their bikes, waved to them. If the garb they wore wasn't so colorful, Joe might not have seen them.

"Let's give them a hand." Without thinking twice, Carl pulled over. Joe got out, holding on to his door with both hands.

"Put them in the bed," he shouted to the trio, indicating their bikes. "We got room in the truck for all of you."

Breathless, covered with dust, eyes wide with fear mixed with relief, the men climbed in.

"You can't know how grateful we are," one said. They were young, in their early 20s. "Wind came up so fast. We lost our way coming down from the hills. Nobody would stop to help."

"Probably couldn't see you," Phillip glanced back at them.

"Our cars are in a parking lot about a mile from here," another pointed. "Can get us there?"

"No problem."

A few minutes later Phillip pulled into the parking lot. The wind hadn't subsided, so he and Joe helped get the bikes out of the truck's bed.

"Maybe you want to hang out here for a while until you can see the road better," Joe suggested, shouting to be heard. They all nodded and gave heartfelt thanks.

"Maybe we ought to take the same advice," Phillip mumbled half to himself, looking out the window.

He edged out of the parking lot anyway, careful to look both ways.

The Mountain Edge Trucking Company boasted a good safety rating. The owners took care of their trucks, made sure all paperwork was submitted to the state's road department accurate and before deadlines.

Work requiring "downtime" of hours such as replacing windshield wipers, changing oil, draining radiators, changing tires, usually took priority.

Other things, like replacing brakes, might take a little longer to schedule. A truck's brakes needed replacing every 100,000 miles, sometimes more often, especially if a truck was driven over high mountain roads with steep grades.

The driver of Semi-Trailer Truck No. 72 was heading home to Rock Springs after three days on the road delivering construction materials to various towns along the Rocky Mountains.

His rig was large, hardly affected by the dirt and blowing debris. The trailer was empty, the driver mindful of the back tires' propensity for shimmying on the road.

He knew the truck was due for a brake replacement. He'd get it taken care of next week.

"I can't believe the wind is worse." Phillip leaned forward over the steering wheel in a futile attempt to see out the windshield. A dark brown wall of dirt was all he saw.

"We should have stayed back there, I don't even see the road where we can pull over." Joe was also craning his neck from his window to the front. "Maybe slow down."

The warning came too late.

The semi driver came out of the storm and plowed into Phillip's truck.

The sound of smashing metal was abrupt as the semi hit the back end hard, forcing the truck a hundred feet forward in a matter of seconds, deflating all four tires. The truck's stability was compromised, it spun around and teetered precariously, threatening to tip over.

Brakes squealed, metal and against metal, lights flashed. The semi kept going, unable to stop. It smashed into the truck again with a sickening Bam! this time on the driver's side, forcing the truck to roll over and over before landing on the passenger side.

The semi finally stopped, its front end crumpled from the impact.

The wind continued its incessant, maddening howl.

CHAPTER 45
THE GLASGOW COMA SCALE

Lacaria got the call. She did not believe what she was hearing.

Phillip and Joe, in an accident? Has to be some mistake, they're in Jackson, she told the person at the other end.

They were on the road, was the response. *The windstorm, a semi hit them, they're at the hospital now.*

"Are you sure you have the right Phillip Ebbers, Joe Ruiz?" She knew the question sounded stupid as soon as she said it.

Skylar overheard the conversation, saw the confused look on Lacaria's face.

Yes, it's them.

"They're OK, aren't they?"

You need to get here, as soon as possible, please drive carefully.

Her heart and hands were shaking. "We have to get to Jackson." She remembered to gather legal papers, insurance cards.

Skylar put her arm around her aunt. "I think Dr. J and Carl are together with Becky. You call them, I'll call Tess, we can pick her up, then we'll leave for Jackson, OK?"

Lacaria nodded, fumbling for Dr. J's number on her phone.

The restaurant was busy, loud with conversations from table to table. Most customers looked up when two ambulances raced by, loud sirens against the annoying sound of the wind.

"Not surprised something bad has happened in this weather," Carl said, paying the bill for their lunch.

Dr. J's phone pinged. Lacaria's voice was thready, the words difficult to understand.

"An accident? Are they OK?" She shook her head at Carl and Becky.

Her free hand flew up, her eyes widened.

"Oh, my god, no."

They raced out the door.

Joe was in the emergency room getting stitches over his right eye. His shirt was in tatters, the paramedics cut it up to insert IVs and take his heart and blood pressure readings.

He sat up and groaned.

"Probably have a cracked rib or two. You're lucky," the nurse told him "Your x-rays came back clean."

"I need to get to Phillip. My son."

"He's in intensive care, they're running scans on him now. You'll have to wait."

"No." he protested, wincing again when he tried to stand up.

The double doors to the ER whisked open, Carl, Dr. J, and Becky rushed in.

"Are you OK?" Dr. J reached him first.

"Glass cut me above my eye," he held a hand up to his bandage. "Phillip took the brunt of it, the semi hit the driver's side. Our truck rolled over a few times, I don't remember much after that."

"How is he, where is he?" Becky looked around frantically.

"They won't tell me. Does Lacaria know?" He steadied himself. "I can't find my phone."

"She called us, they're on the way."

Joe put a hand to his head. "I'm a little woozy."

The nurse guided him back to the bed. "You need to lie down, you're in shock."

Becky told him, "We'll find out what we can."

In intensive care, they asked about Phillip.

"Are you next of kin?" was the polite question.

Carl and Becky exchanged frustrated looks.

Dr. J said simply, "His dad's in the ER, his mom is on her way."

"I'll have to wait for one of them before we can release any information. I can tell you the doctor is with him now, we're waiting for lab results."

They returned to the ER to sit with Joe. They remembered there was another victim of the accident, the semi driver.

"He's already discharged, minor injuries, some cuts and bruises," they were told.

An impatient hour later, Lacaria, followed by Tess and Skylar, arrived.

Insurance forms presented, powers of attorney handed over, they were finally able to get some answers.

A tall, older woman approached, her nametag said, "Dr. Peterson." She sat down with them.

"Sorry for the delay, we have his x-rays. His left leg is broken below the knee, a compound fracture. His left kidney is also damaged. Both will need surgery." She paused. "Once we get in there, we'll take a look at his spleen. Might have to be removed."

Lacaria looked around wildly. Becky put her arm around her, recognizing signs of shock. "You can live without a spleen," she assured her.

Dr. Peterson stood up. "We'll get Phillip into surgery. But," another pause, "this kind of accident, we have to check everything."

Carl leaned back. "Brain injury?"

"We'll know more when we get a CT scan, I'll call a neurologist to review them. It's premature to say anything. Fortunately, there's no visual sign of swelling."

Lacaria doubled over, trying to breathe. "This can't be happening." She spoke for all of them.

Three hours later, Dr. Peterson returned.

"The damage to the kidney isn't bad, we were able to repair it. Fortunately, everything else, including the spleen, looks OK, of course we'll be monitoring everything for the next couple of days. An orthopedic surgeon is with him now, putting his leg back together."

"And the CT scan?"

"It looks clear, but brain injuries are tricky. The neurologist ordered another scan this evening and another in the morning."

"When can we see him?" Joe asked.

"In a while, he's still sedated." She stood up. "The first twenty four hours are crucial. We'll be watching him closely as the anesthesia wears off." She turned to leave, then held back. "Have any of you heard of the Glasgow Coma Scale?"

"You're saying Phillip is in a coma?" Joe asked.

She didn't answer. "I'll have a nurse give you basic information of the GCS. She'll also let you know when you can see him."

Becky, was not about to wait for a nurse, she immediately began to search her phone.

She read out loud: "Doctors use it to measure decreases in consciousness. Eye movement, talking, motor skills are scored as these functions increase, or decrease, or no changes are discernible."

She looked around the room, her heart skipping several beats. Her mom and dad holding tightly to each other. Joe and Lacaria weeping inconsolably. Dr. J held Skylar's hand. The Double B Gang, all here, minus Phillip.

Becky's voice broke. "When he wakes up, as he wakes up, they'll be watching for those things.

"And, we will, too."

CHAPTER 46
THE EMPTY SKY

No pain, nothing hurt, nothing felt. No sense of fear, happiness, hunger. No smells. No memories. Nothing.

Is this death? Is this what dead people ask? Phillip wanted to laugh because he was certain it was, but he did not have a sense of humor, either.

There was, however, the sky. Or, *a* sky. He didn't recognize it. It wasn't blue like a day sky, or black like a night sky. Empty of color. Empty of clouds. Empty of sun.

Empty. Like him. How can that be?

How can that be?

Joe and Lacaria were allowed in to see Phillip for a few minutes.

"We'll be getting him downstairs for another CT scan," the nurse explained. "Talk to him, let him know what's happened. We don't know, he might hear it. It's important he knows you're here."

Joe held Lacaria in a tight grip as they looked down at Phillip, lying on his back, a thin breathing tube protruding from his nose. His face was pale.

The left leg was bandaged. Lacaria asked about a cast.

"A cast will be applied later, we're monitoring for infection. We'll also x-ray the leg again to make sure the surgery was a success. It was a bad break."

"Is he breathing on his own?"

She answered, "Yes. The tube is to make sure he always has enough oxygen. His heart rate is good, too. He's young, and in excellent shape."

Lacaria was doing her best to keep from crying. If what the nurse said was true, she did not want Phillip to hear her sobs. "When will he wake up?"

"He's still sedated, it will wear off shortly." She glanced at her watch. "When he's back in his room, you can see him again, please keep visitors to one or two at a time."

In the waiting room, Joe helped Lacaria to a chair, then returned to tell the others how Phillip looked.

"Now we wait." This was from Carl.

Tess nodded. "I've booked some hotel rooms for the night. Skylar and I will go back and pack some clothes for all of us. Guess we're back to assigning shifts." She smiled "Autumn gave us lots of practice."

Skylar was the only one exempted from a shift, perhaps, it was suggested, she should return to Los Angeles, go home to her sister, causing a moment of panic for the teenager. She was adamant in staying. "I can help at the ranch, do whatever, feed horses, feed Corky.

Please don't send me away."

They agreed, with the understanding she would always be with an adult.

Voices. He heard voices. He *was* hearing voices.

Coming from the empty sky, which meant it wasn't empty anymore.

He wanted to open his mouth to talk. Nothing came out.

He wanted to open his eyes. Where were his eyes? They seemed to be missing.

He fell back into the empty sky.

Good news. The CT scan showed no change.

"We'll have some tests in the morning, but—" Dr. Peterson cautioned, "we may want to transfer him to a hospital in Salt Lake City, to a head trauma unit."

"You can't treat him here?" Lacaria asked.

Dr. Peterson shook her head. "Not to the level he might need. Let's see what happens in the next day or two."

Another CT scan the next morning showed no change.

Joe and Lacaria were at the hospital all the time except for weary breaks to eat or shower at the hotel.

Becky also stayed in Jackson. Dr. Shultz arrived later to give what consolation he could.

Carl assured them he would make sure construction on the conference center stayed on track. "When he wakes up, that'll probably be his first question," he smiled. The word "when" gave them all thin hope.

Second day. No change.

A feeding tube was inserted in Phillip's stomach.

They began to hear more mentions of the hospital in Salt Lake City. The likelihood of transferring Phillip to the hospital hundreds of miles away was becoming more likely, adding to the stress.

"We need to get ready." Joe's tone was soft.

Lacaria nodded. "I'll ask Tess to look for hotels near that hospital. One room. For us. There's no way they'll be able to be there." Her voice drifted off. "We'll be on our own. Looking after our boy."

The couple held each other close, finding the strength they'd always had together, hoping this time it was enough.

Flowers arrived as word spread of the accident. Neighbors, colleagues, friends. There was only so much counter and table space to put them all, many ended up in the waiting room.

The most interesting delivery was a large basket of red apples from Jack Brinkle. It elicited some chuckling with the "it's the thought that counts" comment repeated several times.

"Don't unwrap it," Carl advised. "There are so many, they'll fall to the floor."

The apples were given to the hospital staff, with assurances they would be appreciated.

Morning of the third day.

Another CT scan.

No change.

Phillip's eyes were checked several times, his feet and toes checked for reactions. No flicker, no sign of movement.

"Guess it's safe to say he's in a coma," Becky whispered. By now she had referred to the coma scale a hundred times, knew it by heart.

She was sharing her shift with her father. He came up beside her. "I wish I could say you're wrong. Not sure I can."

"I can't stop crying." She turned away from the bed.

Not sure what's going on, Phillip said out loud. Except it wasn't out loud, his lips didn't move.

He looked up at the empty sky. It seemed to shiver, then there was an explosion of red apples. Hundreds of apples, maybe thousands, avalanched all around him. They were the size of pumpkins! Where did they come from? He ducked, put his hands over his head. *This is a dangerous situation. I'm going to get killed.*

A second later, or maybe it was an hour, the apples disappeared, the empty sky remained red. This *is an improvement. Color. Color is good.*

The pumpkin-sized apples smelled terrible, already beginning to rot.

He tried to step over them.

He realized his legs couldn't move at all. Especially the left one.

Why can't I move?

More apples began to fall from the sky.

Becky felt compelled to be in Phillip's room. If he was to be transferred to Salt Lake, she would go there as often as she could, but it wouldn't be like now, where she could spend as much time as she wanted at his bedside. Days were grim, nights were worse.

Joe left to get some cold drinks. Lacaria sat in a chair, leafing through a magazine, trying to find a normal thing to do, even though nothing was normal about their lives.

"I still don't understand how this could have happened. To us. How can we go on?" She put the magazine down.

"You remember Slash? My horse?"

"Your beautiful black? Oh yes, what a marvel it was to see the two of you. Like poetry in motion, could hardly tell where the horse left off and the girl began."

"I lost him a few weeks before I met Phillip, well, should say re-met him, when he came back from Europe. We grew up together as small-town farm and ranch kids. He called me "Cowgirl" and teased me mercilessly about my long braids." She smiled at the memory. "He was five years older, grew up before I did. When we saw each other again, all those years later, it was so natural and easy.

"He was the first person I talked to about how Slash died, how I felt," Becky continued. "He listened, he understood."

Lacaria squeezed her hand. "He loves you, Becky."

"We've had some problems the last few days." An admission she hated to make. "I'm ashamed of the things I said to him."

"He told me about the argument you had." Lacaria put her arm around Becky. "You said two years ago, he listened, he understood. The other day, he did the same thing. He listened. He understood."

"I don't think I can take it if we lose him. I can't even look up in the sky, all I see is emptiness."

Overwhelmed, Becky put her head between her hands. Sobs turned into a keening sound as Lacaria hugged her as tightly as she could. "He needs all the love we can give him, and that will fill that empty sky."

Whoa. A new sound. Becky? What's she doing here?

Phillip looked around. *Hey! I can move my head.*

He looked at the apples. Didn't she smell their stench? He needed to warn Becky to stay away, she might slip and fall. Or, worse, get attacked by more apples falling from the sky.

Becky! Becky! He shouted, the words a jumble. Or a gurgle. He didn't know which, he kept shouting.

Becky! Get out!

Neither Becky nor Lacaria knew which one heard the sound coming from the bed first.

"You heard him, right?" Lacaria whispered.

Becky nodded. "His eyes are moving under the eyelids."

"Are you sure?"

"Check his right foot, tickle it with that pen."

Lacaria gasped. "His toes moved. I know they did. I'll get the nurse." She rushed out.

Becky squeezed Phillip's hand.

"Ouch."

A whisper. She would have missed it if she turned away.

She squeezed harder.

"Ouch. The apples hurt me."

"What? Apples?" Should she laugh?

His eyes remained closed but his voice was louder. "The apples, you need to get away, don't come in, they're on the floor. I don't want you to get hurt. Ever again."

"Phillip. Open your eyes."

He opened his eyes.

"There you are." She smiled.

He smiled back.

A blue sky opened for both of them.

CHAPTER 47
OLD FRIENDS

Aarón heard the vehicle laboring up the dirt road, the motor lurching its familiar sound.

"We have a visitor," he told the cat, stretched out on a small table near the open door. He scooped ice chips from a portable cooler and poured grape juice into two glasses.

A truck door slammed, Dr. J stepped through the door.

"How's Napoleon?" she asked, scratching the cat's chin.

"Still catching mice and the occasional pack rat." Aarón handed her a glass as she sat on the opposite end of the table from him. In many ways, and in the ways that counted, this little casa was more of a home to her as a child than her actual home.

"It's been a while since I've seen you."

She pointed a finger at him. "That's not true, you saw me the other morning."

He laughed. "I knew the Shoshone part of you saw me."

She looked down, twirling the glass. "If there is any Shoshone in me, it came from your family, not mine."

Dr. J's parents came from the Wind River Reservation but moved to Idaho before their daughter was born to give her as many advantages as they could. Good schools, good medical care. They returned a few times a year, drawn to family, festivals and Shoshone traditions around births and death.

Dr. J was drawn to the colors, the music, from dances and pageants. There she met many cousins and their friends, such as Aarón. He became an older brother, not in blood but in spirit.

He introduced her to his mother and father, important members of the tribe. From them, she learned the Old Ways, the language, and their connection to the earth's magic.

Dr. J became a Daughter of the Earth. She entered her first year of college and set on the white man's path to science. Somehow, she embraced both, and kept true to both.

Aarón's parents were gone these many years; his friendship with this scientist endured.

Today he could tell she was worried.

"I was in town a few days ago, I heard about Phillip Ebbers." It was his way of prompting her to open up.

"We were so worried, weren't sure he was going to recover. He's OK now, making progress, healing. Home.

"But his accident, almost losing him, other things that have happened, I've been thinking about what I'm doing. Why am I doing it? Every success is met with a ton of failure."

She told him about Lily Gulch, the horrible way Juno and Peggy Sue died. "The BLM meeting, filled with so much hatred, lies," she added.

"Was this different than other times?"

"Perhaps it was because I thought the work we were doing at the Double B, the new conference center, the grants, the media attention, was changing minds. Ha! Did I get a rude awakening."

"Isn't there a saying, something about never believe your own press?"

"Funny. Perhaps I've been wrapping myself in a blanket of dreams, thinking I was protected. What an idiot I am."

At this Aarón laughed out loud. "You are Dr. Faith Jergens. THE Dr. J. Ground breaking research, on the covers of scientific journals the world over."

She tilted her head. "You exaggerate."

"I go to the library, keep up on these things. What's *really* bothering you, little sister?"

She counted: "First, the bait trap. Second, Phillip's accident. I feel like something's going to happen, and I am so afraid it's going to be bad. A third thing."

"Now you're being superstitious."

They heard the soft clip-clopping of hooves against stone. Through the door they saw Mosaic at a distance near the spring.

Dr. J stood up. "Is he getting closer to you, more comfortable?"

Aarón shook his head. "No, but he has been acting strange."

"He was with you above the waterfall, wasn't he, watching us release Autumn and Alexander."

"He came for me early, led me there. I can't shake the feeling he's waiting for something, someone. I'm sure I'm just imagining it."

She leaned against the doorframe, knowing if she went outside the horse might get spooked, shy away. She wanted to watch him a while longer.

Mosaic drank from the spring. He shook his head, sending a cascade of water drops into the air.

She sighed, finding deep peace watching him.

"He is so magnificent, reminds me of another horse." Dr. J's words were soft. The thought brought surprising calm to her heart.

Mosaic looked at her for what seemed like a long time.

The horse broke the spell when he moved up the stream, out of view behind a line of trees.

Aarón went outside after Dr. J left to find Mosaic pulling grass and wild flowers in the field.

"You soothed her, old friend," he told the horse. "Perhaps it's what she needed."

He watched Mosaic eat for a few more minutes before the horse trotted away toward the valley, disappearing from view.

The old man would not see the horse again for several days.

Silver Moon stood on a hill, a soft breeze ruffling his mane.

He wasn't sure what he was seeing, or how he should respond.

Autumn and Sheani came up behind him.

"Who are they?" Autumn asked. Below them, close by, two other families were standing on the mountain meadow, fifteen to twenty other horses, stallions, mares, foals, colts, and fillies.

"I don't know," Silver Moon answered. "I think I recognize the roan stallion, he lives across the river."

"Crossing the water with their babies?" Sheani wondered. "A dangerous thing to do. Why are they here? When did they arrive?"

"Last night. I've been watching them all morning. None of the stallions are challenging me. Yet."

From their left, they heard the clip-clopping of more horses coming up the trail from the canyon. A band of four young stallions came into view and immediately sought the shelter of the Ponderosa Pines.

"If anybody was going to challenge you, it would be them," Autumn let the thought drift.

Silver Moon shifted. "I know two of them. We were friends, they were in my family. Father saved them the day when he was taken away."

"Warrior?" Sheani was shocked. "I have not thought of him in years."

"I haven't either," Silver Moon nuzzled her, thinking she might still need comforting after seeing what had happened to Juno and Peggy Sue. "Take the others closer to the cliffs. I need to stay here a while, keep an eye on things."

He did. Over the course of the day, three more families joined the others on the meadow.

By sunset, more than fifty mustangs gathered, keeping their distance, eating, and, it seemed, waiting.

But for what?

CHAPTER 48
STARTING OVER

Becky poured Phillip a cup of coffee from a carafe. He was comfortably ensconced on the larger sofa.

The living room was rearranged before he came home from the hospital, with furniture moved so Phillip, using two crutches, could easily get around. For the time being, this would be his bedroom.

"Mom's bringing omelets and sausage from the Wrangler," Becky said. "We also have orange juice in the fridge."

"I'm going to gain fifty pounds lying here, sitting around until this cast comes off."

"Not for six long weeks," Becky spread out her arms with the word "long" to give it extra impact.

"It's only been two weeks, and I'm tired of it." He rapped the plaster, which was covered with names, sayings, and designs, mostly courtesy of Skylar.

"I think this is supposed to be a dragon," he pointed at one drawing.

Becky narrowed her eyes to look at it. "She hasn't found her inner-artist." They laughed.

"How did your doctor's appointment go yesterday?" she asked.

"They want to do another CT scan in a few weeks, routine. It still bothers me I can't remember a thing about the accident, and hardly anything about the BLM meeting. Dr. Peterson says that's normal."

Quiet grew back between them.

"I wish you can't remember some things from a few days before, too." Becky twirled a strand of hair.

"We haven't talked." He reached for her hand. "And we need to."

"Do we? I said some things I didn't mean."

"You were right about all of it. Being loved, and loving, it's hard for me. I can't blame my grandfather," he smiled, "but I kind of do. Growing up, I was always thinking, wondering, what can I do to make him angrier, hate me even more? Even though he's dead, I still want to make him angry. I even wondered if that's one reason why I'm doing all of this," he waved his hand towards the conference center. "Destroying his ranch, his legacy, everything he worked for. Everything he cared about, because he didn't care about me.

"I'm finally admitting I liked disappointing him, I liked hating him." He shook his head. "Not exactly healthy, right?

A silence hung between them. Becky knew this wasn't easy for him to admit. She also understood he needed to say these things, and she didn't need to say anything.

He continued. "I have a choice to make. I can go on hating him, let him destroy everything I'm doing. Let him destroy me. Let him destroy us." He took her hand.

"Or I can let my hatred die, finally bury it in the ground with him.

What I'm doing here, what *we're* doing here, it's important, it matters. Has nothing to do with him, has everything to do with what is right, what is good.

"I love you Becky, I fell in love with you the moment I walked into the Wrangler two years ago. Looking into your eyes, it was all I needed to see. I hope you still love me," he smiled shyly, "and you're not falling for that Tab guy."

She bent over to kiss him.

"That Tab guy is history, he never meant a thing to me."

"Can we start over? Maybe spend the rest of the summer getting to know each other again?" He held out his hand.

"Hi, I'm Phillip Ebbers. The new me."

"Becky MacKendrick. Nice to meet the new you."

CHAPTER 49
THE DOUBLE B GANG

Lacaria and Joe were in their living quarters. It was early morning, both were exhausted.

"I haven't done any real work in days, I don't think I've been this tired in years," Joe told his wife. "I feel absolutely drained."

She rested her head against his shoulder. "Don't know about you, I'd like to sleep in tomorrow, maybe go out for lunch, get some fresh air, hike up on the east slope above the lake?"

He kissed her. "We'll make it a date."

Skylar sat at the studio's computer, thinking she'd watch more videos, maybe another one of Dr. J's archived blogs.

Several social media pages popped up. People were still angry about

Juno and Peggy Sue, more pictures posted of both horses, Peggy Sue in all her cuteness, Juno the beautiful mare in a peaceful meadow. Skylar understood why people were still upset; she was, too.

She browsed a few more of the websites before opening a desktop folder holding several videos.

A chime rang on the computer. It rang again. And again. An icon appeared under the social media banner *Operation Warrior.*

Curious, Skylar clicked on it. She caught her breath. An image filled the screen.

Can't be, can it?

She stood up and took down some of the pictures of a dappled gray stallion. Looked at the monitor again. Held up some of the pictures at the image on the screen. And raced out of the room.

"Uncle Joe! Aunt Lacaria!" She pounded on their door. "We found him!"

"I'm so afraid to hope for this, there have been so many false sightings." Joe bent down to the monitor, the pictures from the bulletin board in his hand. Yes, a horse, rearing up with a rider on his back, dappled gray. Was it Warrior?

"This is a bucking bronco in a rodeo," his voice trailed off.

"Do some of the mustangs end up in rodeos?" Lacaria asked. "Surely not."

Joe stood up. "They're not supposed to. We've heard rumors, none confirmed."

Skylar enlarged the image. "You told me all rounded-up horses are branded." Skylar enlarged the image, and enhanced it.

Seconds later, the unmistakable rectangle of a brand appeared on the left side of the horse's neck.

"Can you make it clearer?" Joe fumbled through the pictures in his hand. He found the one he was looking for.

"Maybe," the girl whispered.

Joe gave her the picture showing Warrior's brand, taken before he disappeared.

The brand on the computer's monitor grew bigger, at first fuzzy. With a few more clicks, the symbols were almost clear enough to read.

Lacaria gasped. "I'll go get Phillip and Dr. J."

Phillip handed Joe his crutches and eased into the chair. He knew the stakes. Absolute, 100 percent certainty was vital.

"All these years later," Dr. J mused.

"I guess putting up all of those new sites helped," Skylar said, "but maybe all of the attention, publicity, about the bait trap renewed interest, too."

They realized this was the silver lining to Juno's and Peggy Sue's tragic deaths. They were eager to take it.

Joe blew air out of his cheeks. "So, what's the plan?"

"Get him back," Phillip said. "Not going to be simple, or easy, but it's what we gotta do."

An hour later, the living room was crowded.

Phillip looked around. "The Double B Gang is all here."

Dr. Shultz raised his hand. "Plus one, in an unofficial capacity."

"After the last few days, we need some good news," Tess said, putting her arm around Carl.

Joe said, "The person who posted the picture said Warrior is a bustin' bronco in a rodeo. El Paso, Texas, at the town fairgrounds."

"Some of these outfits skirt the Texas-Mexico border," Dr. Shultz explained. "Go back and forth to avoid any kind of inspection or scrutiny. They're generally small, a few animals, easy to load up and get going on the road if they have to leave town quick."

"They could be gone today, tomorrow?" Tess asked.

"Possibly, El Paso is a good-sized town, they might get several performances in, if they're making money," Carl answered. "I remember talking to some associates with the Department of Agriculture. The people running these operations don't like anybody looking over their shoulder. Rarely keep records of any kind and when an animal is used up, well, it goes to a kill pen."

"Who rides the broncos?" Skylar asked.

Joe answered: "Locals, mostly, trying to get the experience for the bigger events. Some follow them around, taking their shots. The winners get a little cash, maybe a trophy or belt buckle. Or a trip to the emergency room."

"We don't know how Warrior's been treated." Lacaria let her words trail.

"Good guess? Not well." Coming from Dr. Shultz, those words carried impact.

The veterinarian had an idea. "I have a friend, someone I went to school with. He's head of the Texas Ranch Animal Board. I'll call him, ask if he'd be willing to pay this rodeo a little visit, a spot inspection. Maybe buy us some time."

Joe folded his arms. "I have some ideas. I can fly there in the morning, find the rodeo and get a feel for their owners, see what we can do to get Warrior out of there. Maybe offer to buy him."

"Might raise suspicions," Tess said, "if they think the horse has special value, which he does."

"I'd still like Joe to get a visual confirmation it's him," Phillip cautioned, "before we go to Defcon 1."

"You'll have to rent a truck, a trailer to bring him back." Lacaria said. "First things first. Let's get you to El Paso as soon as possible. I'll get you a flight out of Jackson in the morning. Book you in a nice hotel, too."

"What if they don't want to sell him, for any price?" Becky asked.

Phillip shrugged. "Then we go to Plan B."

"Which is?"

"I have no idea. If somebody comes up with one, I would love to hear it."

CHAPTER 50
WARRIOR

The dappled gray horse leaned against the rail and hung his head down. After two years, he was used to the saddle on his back, the bit cutting into his mouth, and the noise from the humans, yelling, shouting to one another, to him.

His memories were covered with fog, fragmented. Hard to make sense of it all, no matter how hard he tried.

Was there sweet grass and flowers a long time ago? Other horses nudging him with love and comfort? Maybe, he wasn't sure.

Replaced with panic, fear, anger, those memories washed away. He was with other horses he did not know, crowded together with the same panic, fear, and anger. Humans watching, shouting. Bad hay, bad water. It was hot and he constantly stepped in mud and manure. His mane and tail were soon coated with it.

A rope was thrown around his neck, a searing pain on his neck, another pain in his groin, this one worse. Humans stole his reason for being a stallion away from him, and with it his courage, his reason for living.

He was led out, taken away. He met other horses, had no interest in making friends with them.

A day later, a thing they called a saddle was put on him, cinched tight around his belly, then the jagged bit in his mouth. He was kicked, sticks poked at him, the end of them filled with a fire when it was jammed into his sides.

Day after day he was tormented, objects thrown at him, kicked until he was put in this wooden box, a human mounted him, a door released, and the shouts of humans drove him out.

He was reborn as a bucking bronco. They named him El Diablo. The Devil. Because he hated them, and more, he hated himself.

The fire stick jabbed his side. El Diablo arched his back against the pain.

It was time for him to try and kill the human riding on his back.

CHAPTER 51
THE DEVIL

Joe watched the night's performance with a growing rage.

Earlier, he had entered the fairgrounds with a sense of dread. A sign on the gate announced the rodeo would start at seven p.m., and cost fifteen dollars a person. Twenty with the full-color program, which he paid for.

But it was the posters who drew his attention. All of them featured the dappled gray horse called "El Diablo."

But the pictures were of Warrior.

"The most dangerous, deadly buckin' bronc west of the Pecos!" the posters proclaimed. *"This horse wants to kill any rider, and will if he gets the chance."*

Here was Warrior, rearing up on his hind legs, his head twisted around in obvious fury. Another poster showed him kicking his hind legs in a grotesque ballet, the rider dislodged and tumbling backward.

The program in Joe's hand had the same pictures. Joe wanted to crumple it but didn't. It might be useful in the future. As proof. He knew Lacaria would want those pictures, and he knew what she would do with them.

The stands were full, people chatting, laughing, many with children.

First came the bull riding, normally the capstone event. These bulls were less than enthusiastic, easily ridden to the last second.

Next came goat ropin', one of the more popular events especially with kids. Adult "local cowboys" with lariats chased bleating, terrified goats around the arena, trying to lasso them, most of the time failing. The person with the most success got a trophy and 10 bucks.

At last, nearly an hour later, the main event, the Buckin' Broncos.

El Diablo, the "Killer Bronc" was the obvious draw.

Joe clenched his fist and gritted his teeth. *Gotta stay calm, no matter what I see.*

The piebald was first, bucking in an expected way, the rider stayed on until the bell.

The gate for the second bronc, failed to open on time, two workers struggled with the latch. It gave way, the horse exited, bucking wildly, clearly panicking from the unexpected delay. The rider was dislodged, unharmed, walked away.

"And now! What you've been waiting for! How many of you want to see," an effective pause in the announcer's voice, "El Diablo!"

The crowd roared, some getting to their feet, clapping, whistling, cheering.

Joe watched the chute to his left. He saw Warrior, his body shifting back and forth while the rider lowered himself on the horse's back.

"Guy's gonna get killed," somebody behind Joe laughed.

"I saw El Diablo in Comstock last month," another man said. "He rammed against the rail so hard, broke the rider's arm. Would have been worse if somebody hadn't got him out of there. He's vicious."

"I hope he's as riled up as he was then." Another laugh.

Joe clicked Record on his phone.

El Diablo continued to shift back and forth. His head was low, his back arched.

The gate opened.

The horse spun around backward as though he might re-enter the chute. But, no, he spun around again, back legs kicking up. One more spin and WHAM he threw his entire weight at the wooden rail. Even at this distance, the crowd heard the sickening sound as the wood split, the rider thrown against the broken pieces.

Now El Diablo reared up on his hind legs, front hooves flailing in the air. Down, then up again. Two more spins, another crash into the rails.

Somehow, beyond all expectations, the rider stayed on. Blood spurted from the rider's leg. The cheers and whistles from the crowd were deafening.

Joe closed his eyes. *I don't want to see this. I want to be somewhere else. Anywhere else.* His rage was nearly out of control.

Did it match El Diablo's? How couldn't it? Imagine this horse's pain, suffering, torture, to get to this place. There was no escaping, he had to watch, keep recording.

It would be normal to think by this time Warrior was spent, exhausted. Where was the bell, shouldn't it have rung by now?

The rider hung on, surely he was ready for this to end?

El Diablo lunged at the rail one more time, hit it with his rump, more broken pieces of wood flew into the air. And, so did the rider, landing with a thud in the dirt.

El Diablo charged at him. A gasp went up from the crowd, as the horse's hooves stomped his legs again and again. More blood stained the dirt. A rodeo clown finally ran over, waving the horse away before he could do more damage. A stretcher was brought out.

The bell finally chimed.

El Diablo was finished, he had given the humans a good show, and given himself a tiny bit of revenge.

An hour later, walking casually, Joe had got as close as he could to the pens holding the livestock.

The bleating of goats greeted him in the barnyard.

One of the pens was segmented, holding the bulls. They were a motley assortment of colors, one brown, one white, one red, all with the requisite curved horns. Joe knew a bull was "encouraged" to buck with a flank strap around its middle.

Horses were another matter, and needed more "encouragement." When he found the horses' stalls, he immediately saw what those were.

Four stalls. Four horses. The first horse was black except for white socks. Ears flared, he looked at Joe askance, not taking his eyes off of him while he munched at some hay. Scars, some old, some new, spread across his back.

The second stall held an older horse, a little gray around the muzzle. He might have been a nice-looking piebald at one time. More scars were evident.

A buckskin horse lay prone in the third stall, a bandage wrapped around one of his front legs. Blood was caked around the wound. This horse had not been in the arena that night.

Finally, the last stall.

Warrior. He leaned against the railing, head down, not looking at anything, anyone. Scars on his flank from the cattle prods were prominent. A halter twisted around his head, it looked old and hard. Soars on his mouth spoke to the metal bit, the kind with wire spikes, jammed into his mouth each night.

A broken soul.

"Hey, guy," he whispered, hoping to get a response. "Warrior. Been looking for you a long time."

No response.

Before anyone saw him to tell him he shouldn't be there, Joe quickly took his cell phone out to take several pictures of Warrior. He zoomed in on the brand, confirming it was, indeed the lost horse. He decided not to send the pictures back to Wyoming, not yet.

His heart was broken, why should he break their hearts, too? Until he told them some good news, no reason to tell them anything yet.

CHAPTER 52
DECK OF CARDS

Joe devised a plan. Sort of.

He went looking for the rodeo's owner.

An older man was doling out cash to several men in the fairgrounds' office. Joe recognized them as the riders of the bulls and horses, except for the one who Warrior had put in the hospital. Cheap-looking trophies were on a large table, somebody was taking pictures.

A German Shepherd puppy, only a few weeks old, was on a leash held by a young man in his early twenties. He nodded amicably to Joe.

"Did you see the show?" he asked. "Whadja think?"

Gathering his wits, Joe knew he needed to become somebody else, somebody friendly, a kindred spirit to this world.

"Great organization you got here. Impressive."

"Yeah, my dad, Rollo, he owns this." He indicated the man with the cash.

Joe reached down to pet the puppy. "What's this little guy's name?"

"Antonio, bought him yesterday."

Rollo finished and stepped over to the doorway. Joe sized him up. He was a little paunchy in the jowls, graying hair, maybe close to seventy years old.

"I'm beat, let's go get some dinner. Who's this?" He noticed Joe, the question was abrupt, a little suspicious.

Joe held out his hand to introduce himself by his first name. "Joe. I'm passing through, on my way to Houston. Saw your rodeo here, thought I'd take it in. Glad I did. My uncle owned a rodeo almost like this in Southern California, worked it as a kid in the summers, best job I ever had."

Rollo grinned, he liked what he was hearing. "Nice to run into somebody who knows what kind of entertainment we're giving people. A lot of kooks, nut jobs, want to shut us down. Had a state inspector here yesterday, checking our paperwork. Made us stay an extra day. Heard we abuse animals. We don't, right, Benjy?" He clapped his son on the back.

"The guy who got hurt, was it serious?" Joe asked.

"Nah, broken leg, some bruises, hurt ego. These young rodeo riders, they think they're gonna break El Diablo, we make them sign waivers. They get hurt, not on us. Standard agreement."

"I'll go make sure everything's packed up," Benjy said, looking down. Joe noticed he hadn't answered his father's earlier question about animal abuse. "I'll leave Antonio here if you don't mind." He left.

Joe wondered if the young man felt the way his father did.

Rollo shook his head. "Kids. My only son don't want to have anything to do with this." He swept his hand around. "Rodeos, the life." He sat down at the table, inviting Joe to sit as well.

"I'll be honest, before we got El Diablo, my rodeo wasn't doing good. It's not an easy life, finding what works, getting those stands full. Then I found that horse, and things immediately got better. He's fierce, has never let up. The crowds go crazy. I hoped my son would get excited, seeing how good acts can make you money. If anything, he's worse, always sulking, complaining."

He looked down at the puppy lying under the table. "This dog here. Showed up with it, didn't even ask me."

"Is he your only kid?"

"I have a daughter, she's selling shoes in Houston. Ha ha! Selling shoes is better than this?" Rollo shook his head. "Hard to understand."

"I get it. I have a son, too, little worried about him, he hasn't settled down, yet." Joe was beginning to form the lies he needed to tell. *Bait the line, cast it, reel it in real slow.*

"What do you do in California?"

"I owned a chain of Italian restaurants—a small chain, six restaurants in and around San Francisco."

"Italian?"

"My father was Italian, mom was from Mexico." Joe smiled. "I can speak Spanish, hardly any Italian, unless they talk real, real slow. Which Italians generally don't do."

Rollo laughed. "My mom was from Mexico, too. My dad, German."

Joe raised his eyebrows. "Unusual combination."

"But unlike you, I can't speak Spanish but German? *Wie ein Einheimischer.* Like a native."

Joe stood up. "Best get back to my hotel. Early start tomorrow." A bluff, getting ready to bait the line.

Rollo wanted to talk, he saw a guy who appreciated his kind of rodeo. "What's your business in Houston?" Rollo leaned forward, Joe sat back down.

"I'm looking to buy a business for my son, get him settled."

"What kind of business?"

"Not sure, there are a couple of ideas I saw online."

"Doesn't want the restaurants?"

"I sold them, to a larger chain," Joe smiled. "Gave me an offer I couldn't refuse. But I got to roll it over before the IRS says I owe a bunch of taxes. My accountant's breathing down my neck."

Rollo shifted in his chair. He wasn't about to ignore Joe's "bait" dangling in the air between them.

"You said you like the rodeo life, eh? Maybe your son would, too?"

Almost hooked.

"Are you looking to sell?"

"Maybe, under the right circumstances. The right money." Rollo was cagey.

Benjy returned to say the animals were in their stalls, fed, and watered. "We'll be ready to leave in the morning."

"Sit down, son, this should interest you."

He turned back to Joe. "I have a figure in mind. Two hundred and fifty thousand.

Joe tilted his head.

"What do I get for that?"

"All the stock, the tack, and three haulers."

Joe narrowed his eyes, considering. "Trucks, too?"

Rollo shook his head. "No, not the trucks." He gave a short laugh. "We have to get out of this town, you know?"

"Seems like a lot of money," Joe mused. "Four horses, bulls."

"And the goats. They're all yours.

"Oh, and the dog, you can have the dog, too."

Benjy began to protest, Rollo held up his hand.

Joe felt a moment of revulsion. Rollo would sell his son's puppy? He needed to keep the discussion amiable. "Forgot about the goats." He did not mention the injured horse, did not want to tell Rollo he'd been in the stables checking the animals out.

He moved his fingers over the table. "We seem to be a ways apart, maybe too far apart."

"You haven't told me *your* number."

"Eighty thousand." Joe got up to leave, his heart was pounding. To be so close to getting the horse he wanted, the horse he needed. He decided to bluff. "Maybe going on to Houston is the better idea."

"Wait," Benjy pleaded. "Can you come up, a little?" His look of desperation made Joe sit back down again. *The kid needs this, even if he has to give up his dog.*

Joe made a quick calculation. "I can do a hundred and fifty thousand." *And Lacaria is going to kill me.*

"I like you, you're a good businessman. Let's make it interesting, shall we?" Rollo drew out a deck of cards from a pocket.

"Are you a gambling man? Simple game. Five Card Stud. You win, you get it all for your hundred and fifty thousand. I win, I get your money and keep my rodeo."

Joe's face reflected the numbness in his stomach. Not a good poker face. He nodded.

Rollo dealt the cards, five each, face down.

Joe peeked at his cards, discarded two, Rollo gave him two more.

"Dealer takes one," Rollo leered. "Let's see what we got."

The two men turned their cards over.

CHAPTER 53
TRUST

Rollo seemed congenial enough after he'd lost the game.

Cards dealt, the men turned over their hands. Rollo held three fives, a good hand.

Joe held two aces and two nines.

The better hand.

Rollo was disappointed but seemed to take his loss with a smile and clapped Joe's back.

The fairgrounds manager came in and told them they needed to close up. Her namebadge said Shar.

Joe asked her if they could use a computer and printer. "We need a few minutes, and I don't suppose you know if a Notary Public is nearby?"

The fairgrounds manager fetched a Notary from a nearby "Open 24 Hours" quick cash business, who would, of course, charge triple, for the late hour.

"I'll log into my bank, get the money transferred to you right now, wherever you want," Joe assured.

Benjy didn't wait for his father's response and quickly fished out a bankcard.

Rollo signed the contract and shook Joe's hand.

"All yours, now."

One hundred and fifty thousand dollars richer, Joe figured Rollo would take the money and leave.

But he didn't trust him.

Shar walked with him across the parking lot. Antonio padding along at Joe's side. "You have a rodeo, what are you going to do now?" she teased.

"Glad you asked. I'm going to have to keep the animals here for a few more days, we'll pay your rate, of course. Feed and water. I'll get my people here as soon as I can, and we'll take them all home to Wyoming."

She tilted her head. "You're not in the rodeo business, are you?"

Joe laughed. "No, ma'am, not in the least bit. I have a favor to ask you, and I'll pay extra for it."

She heard his request, didn't need to ask why, and immediately agreed.

She didn't trust Rollo, either.

Joe drove his rental truck into the barn between the stalls. He shut off the engine, got out, and bolted the building's large double doors from inside. This would be a long night. Joe was not going to allow Rollo and his crew to steal the rodeo he'd lost in a poker game.

All of the animals were eating good fodder and fresh water. The horse with the bandage was standing up, a good sign.

Warrior was in the place where he'd been before, as far away from the gate as he could get, against the wall, head down.

"I'm bringing you home," Joe said out loud. "You have a new grandson, you're going to want to see him. I'm going to do everything I can to make it up to you."

He returned to the truck. The puppy was in the front seat and immediately put his head on Joe's lap. He looked up when Joe ruffed the fur between his ears.

"What are we going to do with you?" he asked. "Hope you like Wyoming."

His long search, his quest, was over. Warrior was right in front of him, proof to his success. Why didn't he feel better, relieved? His heart heaved in new grief, and new guilt.

Bending his head, the ol' cowboy finally stopped trying to fight back his tears.

CHAPTER 54
A BARGAIN

"I think we heard from Joe," Lacaria came out of the office. "And I'm going to kill him."

Becky and Phillip were in the living room, finishing a light breakfast. "We kind of like him," Phillip joked. "What'd he do?"

She continued, "He's transferred one hundred and fifty thousand dollars out of one of our bank accounts."

Becky bit into a bagel, gave a small piece to Corky, who sat by her side on the couch. "That is a lot of money," she mumbled around the cream cheese.

"Will the check clear?" Phillip smiled.

"This isn't funny." Lacaria's phone rang. Joe's image filled her screen, his face scruffy and unshaved.

"You look terrible," his wife said. "And you've also spent a lot of money. On what?"

"Had an interesting night. I bought a rodeo," Joe began. "It was a bargain."

Lacaria looked at the transaction amount again. "A bargain?"

"We got four bulls, a bunch of goats, three livestock trailers," he let his words hang in the air, "and Warrior."

Silence. Lacaria put her phone on speaker and directed the screen to the others.

"It's him? Are you sure? How is he?" Becky jumped up.

"Yes, I'm sure, and he's different. I'll send you pictures. I bought three other horses, also broncs. Oh," a picture clicked on the screen, a puppy at Joe's side. "We got a dog. His name is Antonio, I'm calling him Tony."

Phillip reached for his coffee, not sure what to say. A rodeo? Bulls? Goats? A puppy? Joe saw the look on his face.

"No offense, boss, you look like you've been hit by a truck."

"I was. But you look like you've *slept* in a truck."

"Well, I did."

Dr. J came down from her room, Carl and Tess were called at their farm. Becky called Dr. Shultz and wandered into the library with her phone.

Skylar was bringing a tray of fresh fruit from the kitchen, seeing the sudden buzz of activity. "What'd I miss?"

Lacaria handed her the phone, a series of pictures of Warrior streamed across it. Skylar keyed in a code, a few seconds later those images appeared on the large screen above the dining room table.

Carl and Tess arrived as Becky got off the phone with the veterinarian.

"Is it true?" Carl asked. Like the others, he wanted to believe.

Dr. J nodded. "Joe confirmed the brand."

"Now what?" Tess asked.

Phillip was decisive. "We got a job to do. We bring Warrior home."

Joe piped up, his images replacing the pictures on screen. "Easier said than done. I'm not real optimistic about the condition of two of the trailers, axles are rusty, holes in the floors. I don't think they'll make the trip. One trailer is OK. It's large enough for the bulls."

"We have our four-horse trailer," Carl offered.

"The Double B has the livestock hauler on the other side of the barn. Is it road-ready?" Phillip asked Joe.

"It's fine, tires are good, somebody has to check the brake lights when you hook it up."

"I'll take care of it," Carl offered.

"I've got to go, feed the animals and give them water for their day. The goats are getting loud. Call me later."

"Joe," Phillip's voice rose before Joe clicked off. "Hire some security for that barn so you can get a good night's rest!"

Becky came back into the room.

"Dr. Shultz wants us to fly to El Paso, today if possible. Inspect all of the animals, see what kind of paperwork there is, if any. Vaccinations, if any. And we'll be transporting livestock across four state lines." She thought for a minute. "We'll need a couple of days to get it all straight.

"I'm going home to pack, then to the clinic. Lacaria, can you get us tickets out of Jackson, and hotel rooms where Joe's staying?"

Tess left with Becky, saying she needed to get to the Wrangler to ask one of her employees to take over while she was gone.

The doorbell rang.

"You expecting somebody?" Lacaria looked at her watch. "This early?"

Nan Whittier stepped into the living room to a bunch of unfamiliar and curious faces.

"Have I come at a bad time?"

Phillip leaned back. "I forgot about our appointment. I am so sorry. This is Nan, the photojournalist I mentioned to you." He smiled awkwardly and pointed at his leg. "I set this appointment up, before all this happened."

Nan shook her head. "I should have called first."

Dr. J held out her hand. "Things got a little haywire here. You were at the bureau's meeting, weren't you?"

"Yes, got a good story out of it, too." She looked about at the cluttered room. "I can come back another time."

Dr. J exchanged glances with Phillip, both thinking the same thing. *Might be a good idea to have a journalist of Nan's reputation along for this ride.*

Dr. J smiled. "I think you've come at a *great* time. I don't suppose you're free for the next three, four, maybe five days?"

Before she could answer, Phillips' laptop pinged. Joe's video of Warrior's "performance" at last night's rodeo filled the screen.

Seconds after it began, Nan's hands flew to her face. She knew *what* she was seeing, and she knew *who* she was seeing.

"Warrior?" Nods all around. They quickly filled her in on their plans.

With her reporter's instinct, she knew this might be the biggest story of her career.

"Where are we going?"

CHAPTER 55
THREE THOUSAND MILES

"Lacaria, it makes sense for you and Skylar to stay here, hold down the fort. Our eyes on the sky to get us to El Paso and back, let us know if there are any changing road conditions, problems along the way," Phillip told them. He nodded to his crutches. "I can't do much to feed animals and I can't drive to the MacKendrick farm to feed theirs, either."

Lacaria nodded. "We'll take care of everything." She looked down at Corky. "And take care of you, too."

Skylar smiled at the dog "You're going to have a new baby brother in a few days."

"I've been thinking about the best roads to take," Carl keyed up a road map of western states on the screen. "Fortunately, I drove most of them when I was with the bureau, went to Albuquerque several times, less than three hundred miles from El Paso. It makes sense to use the same route to return as the one we take to get there."

"I'll upload photos, videos to our website, transmit them to our members, the media," Lacaria sat down on one of the chairs, nodding to Nan.

Nan agreed. "I'll have several reports every day, interviews, pictures. Some of the nationals could pick this up." She looked at Skylar. "And who better to tell the world you've found Warrior?"

"This is like *The Cavern of Dragon Eggs*!" The teenager ran out of the room to return with the large grease board on an easel and several dry ink pens in different colors.

"We have a quest, a journey to take, this is our Game Board.

She wrote in red letters at the top:

RESCUING WARRIOR
GETTING THERE, AND BACK

"We need our champions, our soldiers. Strengths and skills."

"Liege Lord," she pointed to Phillip. "You have bags of gold to pay for this."

"Guilty, well, less a hundred and fifty thousand dollars."

"Dr. J is our Wizard, a scientist who has all the answers." The teenager smiled slyly. "And the books.

"Carl said he knows the way. He'll be our Ranger."

"Ranger Carl," Dr. J agreed. "Your new title."

A pause while Skylar thought. "Ah, Wizards. Our veterinarians, Becky and Dr. Shultz. A great skill to have for this quest.

"Tess will be our Quartermaster. She has a store. She'll bring lots of snacks for the drive."

"Doughnuts will be good," Carl laughed.

Skylar continued. "Technology. Lacaria. A Mascot? Joe's puppy, Tony."

"What about Joe?" Carl asked.

Another pause, Phillip spoke up. "Our Mage. Our wise one, Joe fits perfectly."

"And me?" Nan wondered. "What's my role?"

"You're our Scribe, of course. You will chronicle these great deeds for the Ages.

"Now, we need tools, resources," she stepped back to consider.

She drew a vertical line down the middle of the board in black.

In blue ink, on the left side, she wrote **Getting There**. On the right side, in green ink, she wrote **And Back**. On both sides were written:

Trucks

Trailers

Drivers

Hotel rooms.

Eats

Phillip nodded at the cast on his leg. "I'm obviously not up for driving a truck. Two of you will each be in a truck pulling our two trailers to El Paso, and drive another truck to pull the one Joe bought."

Skylar wrote on the Getting There side:

Drivers: Three trucks, three drivers. Carl, Tess, Dr. J. Passenger, Nan.

On the Getting Back side:

Drivers: Three trucks, six drivers. Carl, Tess, Dr. J, Joe, Becky, Dr. Shultz. Passenger, Nan.

Carl observed, "Going there, trailers empty, not a big deal, two days tops. Coming back with the trailers filled with a heavy load, we'll need two drivers each truck, in case one gets tired, or stressed. Both could happen when you're hauling big animals. But are we sure we want to bring all of those animals back?"

"I suppose we could give the goats and bulls to somebody in El Paso." Phillip answered.

"What would happen to them?" Lacaria bit her lip. "They might end up in a bad place, and there are the other horses to consider, too."

"Spoken like the soft-hearted woman you are." Phillip waved a hand to the landscape outside the windows. "Not like we don't have a few thousand acres for some goats and bulls to roam about."

Names were added to the Getting Back side:

Becky and Dr. Shultz: one truck

Carl and Tess: one truck

Joe and Dr. J: one truck

"There will be challenges, too." Dr. J's look was questioning, she held out her hands. "What would those be?"

Everybody talked at once. Skylar tried to keep up, writing what they were all saying.

Gas, feed for the animals, the weather.

Fatigue.

Fourteen hundred miles was underscored.

"No, Skylar," Carl said. "We'll be driving almost **three** thousand miles, round trip."

Silence for a few seconds as the sobering thought sunk in.

The change was made on the board, more items were listed.

Trucks break down (groans at this).

Cone zones (more groaning at the thought of road construction delays).

Carl stood up and went to the board. "There's something we haven't thought about. Haul time."

"What?" Nan asked.

"We can't haul livestock in a trailer for more than four hours, five tops. They need to stretch their legs, get fresh air, water, feed. We'll have Dr. Shultz with us and he's going to be a real stickler about that, as he should be. It's going to take us several days to get them back here."

Phillip blew air out of his cheeks, thinking. "The heat of the day, we'll want to travel early mornings. We're going over mountain passes, too. Skylar, put Route down on both sides, and Haul Time on the right side."

"How do you give horses, bulls, goats a break?" Skylar asked. "Let them go free into a field or somebody's backyard?"

"We use fairgrounds. They'll charge, usually pretty reasonable, but we'll have stalls, feed, water, maybe staff to help. We'll want to call today, book them immediately, tell them what's coming."

Skylar underscored the words Haul Time in red ink several times. Her eyes grew large. "We have a lot of phone calls to make."

Nan took a picture of Skylar's Game Board. "Perfect for my first article," she grinned.

Carl sought out Dr. J before he left.

"We haven't talked about the endgame, the 'and then what?'"

She knew what he was referring to. "What do we do with Warrior when we get him back here."

She leaned against a wall, arms folded. ""Like you said, we have thousands of acres. But wouldn't seem right, would it. A field, by himself. Solitude, that might be OK after all he's been through. I honestly don't know right now." She shrugged.

"Maybe he'll let us know what he wants when we get him here. With that horse, anything might happen."

"Pack a bag for me, will you?" Phillip asked Lacaria.

Lacaria was going into the kitchen, Phillip's request stopped her in her tracks.

"You're kidding, right? No way you're going with them. You have to stay here."

He tilted his head. "I'll just sit around here, fretting and driving you crazy. I have to finish this."

"You're not vanquishing dragons or monsters."

He thought for a moment. "In a way, I am."

Lacaria sat down next to him and put a hand on his shoulder. "Your leg is in a cast, you're recovering from a concussion, the surgery. This isn't a good idea."

He pointed to the Game Board. "I'm exerting executive privilege as the Liege Lord. You're overruled."

Despite her concern, she smiled.

Phillip squeezed her hand. "I'll be all kinds of comfy in the backseat, headphones on, listening to music. You know Becky will watch me like a hawk, so will Tess, and," he chuckled, "I'll pull up Skylar's game, check it out."

His next words brought tears to her eyes.

"Don't worry, Mom, I'll be fine."

Skylar was exhilarated. "Leading the charge" to organize Warrior's rescue was heady stuff. It was also tainted with a little bit of guilt over the hack.

Yeah, and worried I might get caught, too.

Maybe what she'd done today might make up for it? The damage, the repercussions?

So far, she didn't feel any better.

Maybe she never would.

CHAPTER 56
TIMING IS EVERYTHING

"We need to make a decision," Dr. J said to Nan and Phillip. "How do we tell the Double B's followers we've found Warrior, and when?"

"There might be some interest."

"How about we wait until we get to El Paso, we'll have more information from Becky and Dr. Shultz, see it all for ourselves," Dr. J suggested. "Announce we've found Warrior, don't say where he is, more information will be coming, that kind of message."

"Good idea, Lacaria and Skylar can set the stage so to speak, and as we begin our trip back, we can stream from our phones. In my business, timing is everything."

Skylar listened to the discussion. "Should we upload the pictures Uncle Joe sent, and that video of Warrior in the rodeo?"

"It's devastating," Dr. J mumbled, "but it's profound. Phillip?"

He didn't need long to think about it. "Yes, we need to tell people what he's been through. Start all of that *after* we leave El Paso."

Nan said, "I told my editors the Double B article is taking a different turn."

"What'd they say?" Phillip asked.

"They're chomping at the bit," she joked. "This trip is going to be different from anything I've ever done. I appreciate the invite."

Dr. J and Carl were looking at the map on the screen. Skylar joined them with a notepad and scribbled as they talked.

"We're starting here," Dr. J pointed to West Central Wyoming. "We're going here." She traced the line to El Paso.

"Wish it was that easy," Carl chuckled. "Shortest distance between two points and all. Colorado gives us the most challenges."

He counted them out, none of them wonderful. "Douglas Pass. Falling rocks are common, not a great road for trailers.

"The alternative is going through Craig to Rifle. I like it better than Douglas Pass. From there we go south through Montrose.

"Another decision, we can go up Log Hill, then down Lizard Head. Or, Red Mountain Pass."

Phillip held up his hand. "No way, absolutely no way."

Carl laughed. "Agree. Our final selection is Cochetopa Pass."

Lacaria frowned, looking at the map. "You have to take the switchbacks up to Gunnison, then down coming back. My sister lives in Salida. It's slow and there's always a lot of traffic, especially tourists."

"The road's been improved some the last few years, but you're right," Carl agreed. "It will be slow going coming back with heavy livestock trailers."

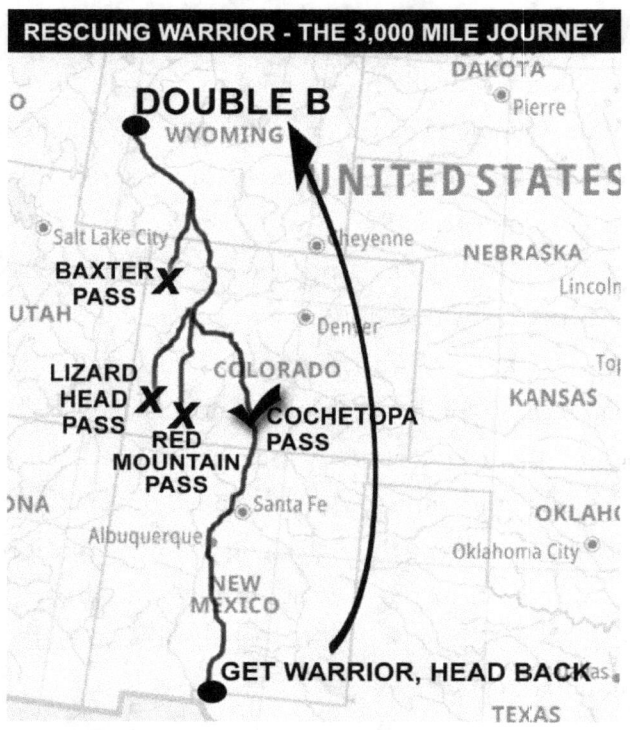

He stepped back to take in the map. "Remember, we're not going be going eighty miles an hour. Fifty or sixty if we're lucky, and any of these passes are going to slow us down."

"What do you think?" Dr, J asked him.

"I'm thinking Cochetopa. We'll be going down it on the way, piece of cake with empty trailers, we'll get the lay of the land for the return trip. We'll have good options for fairgrounds, too. How about we work on those next, you can start making calls."

Tess returned as Carl finished mapping their routes to and from El Paso. She told him Becky and Dr. Shultz were on their way to Jackson to catch a flight to Denver, then on to El Paso. "They'll be there late this afternoon. Joe's picking them up at the airport and they'll go straight to the fairgrounds."

Lacaria came out with a lunch tray. "Phillip insists on going with you," she said, shaking her head.

"We'll take care of him," Tess assured her. "I understand why you're worried."

"These horses," Lacaria looked up at Tess, "how they've changed our lives."

"It does seem we're different, doesn't it?" She smiled. "And we're getting goats."

Lacaria rolled her eyes. "We owned goats growing up. They can be ornery as sin."

"Look at it this way. We'll learn how to make goat cheese. People love it."

"*You* can learn how to make goat cheese. I'll sit on the deck and eat it with sausage and crackers."

"Did you decide on a route?"

Carl told his wife, "We'll spend one night, in Gunnison. They'll be long days, about nine hours each."

"What about coming home?"

"Little trickier because of the haul times. It's going to take us four days. You've been elected Quartermaster, in charge of supplies."

"Way ahead of you. I already have three large coolers and they'll be filled with ice. Plus snacks, fresh fruit, the works, for all of us."

"When do we leave?"

She rolled her eyes at his answer. "We ride at dawn."

Skylar found Lacaria in the studio, her head resting on her hands. "Are you all right?"

"Yes, it's been a long day." She looked at the girl. "Your Game Board is a good idea. Helped us get organized. Thank you."

Skylar beamed. "I can't wait to start our podcasts. Is there anything I can do in the next couple of days?"

"I was thinking it's a shame we don't have the new studio up and running. It is cramped in here, and with the videos coming in, voice overs, editing."

Skylar frowned. "Don't you have all of the new equipment in the garage? Tables, chairs, laptops, cameras?"

Lacaria nodded. "The studio in the conference center is done, all the electrical in."

Skylar smiled. "We have two days with nothing else to do, right?"

CHAPTER 57
PEHNAHO

"The horse with the bandage has a deep wound on his leg, it's infected, I'm dosing him with antibiotics." Dr. Shultz told them. He panned his phone's camera around the stalls.

"All of the horses have scars from cattle prods, teeth in bad shape. We can look at treating them when we get home. The bulls are surprisingly docile.

"Then there are the goats," Dr. Shultz chuckled. "Never my favorite kind of clients, and these are proving to be more than a handful."

"What about the paperwork for the states we'll be traveling through?" Phillip asked.

"Coming along, Becky's taking care of it. Not surprised none of these animals have up-to-date vaccinations. The forms aren't involved and I've assured all state agencies I'll be traveling with you." He chuckled. "Interesting enough, it's the puppy giving us the most problems."

Becky came on to the call. "We have no idea if the dog's been tested or vaccinated for anything. He's at a local veterinary hospital, getting checked out, all his shots. He'll stay the night."

"Look," Joe told them in a joking fashion, "I bought 'em, I did my job, it's up to you all to figure out the rest. Including getting my puppy home."

They left early the next morning. Tess drove the MacKendricks' truck pulling their horse trailer; Carl drove one of the Double B's white trucks pulling the large livestock trailer.

Dr. J drove the third Double B truck, no trailer behind it. Nan was with her in the passenger seat; Phillip in the club cab, his cast propped up.

Well before noon, they reached I-70 at Rifle, Colorado and soon passed various communities before turning east on Highway 50 to ascend the switchbacks to Gunnison where they spent their first night in the hotel rooms Lacaria had reserved for them.

Pre-dawn the next day the trucks left the hotel parking lot. Everyone was anxious, before the day's end they would be in El Paso, and see Warrior for themselves.

An hour later they reached the canyon leading to Highway 114, and Cochetopa Pass, a winding road with large pine trees on either side opening to lush, rolling hills.

"Beautiful country," Phillip said. "Slow going coming back."

"Time consuming, too," Dr. J nodded to the traffic in front and behind them. "Lots of RVS and semis."

The "shotgun" part of the highway was easier, a nice road from Saguache to Alamosa.

A short time later they were in New Mexico, getting their last bearings, the "lay of the land".

Early in the evening, after a long day, the trucks pulled into the El Paso fairgrounds.

Motors were barely turned off before everyone piled out. Dr. J could not wait, she ran towards the barn.

Joe held the door open for her. "Come on in and see our boy."

The lights were on, giving a good view of the inside. Dr. J walked quickly past the stalls, finding Becky and Dr. Shultz packing up supplies.

"We've done as much as we can here," the veterinarian said. "They're ready for the road."

Warrior stood in his spot in the corner. "He hasn't moved much except to eat and drink," Becky told her.

Holding a hand to her mouth, Dr. J approached him, carefully, whispering soft and low. "*Pehnaho*," she said in Shoshone. *Hello. My brother.*

The horse flicked his ears at the unfamiliar voice.

Dr. Shultz sidled up to her. "That's the most reaction we've seen from him. He's stayed in one spot this whole time, in a way a good thing. Was able to get some injections in him, antibiotics. And—" he paused.

She turned to him, the question she wanted to ask stuck in her throat.

"Six vials of his blood are on their way to your lab in Boulder. Should be there tomorrow."

"Oh," she breathed. "I didn't know if I dared ask."

He pointed to Becky. "She's the one who got them. He stood real still for her."

"I got in there quick, before he knew what I was doing. Once I got those six vials, he let me know to forget about doing anything else, and I should be happy with what I got."

"You have such a special touch with horses," Dr. J's compliment was heart-felt. "Six precious vials of Warrior's blood. Analyzed with Alexander's, gets us closer to proving our theories."

Carl held the door open for Phillip, who hobbled in. Tess walked around him to make sure there was nothing in his way to stumble over.

Nan darted about, taking pictures of Warrior, the other animals, and everybody looking at Warrior and the other animals.

"If I start to cry, give me a hanky." Tess held her husband's hand.

"Too late, I've used all of them up."

"I think all of us had given up on Warrior, finding him. Except Joe." Dr. J looked down. "He never stopped looking, never stopped believing."

Carl stooped down to look at Warrior's mouth. "Are those sores?" he asked Dr. Shultz.

"I can't open his mouth, of course, there might be some deep cuts from the bits they used on him. When you watch him eat, it's obvious he's in some pain."

"Can you give him something?" Tess asked. "Maybe help him, even calm him down for the trip?"

"I could, but for the next few days I'd rather have him ornery and standing up rather than dopey and falling."

Before the sun set, they returned to their trucks. Joe introduced Carl to Shar. "She's been a big help, couldn't have done this without her. She let us use computers, phones, gave us access to everything around here."

The fairground manager smiled. "When Joe told me who you were, what you're doing, couldn't help myself. I'm going to miss the excitement."

"We'll be heading out in the morning," Carl told her. "As early as possible."

"I'll have coffee and doughnuts in my office. And anything else you need. You've got a big job ahead of you."

"Don't mind telling you, we're all pretty nervous. In truth? Scared, too. Getting everybody home, without anything going wrong. And Warrior. I guess you could say he's become a powerful symbol for us. Nothing can happen to him. It's all on us."

"I understand, talking to Joe and looking at all of the information about your ranch on your website."

Nan approached, asking Shar for an interview. The two left for the fairgrounds' office.

A van pulled up, a door opened, and out bounded the fluff ball, Tony, sporting a new collar and gleaming tags. He leaped into Joe's arms.

"You two have bonded." Carl ruffled the dog's ears. "He's a handsome little guy."

"He won't stay little for long, look at those paws."

At the hotel, the others checked in, a large table was reserved for them at a nearby restaurant.

"I'm too tired to celebrate," Carl said.

He went over the route for the return trip with Joe, Becky and Dr. Shultz. "Lacaria and Skylar have made all arrangements, payments, and hotel reservations."

The drivers for each truck were assigned for the trip back.

Carl and Tess would drive the goats.

Dr. Shultz and Becky would drive the bulls. Phillip would be in the backseat.

Joe and Dr. J would drive the horses. Nan would be in the back seat with the puppy.

Joe called his wife later from his hotel room. "I'm leaving in a few minutes, gotta turn in the rental truck now that our gang has arrived and hit the sack."

"Are you OK?" she asked. "I'm seeing new wrinkle lines in your forehead."

"I'm bone-tired, and numb, hardly believing this is happening."

Tony jumped on the bed and mugged the phone. "He's a clown, thinks everything's about him," Joe laughed.

"You're already spoiling him. I'd better let you go, get a good night's sleep. One more thing, Skylar and I have been busy, too." She panned her phone around the room showing the large table, chairs, microphones, and audio controls.

"Where are you?" he asked.

"In our new studio. We decided this is the perfect time, and reason, to break it in."

"That's amazing. Everything works?"

She laughed. "We'll find out tomorrow."

CHAPTER 58
LOADING UP

Three livestock trailers were backed up to the barn's chute early the next morning.

The assumption was the bulls might cause the most difficulty. Instead, they walked up the ramp slowly, and gave no problems.

The horses came next, ropes attached to their halters that were fed into the MacKendrick trailer and pulled tight. Carl, Dr. Shultz, and Shar knew they needed to keep a firm hold on the ropes. These were riding broncs and nobody knew if they would load easily, or balk.

And "El Diablo." Would he live up to his name?

They decided to pull him first, he might be more comfortable in the front of the trailer.

Warrior allowed the rope to be drawn out to the chute and that was as far as they got. He stopped, shook his head. This was an all-too-familiar routine, one always ending in pain. He screamed, tried to rear up. Carl held the rope taut and down, not allowing the horse to have his way. Warrior tried again, but his head was forced to stay down.

"He is strong," Carl winced. The horse was giving him a difficult time.

Dr. J talked to the horse. Becky stood on the side, offering him sweet grass from a nearby field, hoping it would help.

"Come on, Warrior, you're going home and there's going to be lots of this for you to eat."

Interested, the horse took a step, then another to snatch the grass from Becky's outstretched hand.

"Hope you have more," Dr. J smiled.

"A whole bag."

Little by little, the grass lured Warrior up the chute into the trailer and to the back stall. There was a unified sigh of relief.

Warrior banged his rump hard against the trailer wall, shaking it on its axle.

"Letting us know who's boss," Dr. Shultz chuckled.

The other horses were obstinate, but gave them no problems. After all, none of them were the dreaded "El Diablo."

The large livestock hauler backed up to the pen holding the goats who were bleating and panicking. Hooves kicked up dirt.

Shar got two of her employees, both younger men, positioned on either side of the gate.

"I know goats," she said as explanation.

Carl inched the gate open, while one of the fairgrounds men shooed the goats up the ramp. Well, tried to.

One of the goats escaped, leaping over the opening. She was quickly caught by the other employee, who promptly set her down on the ramp.

"Always one in every crowd," he grinned, as another shimmied its way through the opening. "Or, two."

All of the goats were finally loaded in their trailer.

"Not looking forward to doing this three more times on the way home," Tess said.

"You wanted goat cheese!" Joe laughed.

CHAPTER 59
A LONG WAYS TO GO

The West Texas city of El Paso. Three trucks, each pulling a trailer, idled on the road outside of the fairgrounds.

Drivers made last-minute checks, ensuring all hitches were secure, confirming the trucks were ready.

Tension filled each of the cabs.

Joe took a swig of water, listening to the motor's low hum. Maybe he hoped the truck wasn't running right. Maybe break down right here on the road. Maybe Phillip or Carl or somebody would decide to wait another day. Maybe another week.

Dr. J watched him. She exchanged worried looks with Nan, who turned her camera on.

"We're getting ready to leave El Paso," she spoke into the microphone. "Fourteen hundred miles between us and home. Four days to get Warrior safe, to his freedom. That is, if everything goes as planned, and nothing goes wrong."

Shar and the fairgrounds staff walked across the parking lot to wave good-bye. They watched the trucks for a few moments, listening to the idling motors. She knew Joe was leading with the horses.

"Thought they were in a hurry to get home," one of the staffers said. "What are they waiting for?"

She shook her head. "Not sure. Maybe a sign?"

The trucks didn't move.

Becky wondered what was taking so long. "Is something wrong?"

Dr. Shultz leaned forward over the steering wheel. "Don't know what it could be."

Carl in the third truck was also having some irrational thoughts. "This is crazy," he said to Tess, "but maybe we ought to wait."

"For what? You're not thinking of changing your mind, are you?" Tess frowned. "We're going home. Now."

Joe adjusted the rearview mirror. He saw Warrior's head through the truck and trailer's windows. The horse shifted his weight, raised his head, and looked at Joe.

His eyes seemed friendly, soft. "I have to be imagining that," Joe whispered. "There is nothing soft about this horse after everything that's happened to him."

Dr. J put a hand on his arm. "Joe, we have to trust ourselves, you have to trust yourself. More important, know that Warrior might be learning to trust us." She smiled. "At least, a little."

The horse held Joe's stare and did not blink. Had he heard Dr. J's words?

The memory of Warrior turning in the roundup's chute, rearing up, looking for his family, trying to save as many as he could hit Joe hard, forcing the air from his lungs. He shook his head to clear it.

Warrior's eyes had not wavered, continued to watch him.

It was Joe who broke the spell. "OK, then, if he's ready, I'm ready. Let's go," Joe cleared his throat, his voice stronger.

He put the truck in gear, and turned onto the highway.

"Have they left, yet?" Skylar asked.

Lacaria shook her head. "This has got to be nerve-racking for them. Such a long ways to go."

Lacaria and Skylar put their headsets on, adjusted their microphones, and logged into the Double B Wildlife Science Center podcast. Lacaria was the host, Skylar was in charge of pictures and videos.

A cell phone chimed, the signal the trucks were finally on the way.

"Good morning members, visitors, and guests," Lacaria began. "Today's podcast is very special, we have the most important show we've ever had.

"As most of you know, for two years our team has searched far and wide for one of our wild mustangs wrongfully taken from us by the United States Government."

(Switch to a picture of Warrior, free and proud, on a hillside overlooking his mares)

"He fought valiantly, trying to protect his family against the horrors he seemed to know awaiting them."

(Switch to twenty-second snippet of the same stallion, captured, rearing up on his hind legs, looking for his family)

"His name is Warrior."

"Joe Ruiz visited dozens of holding pens, stables, corrals, killing facilities, even slaughter houses. Poured over adoption papers. All to no avail.

"A few days ago, one of our loyal podcast members sent us a picture of what might be Warrior. It was a little grainy, taken hastily, it showed a brand, barely legible, from a location in Texas.

"Joe flew to El Paso. Hours later, we received our answer.

"Warrior has been found."

(A pause)

Lacaria cleared her throat, preparing herself for the next segment. "He has been used and abused, humiliated, as a bucking bronco. Tagged as El Diablo, the devil."

(Switch to the rodeo's program cover)

"Our veterinary team arrived in El Paso two days ago. He has wounds in his mouth and many scars from what has been done to him. You can see why."

(Switch to several pictures of Warrior in his stall, then a thirty-second snippet of Joe's video of the rodeo)

"It was urgent we bring Warrior home, to safety and sanctuary. In short, we bought the whole rodeo. They are getting ready to leave El Paso as we speak, to begin the four-day journey home with Warrior, three other horses, four bulls, and a bunch of goats, too."

Lacaria chuckled in her microphone.

"We'll be podcasting updates several times a day. Traveling with them is award-winning journalist Nan Whittier who will be documenting every mile, sending us pictures, videos, and her reports.

The final image filling the screen was a map of Texas, New Mexico, Colorado, and Wyoming. The caption said:

The road Warrior will be taking home.

"Please, wish them good luck, and Godspeed. Their first stop for the night: Santa Fe, New Mexico." She smiled at Skylar and clicked: *Off line.*

CHAPTER 60
THE WORLD IS WATCHING

What was Warrior thinking right about now?

Was he thinking these humans were going to hurt him like all the others had? Was he thinking soon he'd have a saddle strapped on his back, with another chance to hurt a human as much as possible?

Perhaps he appreciated he was getting better feed, fresher and cleaner water than he'd drunk in years, or the soft, encouraging voices of these humans instead of being yelled at or hurt with the fire stick.

Or, perhaps, after he was coaxed out of the trailer, "Why is there a young dog staring at me?"

Dr. Shultz watched the animals as they were unloaded, looking for any sign of dehydration or injury.

"Goats are fine, so are the bulls," he announced to Carl and Becky. He went into the barn while the horses were led out of the trailer. Warrior didn't give them any trouble, he wanted to get in the barn.

"It was a good idea to stop here first, gave us all a feel for those trailers, a short distance, and to give the animals a feel for us," Joe said as they pitched hay to the animals.

Carl agreed. "The next stretch to Gunnison will be a little longer, we'll leave early, miss the heat of the afternoon before we get there."

"I'm looking forward to some great Santa Fe food," Dr. J came up behind them. "Let's go get checked into our hotel. I'll let Lacaria know we're here safe and sound."

"Has anybody seen Tony?" Joe looked around.

"Buffled." The puppy stood on a bale of hale in the corner of the stall.

"Go away," the horse told him, shuffling his front legs towards Tony in a threatening manner. "I might hurt you, I want to be alone. I like being alone."

Tony stood his ground, or rather his bale of hay.

"Midogrrrr."

"You're making no sense, don't you know how to talk?"

"Gipl!" The dog spun around and around, tongue hanging out.

"I do not appreciate getting laughed at, young sir, and I think that's what you're doing."

Tony tilted his head, then lay down. His eyes were soft, imploring. "Sluf."

"If you stay here, make sure you're not in my way. I hope you don't snore."

Dog and horse stared at each other.

"There seems to be a stare-down contest going on," Dr. Shultz laughed.

"Come on, Tony, let's go," Joe whistled. "Time for supper."

The puppy stayed in his place.

"Tony!"

"You can't go in there now, not with Warrior in the way." Dr. Shultz shook his head. "Looks like the pup is making friends."

"I guess he'll be OK, as long as Warrior doesn't stomp on him," Joe mumbled his doubts.

Lacaria uploaded dozens of Nan's pictures of the bulls, the goats, the trailers, and various "people shots." Of course, Warrior and the other three horses comprised the bulk of the pictures. Nan was an excellent photographer and Lacaria was having a lot of fun, especially reading the comments coming in via email and the podcast's message board.

"Bless you for rescuing Warrior!"

"Where can I donate to help?"

"Amazing journey."

"Can't wait to see him back home!"

Skylar came into the studio. "Anything new?"

"They're in Santa Fe. I'm going through our messages."

Skylar opened a laptop. She looked up. "Did you see this one?" She forwarded it to Lacaria who read it out loud.

"Let's go, World! We're on our way!"

"Where are they going?" Skylar asked.

"No idea. Maybe it was sent to us by mistake?" She shrugged, a chime told her Nan was sending more pictures.

Nan texted Lacaria the next morning. "We're leaving Santa Fe." Animals were loaded, bulls docile as usual, the goats having a fit with their loud bleating.

Warrior balked on the rope in his typical manner, when a blur of fur sped past him up the ramp into the trailer.

"Tony!" Joe shouted. "Come out here, boy."

The puppy jumped on one of the tack shelves and sat down. Warrior was blocking the entry. Joe didn't dare scoot past him to retrieve the dog.

Warrior's head shot up and did the most unexpected thing, he quickly walked into the trailer to his spot.

"Horses like dogs," Becky said, "even a horse like Warrior."

There was nothing to do. Tony would ride with Warrior.

"You shouldn't be in here, look, your humans are upset." Warrior was stumped, how could he get this dog out of here.

"Con jibbam."

"Didn't anybody teach you to talk?"

Warrior tried to turn around in the narrow, confining space. He yawned, showed his huge teeth.

The puppy pulled back towards the wall, whimpering, afraid of the big animal in front of him.

"Don't worry, I'm not going to hurt you. If I was, I would have done it yesterday." He glanced at the other horses in the trailer. "Odd," he said. "I've never talked to any of you all these years, and here I am talking to a dog, telling him he's safe."

One of the broncos stopped his chewing on some hay and looked up. "We tried to talk to you, but you ignored us, so we stopped. We don't know what's going to happen to us, could be good, could be bad, but this food is a lot better than anything we've ever eaten." He went back to munching.

Warrior shook his head and whipped his tail around. It was clear he had some fence-mending to do, and there was still the problem with this young pup.

He stepped forward. "I guess there's nothing else to do, I'll teach you how to talk. You're Tony, a stupid dog. I'm Warrior, a very smart horse."

Tony looked up. "Hosp."

"Close enough."

The convoy needed to beat the rush hour traffic. Santa Fe is New Mexico's state capital, busy with tourists and commuters going to Albuquerque and Los Alamos.

Highway 285 is a quirky route, four lanes before Española, a small town where traffic has to slow down, to make a hard right before following the road.

The three trucks followed each other closely.

Traffic ahead of them slowed. "What's going on?" Joe wondered.

Inching closer, they saw the first signs.

Large ones, small ones, hand-painted, makeshift. Held by dozens, perhaps a hundred people on either side of the road, on sidewalks, in driveways. In the highway's median.

YOU'RE FREE, WARRIOR
WELCOME HOME, WARRIOR
BLESS YOU, WARRIOR
WE LOVE YOU, WARRIOR
GO DOUBLE B GANG!!!

Dr. J thumbed her phone to the others. "Are you seeing this? ARE YOU SEEING THIS?"

People were waving, taking pictures. They heard cars honking. Cheering.

Becky rolled down her window to wave back. "All these people, where did they come from?"

"I feel like a rock star," Dr. Shultz chuckled.

The highway led to another right turn as they left Española. They were forced to slow down for a traffic light. There were even more people here, more signs, more honking, more waving.

Nan was in the last truck with Carl and Tess, who was driving the goats. She rolled down her window, waved to a woman holding a sign.

"How did you hear about us?" she shouted. She clicked her camera to audio.

"You kidding?" the woman shouted. "It's all over the Internet, hundreds of social media pages. The whole world is watching!!!"

Lacaria and Skylar stared at the large screen in the studio. "I can't believe this," Lacaria whispered, turning to the girl. "Look what you did."

"I didn't do it," Skylar shook her head. "You did". She waved her hands around. "All of you, the Double B, did this. Warrior, he did this." She laughed. "Nobody can ignore you. Like the lady said, the world is watching."

The scene in Alamosa, Colorado, was even more spectacular as word spread the Double B trucks were on their way. Across the railroad tracks into town, hundreds more people, hundreds more signs.

The Double B Gang got in the spirit, smiling and waving to the crowds.

A state patrol vehicle flagged them down. One by one, the trucks pulled to a stop.

"What did we do?" Carl wondered.

"You folks heading up to Saquache, then over Cochetopa?" the patrolman asked.

"Yes, sir." Carl's mouth went dry. "Are we doing something wrong? We have our livestock papers here, and our veterinarian is in the truck behind us."

"Don't care, somebody else's jurisdiction, want to let you know we'll be escorting you to Gunnison, want you to have as clear a way as possible. Get you over Cochetopa Pass without any problems." The patrolman laughed. "Our supervisor has a real soft spot for horses, and she wants to make sure you have an easy way of it."

He nodded as another patrol car stopped. "I'll be in front, he'll be behind your last truck. Oh, and expect an even bigger reception in Gunnison, your podcast said you'll be there tonight? People are real excited to have you there. Welcome to Colorado!"

The trek over Cochetopa was fast and easy, the patrol cars using their emergency lights only to ensure large semis and slow recreational vehicles pulled over to allow the Double B convoy to pass.

"Piece of cake," Joe shook his head. "That was the worst part. If the rest of this goes like this, I won't get an ulcer after all."

Approaching Gunnison, they saw the words of the patrolman were true. The road was lined with people and cars on both sides, holding signs, waving, cheering, honking their horns.

"There must be two hundred people here." Cheers erupted, signs held high, there was no waning of celebration for Warrior's rescue. Becky rolled down her window to wave to the crowds at a stop light.

She was driving the trailer holding the bulls, Dr. Shultz rode in the passenger seat, double-checking the paperwork they might need. A sound from above made him look up.

A helicopter with a Denver News insignia was overhead.

"Oh, boy," he pointed to it, "look."

Nan, with Joe and Dr. J pulling the horses, heard the copter, too. She texted Lacaria: *We might be getting our national attention.*

Lacaria shot back: *Might? Our emails are exploding. We heard from CBS, they want to know when you'll be available for interviews.*

They were greeted at the fairgrounds' gate by a young man who introduced himself as the assistant manager. "We're trying to keep people's cars out of the lot," he explained, "but we can't stop them from walking in. Public facility, you know. We've asked them to stand a hundred feet away from where you'll be unloading him. People really want to see that horse. And," he pointed to a building, "you got reporters in there."

IN THE DARK NIGHT

CHAPTER 61
CAN'T WE STOP THIS?

Tab sipped his iced tea as he considered the menu. Every morning, and some afternoons these past few days, Tab was at The Coffee Wrangler looking for Becky, hoping she'd be working a shift or at least stop by. So far, she was a no-show.

He didn't ask anybody about her, wasn't sure if she might have told them about their argument after the BLM meeting. It was embarrassing enough without others knowing.

Why was he still interested in her? She was independent, focused in nicer ways than some of the women he knew. They were harsh, brittle, competitive. Becky was confident, down-to-earth, not afraid of being helpful.

And now, it seems, gone. He sighed in frustration. If he could get only a few minutes with her, smooth things over, see that smile again, hear that laughter again.

He was going to buy a new SUV, he had money to get an expensive one, loaded with the latest gadgets, she could help him pick one out, they could drive it back from Jackson, together. His plans made him smile. Just a few minutes with her, that's all he needed.

He checked his phone, time to get to his office. Furniture was arriving today and there were boxes to unpack.

A sudden commotion near the counter got his attention. Nearly all of the patrons crowded in front of it. One of the television monitors flashed a message: "Warrior News!"

There was a cheer as a cameraman announced: "The Double B Convoy has arrived in Gunnison, Colorado!"

The camera panned to a helicopter in the sky, then down to three trucks, all hitched to trailers.

"We have Phillip Ebbers here, and Becky MacKendrick. You've already traveled almost six hundred miles from El Paso, Texas. How is Warrior doing?"

The faces of Phillip, leaning against one of the trailers, and Becky came into view.

"He's doing fine. All of the animals are. It sure helped to have the state patrol escorting us from Alamosa." Phillip waved to the two uniformed men, being interviewed by another reporter.

He continued: "We're hauling them only four or five hours a day, stopping to give them lots of fresh feed, water, and rest every night." He nodded to Becky. "Following her orders."

"You're a veterinary student, right?" the reporter asked.

"After I graduate from the University of Montana," she answered. "Dr. Shultz is traveling with us. He's made sure all of the animals have been inspected, vaccinated, all of our paperwork in order for crossing state lines." (Becky was told by Dr. Shultz to make sure this was mentioned in every interview. "We don't want anybody trying to jam us up with complaints.")

"How long has it taken you to find Warrior?"

"Too long," Phillip answered. "Two years almost to the day. We received a lot of sightings, people with good intentions trying to help, we followed most of them. The good thing about it, however, is our Ranch Foreman, Joe Ruiz, found a lot of mustangs and either brought them to a sanctuary or made sure they were adopted to the right folks."

The next question: "Where are you stopping tomorrow tonight?"

"Rifle," Phillip answered. "The last leg, then we'll be home."

The camera swung to watch four horses being inspected as they exited a trailer.

"Which one is Warrior?" The reporter's voice drew down to a whisper.

"The last one," was the answer. "The dappled gray."

They watched Warrior, emerge from the trailer, head held high. After several days of eating good food, with supplements, his coat was showing a healthier sheen. He adopted a spirited gait as he disappeared into the barn.

"He's magnificent!" the reporter exclaimed. "And very large."

"Sixteen hands," Becky agreed. Phillip put his arm around her, and she beamed up at him.

The reporter faced the camera. "It is amazing what this horse has been through. Wrenched from his family two years ago, watching some of them killed, disappearing into the void of government kill pens, only to be used as a rodeo bucking bronc, with the scars to prove it.

"Now Warrior is coming home, where he will be finally free, and safe."

Those last words elicited a cheer from the Wrangler customers, with back-slaps and high-fives.

There was a buzz of conversation:

"We have to let our friends know."

"When will they get here? Their website will tell us!"

Tab sat, stunned. Becky was somewhere in Colorado?

His cell chimed.

"Are you watching this?" Jack screamed. "We gotta stop this."

"They said all their paperwork is in order, I'll double-check. What about the BLM? Don't they have something about wild horses, who can own them?"

"Already called Ronnie. She's useless. After a year following release to whoever adopts a horse, the BLM don't care. Anything can happen to it. Now you know why I hate the Double B. When you think they're down, there they are, poking a stick in my eye."

Jack clicked off.

Tab sat for several minutes. The television was turned to a baseball game. Customers mingled about, Warrior still the subject of all conversation.

He couldn't get the image of Becky out of his mind. There she was, smiling, at Phillip's side. Happy.

He looked up at the pictures on the wall. Hundreds of horses stared back at him. He'd never seen a horse before in his life except in movies or documentaries, and here he was in the middle of horse country.

Jack was right. Horses were nothing more than stupid animals. He hated them, and he was starting to hate certain people, too.

Especially Phillip Ebbers. And Becky. Had she used him to make Phillip jealous, make him a part of some stupid game? He leaned back, grinding his back teeth.

The more he thought about that possibility, the angrier, and insulted, he became.

Jack roamed around his office, nervous, upset, impatient. What were those people at the Double B thinking? Bringing home an old mustang, who cares? He thought Phillip's accident would have laid them low for a while, maybe several months, but no, here he was on TV, for crying out loud, laughing, having a great time.

Where was their next stop? He remembered. It was also their last stop before home. Only a few hours away.

He clicked a number on his phone.

"Mr. Franklin, you botched the last job I gave you, maybe I wasn't clear enough. You should have driven some *wild* horses into the Double B's lease, I know there were some around, would have been easy enough."

A pause. "I got another job, give you a chance to show me what you can do. Ever been to Rifle? You need to get there tomorrow. Here's what I want you to do."

CHAPTER 62
MAN AND NATURE

As the day wore on, more reporters and camera crew showed up at the Gunnison fairgrounds.

Nan was in her element, arranging interviews to make sure everyone from the Double B Gang was interviewed and photographed. It was amusing to watch Joe describing himself as "an ol' cowboy," refusing to take credit as Warrior's rescuer.

Equally astonishing was watching Dr. J steer questions around to the subject of the government's intentions on removing all mustangs off of public land, no matter the method. She was a professional, and it showed.

"This kind of thing could go to one's head." Tess sidled up to Nan. "All of this attention."

"I saw Carl getting interviewed."

Tess laughed. "He needs media training. He's a biologist, wants to make everything a dissertation on ecology."

Everyone was tired, ready to check into their hotel, eat dinner, and get ready for the next day.

Harold Franklin, with new job orders, was also getting ready for the next day.

They said good-bye to Gunnison the next morning, pleased they were keeping to the schedule: Leave at dawn; haul time no more than four or five hours; unload at their destination's fairgrounds before noon; spend the rest of the day taking care of the animals, and themselves.

One more night on the road, then home.

The crowds grew larger as they passed through Western Colorado towns. Several cars with more reporters joined them, trailing along, stopping for photo opportunities, interviewing some of the people holding signs.

Back at the Double B, Lacaria and Skylar were kept busy cross-linking and uploading.

"There're so many articles, pictures, videos, it's going to take us weeks to go through it all," Lacaria said, "but I'm not complaining." She looked up. "For months this was a lonely job, who was listening? Watching? I always wondered if anybody cared."

"I don't think you have to wonder about that anymore, Aunt Lacaria." Skylar was sincere. "We're reaching thousands, maybe tens of thousands. I guess you could say Warrior has put the Double B on the map."

The older woman nodded. "And the plight of the wild horses front and center, too."

Rifle, Colorado. Their last stop before home.

Keeping to their well-oiled schedule, and with the efficiency learned from the last few days, the goats were unloaded from their trailer into an outdoor holding pen first. The bulls lumbered down a ramp into a canopied area.

Carl backed the horse trailer up to a fenced corridor. He and Tess opened the door, the four horses were led out to the barn.

"I can't believe how Warrior's come around," Tess said. "He's no trouble at all."

"I think this little guy's got something to do with it," Carl watched Tony follow Warrior, then scoot under a rail to find Joe.

"Letting him stay with Warrior must have done the trick." Joe picked the puppy up.

"Last night on the road," Tess said. "I'm exhausted. How about we treat ourselves to a nice dinner, celebrate a little? We deserve it."

Almost midnight, a lone figure jumped a fence near the barn. He walked around for a few minutes.

"Shoot," Harold said to himself. He thought the Double B trucks would be parked nearby, maybe still hitched up to the trailers. He didn't realize *all* of the Double B Gang needed *all* of their trucks to get to their hotel.

Math was hard for Harold.

He carried a small sack. Nothing like sugar in a fuel tank to gum up the works. Of course, Harold would have been stymied at this venture as well. All of the Double B trucks had locking fuel caps.

Logistics were hard for Harold.

He set the unopened sack near one of the trailers, a knife appeared in his hand.

"Stop them, or at least slow them down," were his orders from Jack. Flat tires would do the slowing-down part. It was the only plan he could come up with.

Twelve times he bent over to stab twelve tires, four tires for each trailer.

Not only slow them down, cost them some money, too.

Jack should be happy with him. Yes, sir, he did his job, and didn't botch it.

Carl and Dr. Shultz surveyed the flat tires the next morning, shaking their heads. "Deliberate," the veterinarian said.

The assistant manager handed them the sack of sugar. "Found this, you don't suppose somebody was going to put it in your trucks? Who would do this?"

Phillip caught the question as he hobbled over. "We have some people in Wyoming who don't like us." He shrugged. "But this seems extreme."

"There are a couple of trailer sales here," the staff member said. "I'll call them right now, we'll get you new tires and on your way as soon as possible."

Joe called Lacaria. "I'll put it on the Internet right away," she said, "people will be really interested in this. There're not going to like somebody messing with the Double B Gang."

Tab was in his new office, moving various pieces of furniture in place. His cell chimed.

"Have you looked into stopping the Double B, taking those animals across state lines?"

"Yes, sir, I did, and it seems all is in order. There's a veterinarian traveling with them, and the state agencies seem content."

"At least I slowed 'em down a bit, maybe we've lost this battle, not the war."

Tab was about to ask how, exactly, Jack "slowed 'em down a bit," when the call ended.

He opened his laptop to the Double B's podcast, bright red headlines were on top of the screen.

"Trailers sabotaged!"

"Tires slashed."

"Nothing will stop us!"

There were shouts of outrage and anger from dozens of viewers, ranging from "Hope they catch them," to outright threats. "If I catch whoever did this, they'll regret it."

Tab groaned and sat down heavily in his chair. He wasn't altogether certain the kind of man Jack Brinkle was, but he was starting to get the idea.

He'd wondered about the pictures paraded at the BLM meeting, of the hoof prints in the dirt on the Double B's lease. Sloppy, getting somebody to vandalize that test area with a shod horse.

Now, this.

"Not smart, Jack, not smart at all," Tab muttered. "I think you need me more than you know."

The convoy left the Rifle fairgrounds just before one o'clock. A distant sound of thunder greeted them as they turned onto the highway.

As usual, Joe took the lead with the horse trailers. Dr. J was with him. Tony was in the trailer with Warrior.

Carl drove the truck pulling the goats, Nan was in the passenger seat, Tess in the back.

Dr. Shultz and Becky drove the bulls, Phillip in the backseat.

"This put us behind, but we'll be home late this afternoon, before dark," Joe said.

Dr. J agreed "It will be good to get the animals unloaded, fed, settled down."

The screen on the truck's dashboard pinged, the other Double B Gang members appeared, concern on everyone's faces.

"Maybe we should have stayed an extra night in Rifle?" Becky wondered. "It's pretty warm, almost ninety degrees."

Dr. Shultz said, "If nothing else happens, we should be OK. A little out of our haul time margins but let's stay the course, get everybody home." The veterinarian's words were reassuring.

""The horse trailer has air conditioning, I'm a little worried about the heat for the bulls and goats." Carl frowned. "Traveling every morning, we've avoided it."

"It's starting to rain," Phillip pointed to the windshield. "That will cool things down, hope it keeps up."

The rain did "keep up."

State Highway 13 from Rifle to the Wyoming border is prone to wind, wildlife crossings, and mudslides.

Nine Mile Gap is a winding, narrow mountain road, forcing traffic to take it slowly. The towering hills are prone to sending cascades of rocks and dirt down on the road, quickly cleaned up by state road crews to send traffic on its way.

This morning might have been no different, except a heavy rain the week before still saturated the top of the hill, leaving pools of water now overflowing with this morning's rain.

Mud began to flow, sending small rocks crashing into larger rocks, and down they all came onto the road.

Travelers in both directions were forced to stop. Fortunately, no vehicles were damaged, no one hurt.

The highway was closed.

Lacaria called all of them for an on-screen conference. "Just talked to the state road department. They don't know when they'll have it open."

Nan checked her video camera batteries, ready to start streaming back to the Double B. This was real-life drama, at her fingertips, and she wasn't about to miss it.

"Traffic's getting backed up behind us." Joe counted ten vehicles in his sideview mirror.

Dr. Shultz's image appeared on the screen. "Man and nature conspiring against us."

"Can we back up?" Phillip asked. "Meeker is only a few miles away."

Tess answered, "Pretty steep drop-off on the other side. The livestock trailers are long, they don't exactly do U-turns. I think there was a pull-out two miles behind us, can we back them up that far?"

"I can do the horse trailer, but the other ones? Take some skill on this wet road." This from Joe.

"Visibility isn't great, either." Dr. J chewed her lower lip.

The minutes ticked by. Trucks were turned off to save fuel; the worry about the animals would not ease.

It had been almost two hours since the animals were loaded, they were still more than three hours away from home. A decision needed to be made. But what could they do?

The rain came down in sheets, pelting the trucks and the roofs of the livestock trailers.

The District Manager for the Colorado Department of Transportation was sixty miles away in Yampa, meeting with county commissioners when he got an urgent call from one of his crews.

"Sorry, gotta take this, the road going over Nine Mile Gap is washed out."

He listened, asked a few questions.

"This is that horse from Wyoming, right? Do what you have to do, but do it safely," he told the crew, giving them permission.

"Take a lot of pictures, anybody got a video camera? There're streaming this on their website? No reason the state patrol has to get all the glory, right? This'll be great PR for us."

He hung up and returned to the meeting. "Is there a monitor around? You're about to see something pretty interesting."

Lacaria appeared on the trucks' dashboard screens. She was smiling. "Guys? I think we're getting some help."

A truck with CDOT insignia pulled up to Carl's truck. A woman in a rain poncho and hard hat motioned for him to roll down his window.

"We're going to get you through, on orders from the chief. It might be tricky, come around on this side of the road. and follow me."

The Double B trucks came up to the mudslide. Several cars and large equipment were already there, flashing lights, men waving and shouting to each other.

Two men joined the woman, conferred a few moments, then sloshed through water and mud to Carl's truck.

"We're bringing in two bulldozers from the other side," informed one of the men. "They're going to push as much as they can off the road, then stay there to dam up anything else coming down. The road's going to be real bad. Rough. Slippery. I want you through there in less than five minutes. I don't want my guys there any longer in case that hill comes down. Can you do it?"

Carl didn't need to be asked twice. "Can and will."

A few minutes later they heard the rumble of the two bulldozers, watching with awe as the huge machines pushed large rocks and several feet of thick mud over the edge of the road.

Men waved them into position, one after the other, to provide the barrier between the hill and the road.

Nan held her camera out the window as far as she could without getting wet. "I'm getting this live on video, sending it back to the ranch."

Carl's truck was first, made it easily, the weight of the bulls probably helping the tires get traction. He pulled to the side, and got out. He didn't care if he got soaked. He needed to see the others get through safely.

The goat trailer was next, driven by Dr. Shultz. It almost stalled when it hit a mound of mud, but he revved the truck a little and got through, pulling alongside Carl. He also got out, as did Becky, to watch Joe.

In his truck, Joe said to Dr. J, "OK, let's do this thing. How many tons of horses do we got back there? Maybe the weight will help us like it did Carl with the bulls."

"Two tons, maybe a little more? As long as they don't shift." Dr. J's laugh was nervous. She leaned over to plant her hands on the dashboard. "I'm gonna hold on for dear life."

Joe set his jaw, and gunned the truck forward. "Now or never."

Almost immediately the trailer slid towards the side of the road, the steep embankment inches away.

Joe's stomach felt like it was sliding with the trailer.

"Don't shift, don't shift," Dr. J gasped, convinced the horses could hear her. And, obey.

The trailer stopped with a moan on the brakes. Joe glanced at the work crew. They were thinking either the trailer would tip over, or jack-knife. Either possibility was disastrous.

He knew what he had to do; he also knew nobody would expect it.

He put the truck in reverse, and backed it up!

The men held up their hands to stop him. Joe ignored the gestures, his eyes never leaving the sight of the trailer in the sideview mirror.

He pulled a hard right on the steering wheel.

The trailer groaned, metal against metal. Its tires spun, mud shot up and out. The trailer shook.

Joe took his foot off the brake, the truck following the deep ruts the trailer made. With gentle taps of the steering wheel, Joe guided the truck to a straight line with the trailer.

Once he was satisfied, he put the truck into low gear and drove it as close as he could to the bulldozer. The truck escaped the mud, the trailer with it.

He could breathe again.

Members of the road crew applauded, shaking their heads in disbelief.

"Guess this ol' cowboy still got a trick or two up his sleeve," he grinned at Dr. J.

"Probably a lot of tricks up his sleeve." She leaned back, wiping her still-shaking hands on her jeans. "But, I'd rather you not show them to me, like, *ever* again. Agreed?"

Warrior's legs almost gave out on him as the trailer shook. Tony was dislodged from his shelf with a surprised, "Yip!"

He looked at the other horses, all of them whale-eyed, heads down.

"It's OK," Warrior assured them, surprised at his own words. Probably because he wasn't that sure himself.

The trailer stopped, then they felt it move again, easier, smoother. They heard humans cheering.

"I think you should stay on the floor, behind me," Warrior told the puppy. "Safer there, just for a little while."

Despite the rain, video of the bulldozers and trucks plowing through mud was clear enough to give all viewers a taste of the effort the Double B Gang was making.

The trucks turned onto I-80 and a short time later onto Highway 191, the final leg of the trip. In every cab, there was a collective sigh of relief.

"It's going to be almost dark when we get there," Carl noted.

Phillip called Lacaria. "What's it looking like at the Double B?"

"Kind of chaotic, lots of cars and trucks on either side of the highway, people standing around, waiting for you. Playing music."

"Do you think you can ask them to pull away as far as possible, no honking horns, stay as quiet as possible until we release Warrior? We'll let them know when it's done."

"I'll sure try."

CHAPTER 63
FAMILY

On the crest looking over the north field, dozens of horses stood in the silhouette of a stunning sunset, watching the lights of the trucks get closer.

"Why are we here?" Autumn asked Silver Moon, nuzzling him.

"I don't know." He looked at the other horses. "It is very odd."

They heard the clopping of hooves behind them and turned to see a large stallion galloping towards them.

"Another stranger," Autumn said.

Silver Moon faced him. Was this a threat?

"Who are you?"

"Mosaic."

"What are you doing here?"

Mosaic tossed his head. "I've been watching all of you. Now's the time."

"For what?" Autumn nickered.

Mosaic didn't answer. He passed them to make his way down the hill.

Autumn turned back to the others. "Sheani, stay here with the little ones. Sandy will help you. Whatever is going to happen, I don't want them nearby."

"Are we alarmed?" Sandy asked.

"I don't know," Autumn answered. She turned away to follow Silver Moon.

Alexander nudged his way to his sister's side and called out. "Papa? Are you going to be all right?" There was fear in his voice.

Silver Moon stopped, then returned to his son. "Yes, I promise we'll be back, all of us will. Don't worry."

One by one, the trucks pulled into the road leading past the Double B's ranch house, headlights charting the courses they took. The one carrying the bulls swung to the right, the one carrying the goats swung to the left.

All of the drivers got out and ran after the truck carrying the horses as it entered the north field. It stopped near the gate leading up to the meadow.

Ronnie drove her car slowly on the county road. "Sheesh, what are these people doing here?" She rolled down her window and asked a woman standing next to her car. "What's going on?"

"They're bringing Warrior home, we're here to see it. They've asked us to park aways back, no lights, be quiet as possible." She smiled. "This is a sacred moment."

Ronnie rolled her window up and shook her head. *There must be a three hundred people here, maybe more*, she thought. All for a stupid old horse. But, she smiled with satisfaction, ammunition to use against the Double B for their sanctuary. Wouldn't attract lots of people? Right here, in front of her, was the proof she needed to stem that argument.

Carl and Becky joined Joe and Dr. J at the back of the truck to open the doors and pull the ramp down onto the ground. Dr. Shultz was close by, watching the horses to make sure they were OK; Nan, of course, had her camera ready.

"There's Silver Moon," Carl pointed. "Autumn's with him, who's this other stallion? Anybody know?"

Dr. J couldn't believe her eyes. "Mosaic. He's not a horse from the high meadows." As though he heard his name, Mosaic looked at Dr. J, considering her with his large, brown eyes. He did not seem at all surprised to see her.

"Look at all those horses," Joe pointed to the incline above the road. "Where they heck did they all come from?"

Phillip hobbled to the fence line where Lacaria and Skylar were.

Becky suddenly ran to the gate. She opened it.

"What are you doing? Get back here," Phillip shouted, motioning with his hands.

She shook her head. "They trust me. Get Warrior out. Now."

The first three horses emerged, galloping a short distance before turning to watch.

Warrior stayed in the trailer, stubborn, shaking, not moving.

Tony sprinted across the trailer's floor, stopped with an upraised paw and looked back as if to say, "Come on. Let's go." He yipped, then barked before Joe scooped him up.

"You did a good job helping us get him here," he told the puppy. "Now it's up to us." He handed him to a smiling Lacaria. "Meet your new mom."

"He's always been so eager to get out of there." Dr. J motioned to the Warrior. "Let's go, boy, you're home."

"Oh, wait." Joe sprinted back to the trailer and opened the small window. Taking out a pocket knife he reached in and with one swift motion, cut the top of Warrior's halter. It fell to the floor.

The horse looked surprised, free of the stiff, rancid leather at last. He shook his head.

"You're truly free now, my man," Joe whispered.

Becky kept the gate open.

"Come on, Autumn," Becky called.

The palomino paused a second, then charged through the gate.

Mosaic ignored the smells of strange humans and followed her.

Silver Moon stopped, immediately assailed with a familiar odor. Head down, cautious, he walked into the field towards the trailer.

"Father," Silver Moon said.

Warrior wasn't sure what he heard. He shuffled, his hooves making an echo in the trailer.

The stallion moved into the field. "Father, it's me."

Warrior answered, "I chased you away. Didn't I?" He was confused, memories clouded by pain and hatred. "I've changed. I'm different."

"I am, too," Silver Moon said. "This is Autumn, my first mare."

She greeted him. "You're Warrior."

Warrior stepped out of the trailer. His head shot up when he saw Mosaic approach.

"Brother? Is that you?"

Mosaic touched Warrior's neck. "Brother." They stood together for a time, breathing each other in, getting to know each other again after so many years.

Has the world stopped turning? Becky wondered. The summer air shimmered, the sunset so vivid in oranges and reds, promising a deep darkness.

The dozens of horses on the hill, they could be ghosts, they stood so still.

She could only guess what might happen next. The gate stood wide open; she stayed between it and the fence.

His legs still shaking, Warrior began to follow the others. He saw Becky and balked. "There's that human here."

Silver Moon stepped to Warrior's side. "That's Becky. She's _our_ human."

Warrior stared at Becky. "I'm not sure. She gave me flowers, but I don't trust her."

"Where else can you go?" Mosaic asked. "Do you want to stay here?"

"No. All I see are humans."

"That's not true," Autumn turned. "Look at all of the horses on the hill, watching you. They're your family, Warrior. We want to take you home."

Silver Moon looked at Mosaic, who nodded. "We're going somewhere safe. All of us."

Warrior began to move again, but faltered. "I'm having a hard time finding my running legs."

Autumn touched his neck. "I understand. When I came here, before I met Silver Moon, I did not know what it felt like to run, either. We'll take it slow."

She led the way. Warrior followed with a slow plod, Mosaic close behind. Silver Moon watched, letting them get a short distance away before following. He stopped and shuffled his front legs. *This human, why does Autumn trust her? Can I?*

He galloped towards the gate.

Becky closed her eyes, reached through the slats, held her breath, held out her hand. She would never be this close to the stallion again.

I have to touch him.

His size, the muscles in his neck, the strength of his back and flanks were overwhelming. She felt thousands of generations of horses, all watching Silver Moon.

"You are what we've become," they seemed to say, "what we are meant to become. You must live, survive, without you we are nothing."

Am I hearing those words? Becky asked herself. *I have never been this frightened in my life, I can't breathe. So much power!*

Did he feel her touch? Hear her gasp? He gave no indication, no acknowledgment, did not shy away, stayed the course, an urgency to get his family to the wild lands above.

Becky opened her eyes. She watched him gallop to the top of the hill, blending in with the others. *Did that really happen?*

When she looked down at her hands, she knew it had.

Seconds later, all of the horses disappeared in the dark night.

From the road, cheers rang out across the fields of the Double B. Lights flashed, horns honked.

Becky closed the gate and walked over to Dr. J.

"You might be able to use this. It's fresh." She made no attempt to stop crying.

Her hand clutched several strands of Silver Moon's mane.

Dr. J's eyes filled with tears. "Such a way with these horses."

Carl took the hair from his daughter's hand, a lump in his throat.

They joined the others from the Double B Gang gathered at the fence.

Job done.

Warrior was home.

GETTING WARRIOR HOME.

by Nan Whittier, Scribe
Exclusive for The American News Journal
Part One of a Series

Warrior is home. And has disappeared.

We don't know where he's gone, perhaps we'll never know, perhaps we're not supposed to know. We know he is with his family, his son Silver Moon is taking care of him.

I watched as he was greeted by the famous stallion and his mare Autumn, and a host of other horses who for some reason felt compelled to watch this reunion from the top of a hill, before themselves disappearing in the dark night.

This was magic.

Last month I was invited to report and document what it took to find, and get, Warrior home. I traveled with the people of the Double B Ranch almost three thousand miles, from western Wyoming to El Paso, Texas, and back again.

We weren't alone, as many of you know. So many people helped us from fairgrounds managers and staff (a special shout out to Shar in El Paso!), to state patrolmen who escorted us over a high mountain pass, and the brave operators of bulldozers in Colorado staving off a rockslide so that we could pass.

And, many of you, hundreds, perhaps thousands of you, lined roads and highways with your signs and love. You were noticed, and appreciated.

More magic.

In the coming days, this series will give you all of the details, the "behind the scenes" moments (there were many) and introduce you to the Double B Gang, the extraordinary men and women who brought Warrior home.

I hope you come along for the ride.

Trust me, it was an epic journey.

A Word about Words

In the equine community, a newborn horse, male or female, is called a foal. A yearling is horse of either sex that is between one and two years old. A colt is a male horse under the age of four while a filly is a female horse, also under the age of four, even though both are considered adults.

While I have attempted to stay true to this terminology, there are times when I have used the words "stallion" and "mare" without explaining relative age.

IN THE DARK NIGHT

ABOUT V P FELMLEE

Vicki Felmlee is a former newspaper reporter and editor. She has written extensively for several magazines and is a board member of Women Writing the West.

She is the author of The Abandoned Trilogy: *The Amazing, Interesting, Dangerous, and Somewhat True Adventures of Prince Tadpole & Princess Clara*; *Good Boy Ben*; and *Autumn and The Silver Moon Stallion*, the 2024 Silver Medal Winner, Willa Literary Award for Young Adult Fiction.

She lives in Colorado, with her husband and an assortment of dogs, cats, and chickens.

In the Dark Night is her fourth novel.

Learn more about her upcoming books in the Double B series, *The Color of Fire* and *The Promise of a Thousand Sunsets* at vfauthor.com

©Deb Little, Photography

The Color of Fire

by V P Felmlee

Book 2 of Wyoming's Double B Ranch

COMING EARLY 2025

Deb Little, Photography

Deb Little, an Ohio-based photographer, set out to find and photograph the wild horses of the Pryor Mountains more than twenty years ago. What she found fed her need to capture their beauty with her camera and inspired her to tell the stories nestled within the lives of these incredible Mustangs. Following and photographing them over two decades has allowed Deb to know the many generations that make up the vitality of these wild horses.

Deb has since added other wild horse ranges in her travels to create photos. However, the Pryor Mountains, nestled on the Wyoming/Montana border, will always hold a special place in her heart. Deb's Photo Fusions, as seen on the cover of *In the Dark Night*, are fine art pieces that explore the treasures found deep within the heart of wild horses. More of her photographic art can be found at www.deblittle.com.

The Storm Within

©Deb Little, Photography

IN THE DARK NIGHT